CROOKEDWOOD

Liza Costello's first novel *The Estate*, an earlier version of which was released by Audible, was published in 2021 by Hachette Books Ireland. Her writing has appeared in many places, including *New Irish Writing* and *The Stinging Fly*, and has been broadcast on Irish national radio. She has also been short-listed for a number of short story and poetry awards, and was winner of the 2011 Dromineer Poetry Prize.

Liza lives in County Westmeath with her husband, John, and two children, Martha and Brendan. *Crookedwood* is her second novel.

CROOKEDWOOD

LIZA
COSTELLO

HACHETTE
BOOKS
IRELAND

First published in Ireland in 2022 by HACHETTE BOOKS IRELAND
First published in paperback in 2023

1

Cataloguing in Publication Data is available from the British Library

Paperback ISBN 978 1 52935 016 6
Ebook ISBN 978 1 52935 014 2

Typeset in Georgia by Bookends Publishing Services, Dublin
Printed and bound in Great Britain by Clays Ltd, Elcograf, S.p.A.

Hachette Books Ireland policy is to use papers that are natural, renewable and recyclable products and made from wood grown in sustainable forests. The logging and manufacturing processes are expected to conform to the environmental regulations of the country of origin.

Hachette Books Ireland
8 Castlecourt Centre
Castleknock
Dublin 15, Ireland

A division of Hachette UK Ltd
Carmelite House, 50 Victoria Embankment, EC4Y 0DZ

www.hachettebooksireland.ie

For my sisters
Anna and Emma

She listened anxiously; the sounds were distant,
and seemed to come from a remote part of the woods.

— Ann Radcliffe, *The Mysteries of Udolpho*

PART I

1

Weeks later, pinned against the bracken floor by the weight of his body and knowing she's about to die, Sarah's mind will go back to this evening in her mother's warm kitchen, when there are still a couple of weeks before the clocks go back and she has come down from Dublin. It will go back to this very moment, when she is looking out the window above the sink and taking in the darkening network of fields, slash of red to the west of the navy sky, dusky low-lying mountains at the horizon and, to the east, peninsula of wood that borders their land, all feathery outline and chalky black interior. And the thing that will come to her, with a stunning clarity, is that standing here in the kitchen, she already knows everything. She knows what happened to her in the woods all those years ago and she also knows what she did there. She knows what he's planning to do and why he's planning to do it. And, nestled within all this, another sharp truth: that on this March evening in the old, familiar kitchen, she has never been closer to claiming this single life of hers.

She knows all this and yet she does not know it. Because some memories, she will understand, get hidden as soon as they're formed, secrets within you until you're ready and they start to stir, until eventually you can see them. Just as they have started to stir inside Sarah this evening as she stares out the window, her gaze lingering on the woods, until Nancy clatters a handful of cutlery into the rickety drawer under the draining-board. And she looks around and asks her mother, 'Is everything okay?'

'What would be wrong with me?' answers Nancy.

'Nothing.' Sarah returns her hands to the water, runs the J-cloth over a plate, passes it to her mother.

'You're the one who's had her head in the clouds since she walked through the door.'

Sarah makes a face, as though to say, *Really? I didn't notice.*

'Is there anything wrong with *you*?' Nancy asks.

'Nope.'

'There's nothing stopping you driving back up, if you're worried about the restaurant not surviving without you.'

'Of course not.'

'Their number-one vegetable peeler.'

Sarah roots around in the sudsy lukewarm water until her hand finds a glass.

'I said I'd come down for the meeting with the solicitor,' she says.

Nancy frowns at the glass Sarah has handed her, rubs at a

spot on it with the tea-towel. 'I told Kathy you'd take a class for her on Sunday morning,' she says then, as though this is nothing. 'Seeing as you're down.'

'In the Garden Project?'

'Where else? She's some funding application to get in and she's down on volunteers.'

'My garda vetting for the place was ages ago – it must have expired.'

'March 2004 you last got it. So until March 2007. One month to go.'

Sarah stares at her mother.

'What? Ring her so and tell her you don't want to do it.'

'I'm not doing that.'

'It didn't occur to me you might have other plans.'

'I'll do it. It's fine.' A deep breath. 'It'll be nice, actually.' She takes care to keep her voice light. 'I thought I'd go to that open house as well, while I'm down, about the new development by the motorway. That's on tomorrow, isn't it?'

'Where did you hear about that?'

Sarah blinks. 'Ursula told me.'

'I thought you didn't see those girls any more.'

'I saw them that night I was out at Christmas, remember?' She searches for more dishes but the grey water is empty. 'She gave me a ring last week.'

'Did she?'

Finds the plug, pulls it. 'She did.'

'Well, the more support we get, the better, I suppose.'

Nancy takes the J-cloth from Sarah, starts wiping the draining-board.

'You're against it, then.'

'Of course I'm against it.'

'You don't think it sounds good? There's going to be a playground. Café. Supermarket. Crookedwood could do with a supermarket. And some of it's going to social housing. Most private developments don't bother with that.'

As she speaks, she takes out the broom and starts to sweep the floor. Pretends not to notice Nancy is staring at her.

'You seem very familiar with it.'

'There's a website. I just had a quick look.'

'A website. And you believe, of course, everything it says.'

'I don't think he can lie about it.'

'You're not saying any of that tomorrow?'

Sarah looks at her, surprised to be asked. 'I'm not *planning* on saying anything,' she says carefully.

'If that goes ahead, Crookedwood will turn into one of those commuter towns within the next couple of years. Choked by traffic.'

'I thought there were guidelines to stop that sort of thing happening.'

'The likes of Neil Hart will always find their way around guidelines.'

'I remember you once saying that Neil Hart' – she is careful to use his full name too – 'was not cut from the same cloth as his father.'

'I don't recall that.'

'That first summer I worked in his pub, before the Leaving Cert. He drove me home once, because I wasn't feeling well and you said he was a decent skin.'

Nancy considers this. 'That was a long time ago.'

'Ursula said,' continues Sarah, 'his father gave him that bit of land years ago, long before the motorway was even planned, when it was next to useless. And his brother getting all the good land. Why shouldn't he take advantage of the fact it's now worth something?'

'Because it's not in the interests of the town,' says Nancy.

'I wouldn't mind if it was going to be like one of these developments you see springing up outside Dublin. Miles and miles of houses without so much as a corner shop between them. But this is totally different.'

'I've the old committee back,' says Nancy. 'From the campaign against that housing estate on that site they couldn't drain properly.'

'Really? That's the first I've heard about it.'

'Sure, you haven't been home since this whole thing got launched.'

'You should have won on that one,' Sarah acknowledges.

'There isn't a soul in this town who doesn't see now we were right about that. And the cost of not listening to us. Neil Hart knows he's a battle on his hands with this. He's going to lose too, even if he does have that little politician on his side. We've a petition going into the council. Nearly three hundred signatures now.'

'Wow,' says Sarah, genuinely surprised.

'Yes, wow.'

Still, Sarah wants to add, that doesn't mean you're *not* wrong. Because nothing could be clearer to her that, in this instance, Nancy is as wrong as wrong could be. Saying so, however, is probably all that's lying between them ping-ponging bitter words at each other until Sarah retreats upstairs to her freezing little bedroom, like she's sixteen years old again. So she casts her mind around for something, anything, that will bring them back to safer ground.

'David Fitzpatrick came into the restaurant last week,' she says. 'You know, he used to live here before they moved.'

She almost mentioned this over dinner, but managed to do without it then.

Now, Nancy's eyes widen, as Sarah knew they would. 'David Fitzpatrick. As in the TD's son?'

'That's him.'

'His father's a junior minister now. For planning.'

'I didn't know that.'

'Well. And. How did you know he was there? I mean, you must have been back in the kitchen.'

'He'd seen that article in the *Chronicle* about me working in the restaurant. He asked the waiter if I was on.'

'So you came out to them. And was the father with him?'

'Friends. Someone's birthday.'

'And what did he say?'

'The usual stuff.'

'I don't remember you ever mentioning him. But he remembered you.' Nancy is looking at her closely. 'How did you find him?'

'Fine.'

'What were the friends like?'

'Fine.'

'Well, someone must have said something.'

'He asked about the restaurant.'

Nancy makes a face. 'What's he doing with himself?'

'He works in advertising. I think that's what he said.'

'Doing what?'

Sarah shrugs.

'Does he still play football?'

'I didn't ask.'

'He was one of the best players in the under-18s, that lad.'

Sarah returns to sweeping the floor. Because she has just remembered how one minute she'd been making small-talk with David Fitzpatrick, and the next, she'd been taking in the sight of Neil at the door. It had used up all her willpower to go back into the kitchen, knowing he was sitting at a table out there waiting for her. To keep going until the last order was done.

'Will you see him again?' asks Nancy.

'What?' says Sarah, her face filling with heat. But then she realises. Nancy is still talking about the minister's son.

'God, no. Why would I? I'll finish up here, Mam. You go on into the sitting room.'

Nancy leans against the bar across the range and folds her arms. Like a sulking child, thinks Sarah.

'It's a pity the dinner was ruined,' she says.

Sometimes, Sarah suspects the kitchen is so small that she and her mother can't be in it together for long without one of them reading the other's mind. 'Dinner was fine,' she says. Chicken kievs cooked from frozen. Watery potatoes and cold peas. 'I wish you'd let me cook a meal sometime, though.'

'Sarah. I know you hate me saying this.'

Sarah closes her eyes.

'But there's nothing stopping me phoning Cormac Hart first thing Monday morning and telling him the sale is off. Not a thing.'

'I've told you a million times,' says Sarah, her stomach tightening, like it always does whenever this happens. 'I don't want you to do that.'

'You still want me to sell your heritage.'

'Yes,' says Sarah. 'I do.'

'This place. That started off as a bare few acres. Built up over the generations by the blood, sweat and tears of your ancestors. That's what you're telling me?'

Nancy's hands are on her hips. Her eyes ablaze.

'That's what I'm telling you,' says Sarah.

'And that would be fine, if I believed you.'

'Why would I lie about it?'

'I'm not saying you're lying, exactly. I'm saying you don't know your own attachment to the place because it's always been here, you see. There's a difference.'

'Not this again.'

'I remember you out there with your father when you were small. You won't remember it but it's in you. And once it's gone, you'll never be able to come back here again.'

'I understand that.'

'You think you understand it.'

'There was an economist on the radio the other day,' says Sarah. 'He said there wasn't a single financial basis for being a small farmer in Ireland. Not these days.'

'What does he know about it?'

'A lot, I imagine.'

'Don't I know the struggles involved? Didn't I see your father hold down that insurance job on the side? But we'd be doing it differently.'

'Mam. Don't start.'

'We could have this place certified organic within two years. Joe was saying the market in China is going to keep growing.'

'I know. You already told me that. I don't want to, though.'

'High-end restaurants, like your place. You'd keep a link that way, you see. Isn't it all part of the same thing when you think about it? You'd be in charge of providing the best beef. Isn't that what you're always saying, that it's all about the quality of the ingredients? What more important role could there be for that kitchen?'

'I don't want it, though,' she repeats.

'You'd have the house to yourself. I said before, I'll move into your granny's place in the morning, no problem. You'll be able to do it up whatever way you like. Get your wall windows. Didn't you say to me once the view out there was wasted with these small windows? Imagine doing it the way you'd like it.'

'You couldn't live there.'

'A lick of paint.'

'I don't want any of that, though.' This time, she says it so quietly, it's as though she doesn't mind whether or not her mother hears her. As though it makes no difference either way.

'Well, you can't tell me you prefer what you're doing. Chopping carrots and gutting fish.'

'I've been a station chef for the past year. You seem to keep forgetting that.'

'I don't forget it. I just know, unlike you, it doesn't mean anything.'

'Jack said—'

'Jack said. Has he given you a permanent contract yet? You see.'

'I'm next in line to be sous-chef. That isn't bad, considering I started as their dishwasher five years ago.'

'Jack will promise you the sun, moon and stars because you're a good worker. Fill your head with this notion of some exciting career. He's making a fool of you, that's what that man is doing.'

'He's not making a fool of me. He reckons the sous-chef we have now will move on this year. He told me this only the other day.'

'You don't even have any friends up there.'

'I've friends in the restaurant.'

'That doesn't count.'

'Why on earth would that not count?'

'It just doesn't.'

'Well, what friends would I have down here?'

'What friends would you have? Who wouldn't be your friend down here?'

By now, the pane of glass above the sink is black, reflecting, like a mirror, Sarah's face back at her, which strikes her as foolish and lost-looking. Leaning over the sink, she presses her forehead against its coolness until the bright kitchen light is behind her and, instead of herself, she sees a faint trace of red still left in the sky, the outline of trees.

'It's all right for Jack,' Nancy continues. 'He comes from money. I know you don't like hearing that but it's the truth. This is yours, Sarah. It's your place in the world. Why should it always be the men who keep the line going on a farm? We'd be breaking the mould, you see. Don't forget that. It's more exciting surely than any restaurant.'

It's as though she has never trundled out this argument before.

'I think I'll go for a walk,' says Sarah, her breath clouding the glass as she speaks.

'What did you say?'

'I said, I think I'll go for a walk.' She takes her jacket from the back door, pulls it on.

'A walk?'

'Just a quick one. After the drive down.'

'Where in the name of God are you going to walk to at this hour?'

'Down the field and back. I won't be long.'

Strictly speaking, she's no right to walk through their land. But Pat Doyle, the dairy farmer who rents it from Nancy, who is supposed to be buying it from her, will still be keeping his cattle in the shed at this time of year. Anyway, it's not like he'd care about such a harmless trespass.

'It's too dark,' says Nancy.

'There's still a bit of light.'

'Are you meeting someone or something?'

'Meeting someone? Who on earth would I be meeting?'

'Sure, I don't know what you do be at.'

'Of course I'm not meeting someone.'

'Well, wait at least and I'll get my wellies,' says Nancy, looking fretfully at Sarah's Converse. 'Your feet will be soaked in those things.'

'I'll be back in no time.'

'Oh, suit yourself. You always do.'

'God. It's a short walk after dinner.' And before her mother answers, Sarah steps outside, shuts the door behind her. A bit too sharply maybe. But she didn't slam it, she tells herself, as she crosses the yard. She definitely didn't slam it. Arms folded against the cold, she walks past the outhouses, one with its tin roof half caved in, the door of another jammed open and clearly rotting, weeds growing in crevices of the flagstones, the small granny flat Sarah's father had adapted from one of the outhouses. Then she's over the gate and in the field, which, though it's spring, still has the raggedy-haggard look of winter, the grass dead, branches in the hedgerow bare, any new buds that might be in there hidden by the dark. As she walks, the evening birdsong builds to a frenzied climax, the sharp night air cutting through her thin jacket and the dew seeping into the fabric of her shoes and socks. But she doesn't stop until she's about halfway down, where the land plateaus and she can see the little gully along the far end between the field and the trees and behind her, all that's visible of the cottage is its outline, the small square of light that is the kitchen window.

It started when Sarah was still in secondary school, this idea of Nancy's. She has been fighting it for so long now, the same argument playing out year after year, it's hard to know any more. Sometimes, especially lately, she's found herself wondering if the future Nancy imagines, with the two of them running the farm, *is* what she ought to want. Or maybe she does want it, but just can't see it. That line about supplying the restaurant with organic beef, about still being part of it, that's new. She has to hand it to her on that one.

The awful sliding feeling is back, of everything dissolving. If she had felt this in the cottage, she might have agreed then and there. If only Neil was with her now. He could always make it go away.

She turns her gaze back down the field, towards the motorway, only a couple of fields away and visible from her raised vantage point. Or, if not the motorway exactly, the lights that mark the slip road onto it, the moving headlights of passing cars. Then she looks upwards, at the thin scattering of stars in the sky, and does what she used to do as a kid – stares and stares until more stars reveal themselves, thin, faraway ones that might no longer exist. When she catches sight of a moving one, she feels the old thrill of seeing a shooting star, until she sees it's moving too slowly for that, its course and pace too mechanical. It's just a satellite, drawing its boring line. Still, she closes her eyes and makes herself imagine it: going into the restaurant kitchen in the morning, doing the inventory and then later, when everything's been prepared, testing new dishes on the menu with the staff. Talking the waiters through them. Then during service, being everywhere and anywhere, making sure everything is served just so. And after it all, looking over the menu, putting in orders for the following day, maybe even making the odd suggestion, tweaking a dish here or there.

If Neil hadn't asked this favour of her, she'd never have come down. If it hadn't seemed to mean so much to him, she *would* have made him see – that her saying a few words in favour of his development won't make the slightest bit of difference at this open-house thing. Surely by now she's seen as an outsider in Crookedwood. If anything, people won't like her speaking against her mother, who is so well respected. This seems to her even more valid a point after what Nancy has just said about her campaign.

But it's not as though she didn't try. And it's not as though he has ever asked a favour of her before. And it's not as though she isn't completely crazy about him. Before he'd shown up in Dublin, unbelievably only two months ago, her life outside the kitchen *had* been unsocial, besides the odd work night out. Nancy had a point there. When she wasn't sleeping, time was a problem. How to fill it? What to do with it? Over the years, the long hours in the restaurant made it increasingly difficult to go out at night and there always seemed to be problems meeting up with people during the day, between them being at work and her catching up on her sleep. As the years went by, she'd missed more and more of the lives of college and school friends until, without her noticing it, they weren't in hers any more. Everything whittled down to the restaurant. That night at Christmas had been the first time in years she'd been out with non-restaurant people.

But now, if she isn't with Neil, she is planning what they might do the next time he gets up. Or they are talking on the phone or, more often, texting. Or she's simply daydreaming about him. She can fill hours doing that.

By the time she reaches the bottom corner, where the gully separates the field from the woods, the cold is bone-deep, her feet are numb and the darkness is almost pitch, the birdsong all but petered out. Even this close, the trees have become almost indistinguishable from each other, huddling close, as though guarding a secret. Stepping over the gully and in under them, waiting in the deeper darkness for her eyes to adjust, Sarah wonders if Nancy's reaction would have been any different earlier if she'd known one small fact about her daughter and the minister's son. Not that she'll be telling her about that. Not once has there been a conversation about sex between mother and daughter and, as far as she's concerned, best to keep it that way.

She has just taken a second careful step on the hidden, gnarled ground, hand on tree-trunk for balance, when she feels the dog's eyes on her. She feels them, even before she turns her gaze and sees them, by her hand, and his hot breath hits her skin. Then, its body slowly revealing itself, still and tense with the task of observing her. Lean and thick-necked, hair tight to its skin, jaw slightly open, so she can just make out the dull gleam of teeth. One of those restricted breeds, like a pit bull or a Rottweiler. A pit bull, she thinks.

Ssh.

Attaboy.

Good boy.

She says the words in her mind, not daring to make a sound. The dog stays silent too, not even a low growl from him as Sarah's eyes flit across the darkness and she tells herself that, at any second, the owner will appear, breathless and full of apologies. But even as she thinks it, she knows this is not someone's pet.

This is someone's weapon.

Then, a man's voice, coming from the hollow, a few steps further in. Young and full of panic. 'You don't want him on ya.'

As soon as he speaks, the dog whines, thin and high-pitched. He pricks his ears, moves slightly closer so the breath is hotter on her skin. When she hears a woman's cry, thin like the dog's, it takes a moment to realise it's coming from her. It stops in the same moment as an urgent rustling starts up somewhere close behind her. A frightened animal, she thinks, making its escape. All the time, the dog stays right there, still waiting for some signal.

And then – footsteps, from the hollow. They're coming in her direction. When the man emits a low whistle, and the dog cocks his ears, lets out a quick yelp, Sarah is suddenly moving – one backward step, then turning and running across the gully and back up the dark field, towards the bright yellow square that is the kitchen window. For those first few seconds, she hears nothing but her own feet against the grass but then comes the sound of the dog's heavy breathing and the heavy thud of his paws, and then, behind him, footsteps. She runs faster than she knew she could, but all the time their sounds seem to grow closer and torchlight is wildly swooping across the ground, first on one side of her, now on the other. It scuffs her briefly as she climbs the gate but it's not until she's at the back door, her fingers on the handle, that it's on her again.

This time, it stays there.

Sarah puts a shaking hand over her eyes, squints into the light. 'Who the fuck are you?' she yells, her heart knocking furiously inside her.

The light goes out.

2

The small detached building on Church Street is more like someone's bungalow than a cop-house, with its neatly mown square of lawn out front, frosted-glass panes in the door. The place has always been as likely to be closed as open, the shadow of post often visible beneath the letterbox, through the glass. But this morning, a police car is parked outside, and since Sarah has pulled up, a couple of people have gone through its door, both re-emerging minutes later.

She turns on the radio, to indignant, defensive voices talking over each other. She changes the station before catching what they're on about. Now Beyoncé is singing about a beautiful liar. Sarah looks ahead, at the blue signpost for the motorway there at the end of Church Street. It would take exactly one hour and twenty minutes to be back in the city, another ten or so to get to the restaurant, depending on traffic. Right now, it would still be empty, the floor and steel surfaces clean and shining, ready for the porter to show up and start prepping vegetables, a job she did herself for years.

Neil's voice had echoed her panic when she called him the night before, after failing to get through to the station. Of course, she must have sounded deranged, babbling about a scary dog like that, and being chased by that guy. She'd been so frightened, her teeth had literally been chattering inside her, something she hadn't known could actually happen, her heart's wonky beats paining her chest. It was only when she'd finished muddling through what had happened and he'd gone out to the back room behind the bar to talk some sense into her, that it changed, to soft and reassuring. She'd probably just encountered some kids messing around, he'd said. Maybe someone using. A teenager from the Heights, that's all it'll have been. She should make sure the doors were locked, the windows all closed, and then she should get a good night's sleep. Everything will seem better in the morning. I wouldn't even tell your mother, he'd said, especially with her moving soon. Go into the garda station in the morning, if it makes you feel better, but I'd put money on you never seeing that guy again, or his charming pet.

As soon as he'd spoken the words, she'd heard the truth in them. She'd been able to take a hot shower, drink a cup of tea. Then she woke Nancy, who'd been sound asleep in her armchair by the fire all that time, her mouth slightly open, her head leaning painfully to the side.

'Mam.' Gingerly, she'd put a hand on her mother's shoulder. 'Mam.'

Nancy's eyes opened, as she took in Sarah, her expression all effrontery. 'This is what happens now,' she'd said. 'I lie awake all night and then I drop off in the evening.' She glared at Sarah, as though she was somehow to blame for this new, unwelcome development in her sleeping patterns.

'You're all right.'

'How was your walk?'

'Fine. Tiring. Think I'll get an early night.'

She really had thought she was fine. Or, at least, if she was still rattled, it was nothing that, as Neil had said, a good night's sleep wouldn't solve. Yet here she is.

A sudden loud rap on the window. It startles her so much she screams, her hands flying to her face. But when she looks out, she sees it's just Ursula Hart, Neil's cousin and Sarah's old schoolmate, grinning in at her. 'Demented-looking' comes to Sarah's mind as she lowers the window.

'What are you doing sitting here at this hour?' asks Ursula.

'Avoiding my mother,' says Sarah, grimly.

'Oh, you're priceless.'

This is how it's always been between them – Sarah rising to the bait of being slightly shocking, because that's what is required to make Ursula laugh. Even after things vaguely and inexplicably soured between them, back in their Leaving Certificate year, they still always seemed to fall into this way of being with each other.

'It's great to see you down,' she says, as Sarah gets out of the car. 'Time for a quick coffee?' She nods towards the hotel up the road.

Sarah checks the time. The open house isn't for another couple of hours. But the thought of coffee with Ursula fills her with dread. Any time she's encountered her since school, she's always come away feeling like shit.

She makes a face. 'Nancy wants me to help her go through this paperwork for selling the farm.' She rolls her eyes.

'Ah, come on. You can do a quick one for an old friend, surely.'

They order their coffees at the hotel bar before returning to the lobby, where they take a table under a huge flatscreen television, the only addition to the room since Sarah last set foot in the place, back when they were in school. The black leather armchairs are still there, the ugly patterned carpet, the fish tank set into the wall, and even the creepy, unsmiling mannequins in glass cabinets displaying clothes from the town's only and very stuffy boutique down the road.

'I feel like I'm sixteen again,' she says.

'We should have ordered a plate of chips between us,' laughs Ursula. 'Remember we used do that, the lot of us.'

She doesn't think she's imagining it. Ursula's making a real effort to be friendly.

'It's a wonder we were never barred.'

'So, my lovely. What brings you home?'

'Just helping Nancy with the sale.'

Ursula nods. 'Thank God she's moving out of that place. I know you won't take offence with me saying that.'

'It's for the best.'

'She's finally dropped this idea of the two of you keeping on the farm, then?'

'I wish.'

'What?'

'Just yesterday evening,' Sarah admits, 'she started on about it again.'

'But I thought it was sale agreed and all that.'

'It is.'

'She's mad. Sorry, I know she's your mother.'

'No. I don't know what to think, to be honest with you.'

'You're not considering it.' Ursula's voice is pure astonishment.

'I'm not considering it,' says Sarah. 'Of course not.'

'But?'

'I dunno.'

'It would be pure madness. The two of you living there.'

'She'd be in the granny flat, she says.'

'Jesus fucking Christ.'

'I know.'

'Well,' says Ursula. 'Once the sale is through, she'll have to let it go.'

'It's hard to believe,' says Sarah.

'Just hang in there. Christ.' Ursula shudders. 'Is the toilet still in an outhouse? I know you won't mind me asking.'

'No. That was ages ago.'

'The spiders.'

'Dad sorted that out.' She has a memory of her father standing among bricks at the side of the house, a cement-mixer beside him. She's not sure if it's a real memory, though, or just a memory of a photograph she knows is in one of the albums at home.

'Ah. Your poor dad. What age were you again when he died?'

'Seven.'

'Seven.' Ursula shakes her head. 'He'd be so proud of you now. People like your family. Salt of the earth.'

'I don't know about that.'

'You can stop doing the modest act. I saw that article in the *Chronicle*. What was it? "Crookedwood girl cooking up feasts for Ireland's A-list celebrities".'

'As if Ireland has any celebrities. Let alone A-listers.'

'It's fantastic. I'm proud of you.'

'Ha.'

'Honestly. This place has gone to pieces. Paul said the amount of drug-dealing cases they have coming in from the Heights ...'

'I forgot he's a guard.'

'Why? Have you need of one?'

She's obviously thrown it out as a joke but when Sarah doesn't smile, Ursula's expression changes quickly. 'Did something happen to Nancy?'

'Not to Nancy.' She looks at Ursula. 'It's probably nothing.'

'Go on, spit it out. A problem shared and all that.'

So for the second time, Sarah describes what happened in the woods. It's easier to recount now that it's daytime – the walk down the field, the way the dog had seemed to appear out of nowhere, how he and that guy had followed her home, the torchlight on her face.

'I honestly thought at one point he was going to catch up with me. And his horrible dog. It really felt like they wanted to hurt me.'

'Jesus,' says Ursula.

'Right?' She just catches herself before she says what Neil thought had happened. She had almost said his name. *Neil reckons* ... 'What do you think?' she says.

Ursula looks at her closely. She always did have a sixth sense for gossip. And then, for the first time, it occurs to Sarah that maybe Neil has told her. Despite the twelve-year age gap, the two of them have always been very close – more like brother and sister than cousins. But as soon as the thought enters her mind, she dismisses it. There's no way he would have told Ursula without letting Sarah know.

Ursula frowns, as though trying and failing to make some sense of what she's just heard. 'Was anyone else down there?'

'I don't think so.'

'Did he say anything?'

'He said, "You don't want him on ya."'

'Oh my God.'

'It was weird though. I could have sworn he didn't know I was there until he said that. It was almost like he was talking to someone else.'

'I thought you said there was no one else there.'

'There wasn't. At least, there didn't seem to be. He must have been talking to me.'

'Did you tell Nancy?'

'No. You know how paranoid she can get.'

'No point in worrying her over nothing, I suppose.' Ursula looks at her. 'Is that why you were sitting across from the station earlier?'

'I suppose so.'

'Why didn't you call them last night?'

'I did. No answer.'

Ursula tuts. 'That place is gone to the dogs. Paul says a station in Dublin would never get away with how it's run.'

'Probably not.'

'I tell you what. He's on today but I don't think he's at the desk. Why don't you come over first thing in the morning and tell him about it? Just informally, like. He'll have a better idea than me.'

'It'll just be a fuss over nothing.'

'It's hardly a fuss.'

'I'd feel bad if he's not working.'

Ursula adopts a mock-formal tone. 'A member of An Garda Síochána is never off duty.'

'It won't be first thing. Nancy's me roped in to teach a class in the Garden Project.'

Ursula stares. 'You're not serious.'

'I know. She thinks she can just volunteer my services to anyone.'

'Say no.'

'Oh, they're down on volunteers or something. Kathy has to get some funding application in.' She shrugs. 'I've done so many of them over the years, I could do it with my eyes closed, in fairness.'

'What time's that on at?'

'Half-ten.'

'You're too good, that's your problem. You're too nice.'

Sarah gives her what she hopes is a wry look. 'How's life with you anyways?'

'Oh, same old same old, day in, day out. Sometimes I think I should have stayed in Australia. I'd probably have gone back there, if I hadn't met Paul.'

Ursula went to Australia straight after school. Despite being the brightest girl in the class, she'd never bothered much with studying, only scraping through her exams. As far as Sarah knows, she passed the years over there working in a shop. Her parents' fury the talk of the town at the time. But Ursula had always seemed to Sarah like someone for whom things would work out.

And then she'd moved home, and, to the best of Sarah's

knowledge, temps in an accounting office in Dunlone. Started going out with Paul when he got stationed there in Crookedwood.

'He seems really nice,' says Sarah. It's only a white lie. She met him that one time over Christmas and it's not like she's any reason to think badly of him.

'He's not the worst. Even if he is from Dublin.'

But a change has crept into Ursula's voice. When a young guy comes out with their coffee on a tray, Sarah waits for her to start chatting to him – she's always known everyone in the town – but she just watches him put the cups, sugar bowl and milk on the table.

'Have you set a date?' asks Sarah.

'What?'

'For the wedding.'

'Oh. No, not yet.'

'No rush, I suppose.'

'Exactly.' Ursula pours milk into her coffee. 'I still can't believe Nancy did that.'

'The Garden Project? That's nothing.'

'As long as you don't let yourself get sucked back into small-town bullshit. You know that thing they say about lobsters, pulling each other back down.'

'You might make that point to Nancy when you see her.'

Ursula gives her a curious look. 'Mind you, you always *were* harder than you look.'

'What?'

'Oh, yeah. In school.' Ursula shakes her head. 'All butter wouldn't melt. But when it came to the crunch.' She sucks air between her teeth.

'I don't remember being like that.'

'It's a compliment.'

A classic Ursula compliment.

'Cheers.'

'Oh, my God. I've just had an idea.'

'Yeah?'

'There's no need to sound so suspicious. When are you back to Dublin, did you say? Not until Monday?'

'Straight back after the meeting with the solicitor Monday morning.'

'Cormac?'

'I always forget he's your cousin too.'

'There's a session planned here for the under-21s team. Why don't you come up to the house and talk to Paul, and then we'll head out? I'll say it to the girls. We could have a little reunion.'

Sarah pretends to think about it. 'I'd better not risk it. I'm on in the restaurant Monday night. It's bloody hard enough not to screw up without a hangover.'

'Ah, come on.'

'Sorry.'

Ursula makes a sad face. 'Surely you're allowed one hungover shift.'

'Afraid not. I won't burden Paul with all that rubbish either. I really don't think there's anything to worry about now.'

'All right,' says Ursula. 'If you're sure?'

'Thanks all the same. And now I'd better head. I don't want to give Nancy another reason to be annoyed with me. I said I'd give her a lift to this open-house thing.' Another white lie. That morning, she hadn't chanced even mentioning the open house to Nancy. She'd managed to nip out after breakfast without Nancy even noticing her going.

'What – Neil's thing?'

'I thought I may as well go, while I'm down.' Sarah starts putting on her coat.

'The sooner it's over, the better,' says Ursula. 'I've never seen him so stressed out.'

'That bad? I heard he's a strong case.'

'Oh, it couldn't be stronger. Jobs. More housing. A supermarket instead of everyone having to use that stupid Spar all the time.'

'I agree with you.'

'But there's all this local opposition. Which has seen an end to smaller developments than that. And then, of course, there's Jane.'

Ever since Neil met his wife Jane, Ursula has blamed her for everything that's gone wrong in his life. When she was younger, Sarah had always felt it seemed unfair, despite the horror stories about Jane – a case of Ursula being blinded by her love of an adored older cousin who was once the county's rising football star, the world his oyster, who now has to deal with the indignity of having a crazed alcoholic for a wife.

Now she picks a ball of lint off the sleeve of her cardigan, rolls it between finger and thumb. 'What about her?' she says, as lightly as she can manage.

'The drinking is out of control.'

'Hasn't it always been?'

'Lately, it's different. He's at his wits' end with her. She keeps wandering off drunk out of her skull. The other night, he found her out your road. Completely out of it. Someone could have run her over.'

3

By the time Sarah gets to the community hall, the grey plastic chairs are almost all taken and there is the heavy smell of damp coats and the drone of conversation that's gone on longer than it's wanted to. The table at the top of the room is unoccupied, the white screen behind it blank, above it a clock reading ten past three. Scanning the rows, the first person she spots is Ursula and then Nancy, about two rows further up. Beside Nancy sits Joe, Sarah's godfather and uncle on her father's side. Between them, an empty seat.

Sarah takes one of the few remaining chairs at the back of the room, just as Nancy looks around. She keeps her gaze on her feet and when Nancy hisses her name, she takes out her phone, frowns at it. She keeps frowning at it when Nancy calls her name, this time clearly above the hum of other people talking. She would have kept frowning at it had a couple of people not turned and glanced at her, forcing her to look up and acknowledge her mother.

Nancy is pointing at the chair beside Joe. Sarah looks a moment, even half rises out of her seat, as though intending to move, then sits back down, shrugging. She's fine where she is. *Chat you after*, she mouths. Then she nods at Joe, whom she hasn't seen since Christmas, whom she used to see almost every day. He nods back distractedly, turns around.

Her heart is at its wonky hammering again. It started up when she was in her car, eating a sandwich she'd bought from the Spar for lunch after coffee with Ursula so she wouldn't have to go home, and it hasn't stopped since. It's been coming or going for the past month or so. Thump, thump, long pause, *thwack*. Like it's trying to escape her ribcage. It comes on every now and then, seemingly out of the blue, usually taking hours before it goes back to normal. Thump, thump, pause, *thwack*. An ectopic heartbeat, the doctor had called it. Perfectly harmless, he had said, though it can be a symptom of anxiety. He'd suggested a mild sedative but she'd said no, thanks. She didn't need it. She was just glad there wasn't anything seriously wrong with her.

The door at the back of the room suddenly scrapes open noisily before slamming shut. But turning around, she sees it's just a couple of men. She's not sure if she would recognise Jane Hart anyway, if she did walk through that door. She could probably count on one hand the number of times she's set eyes on her since she and Neil married, the year Sarah finished school. Once in the newsagent. A couple of times at Mass, back when Nancy could still make Sarah go. Once, she saw her at the bus stop, clearly drunk and arguing with someone. Then there was the time Sarah had shown up for a shift in the pub to find her laughing horribly at Neil as he was trying to coax her back upstairs. 'You're such a big man,' she was saying to him. Always on her wrist a thick silver bracelet in the shape of a snake, which people said was a gift from a man she'd had an affair with. It had clanked noisily on the bottles that time she came down behind the bar when Sarah was on her own there, closing up, and helped herself to a bottle of gin without saying a word, without even looking at her. A petite woman with a delicate face, blonde hair hanging thinly. Anger coming from her like a smell.

Not that there's any reason to fear Jane Hart showing up. It can't mean anything, what Ursula said about her being out their road, she knows that much. Otherwise Neil would have told her. It's just a coincidence, and not even a big one. At the same time, she wishes she could talk to Neil about it. She had tried calling him, even though she knew he'd be busy preparing for this and she ought to wait until it's over. So it hadn't come as a surprise when he hadn't answered, though she had been disappointed, even after the text that came minutes later – *Call you soon xx*. Now, she reminds herself how important this thing is to him. She reminds herself of her own feelings about the development too, the genuine value to the town she sees in it. She wouldn't be able to speak in favour of it if she didn't think it was a good idea. But if it wasn't a good development, Neil wouldn't be Neil. He would be someone else, someone she would never fall in love with.

The door bangs shut again and this time it is Neil in the doorway, beside him Paul Walsh, the town's local councillor. It's the first time she's set eyes on Neil down home since their thing started, and the slight catching of her breath happens, as it always does when she sees him anew, even with her heart now doing its wonky beat. The instant wish to have some part of her body touching some part of his. Every time, she gets this feeling. He could be folding a napkin. He could be taking off his glasses and putting them back in their case. He could, apparently, be standing in a doorway, taking in the room, looking tired and ill at ease, despite the pressed suit and clean-shaven face. When Walsh leans towards him, whispers something into Neil's ear, it comes to her that the last time her mouth had been that close to that ear, she'd traced its outline with her tongue and he'd taken her hand and pressed it into his crotch, held it there as he hardened against her.

Now, as he passes he shows no sign of noticing her. But, then, he shows no sign of noticing anyone, his jaw tightly set, as though he's clenching his teeth, a sheen off his forehead, his shoulders all tight-looking under his blazer. Absently, he pushes his hair back from his face as, at the table, he opens his briefcase and his hands fumble connecting his laptop to a cable. It seems to take ages for the image to appear on the screen behind him of a pleasant square in front of the entrance to a shopping centre, a woman pushing a pram across the pedestrian crossing, a row of young trees.

Smile, she wants to say. *My love*, she thinks, a wave of tenderness for him falling over her. *Relax. You've nothing to worry about.*

Paul Walsh stands then, taps his microphone and clears his throat, smiling around the room, and she feels a swell of dislike towards the man. Nancy was right. There really is something wheedling about him, as he welcomes everyone and says that it stands to the community spirit of Crookedwood that there's such a good turnout.

'As most of you probably know,' he adds, 'I happen to be personally in favour of Neil Hart's proposed development. I think it will only be a good thing for our little town. But as its only local councillor, it's highly important to me that everyone here gets their say, and that we have a fair and open discussion. Now, I think it safe to assume that everyone here is acquainted with this man. If he hasn't served you a drink at some point, you'll have seen him score a winning point back in his youth.'

When Neil stands then and looks out at the crowd, there's wariness in his expression and when he starts to speak, his voice is hoarse and he interrupts himself to cough. A couple of sentences in, he stops midway and looks around him, as though he can't remember what he has just said, let alone what he meant to say next. But when he does speak again, his voice is clearer, more assured. It's like watching him turn back into himself. He gets to his last slide without stumbling over his words once.

'So, that's my pitch,' he says. He's not looking at his notes now, but out into the crowd. 'I think I've knocked on every one of your doors at this stage, so it's not like any of what I've said is news to anyone. I would just ask you to remember this is my little corner of the world too. If there was the slightest doubt in my mind that this development was anything but a good thing for Crookedwood, I wouldn't be standing here in front of you all. Thank you.'

The applause is loud as he sits down, even if not everyone joins in. Sarah knows her cue – raise her hand and wait for Walsh to ask her to speak. Nancy has hers raised too, as have a few others.

'Rory Fox,' says Walsh, directing the young man with the mike to the farmer whose land lies adjacent to Nancy's farm, a well-liked and respected member of the community. When he speaks plainly of his own support for the plan, there is the feeling of people listening, even a scatter of applause when he sits down, hands over the mike.

'Thanks, Rory. The young lady at the back there.' He's looking at Sarah. 'You had your hand up.'

Sarah is surprised, just as she was surprised that he went to Rory Fox first. Nancy is sitting closer to the top of the room, and her hand had shot up before anyone else's. But she stands as the young man walks towards her and passes her the mike, which she takes in her hand, looking around at everyone as the room fills with the ragged sound of breath.

'Thanks,' she starts, fixing her eyes on the councillor. People are turning in their seats to take in who's speaking. She can feel Nancy and Joe stare, even though she doesn't dare look their way.

Just sound natural, Neil had said. Say what you actually believe to be true. It had seemed like such a small favour when he'd said that. It had seemed almost nothing.

It *was* almost nothing.

Is almost nothing.

She looks around at the crowd. Tries smiling but it feels false. She clears her throat. 'Just wanted to give my tuppence-worth, even though technically I don't live here any more.' Her heart is going nuts but her voice comes out calm enough. If she could just put her hand on her chest, press against her ribcage, push it back into place. 'I've heard the arguments opposing this development.' She looks at Nancy. 'And I have nothing but respect for where they come from. But what strikes me about this plan is how considered it is. The town needs a supermarket. A café would be nice. There's a playground, the houses are planned at a good standard. Some of them will be social housing. The only thing in front of us is this specific plan, and I think it's a good one.'

She hands back the mike, sits down. As discreetly as she can, she presses her chest.

'Nancy Flynn,' says Walsh then. 'I know you have strong views on the matter.'

Nancy stands. 'Well,' she begins. She looks back at Sarah, as though still trying to process what just happened. Then she turns back to the councillor. 'I have here a petition with the signatures of almost three hundred people—'

'I tell you one thing,' Walsh cuts in, 'I'd not like to be at the Flynns' dinner table this evening.'

People laugh, some loudly, others with unease.

'Sorry, Nancy,' he says, but he's still smiling around at his own joke. 'Go on. We're all ears.'

Nancy waits for the laughter to die down. 'Well, I agree,' she says then. 'I agree that on its own there is nothing objectionable about the plan. The problem,' she adds, raising her voice to an even higher pitch, 'is that that is *not* what we're looking at here. What we're looking at is the beginning of the end for our town as we know it. Once this gets the pass, what is coming next? It won't be long before we've a ring of ugly developments around the town.'

'Well, now, Nancy, I think you'll find there are guidelines against major retail developments by a motorway.'

'Those guidelines,' Nancy is almost shouting now, 'are not

worth the paper they're written on. Not in this country. We can't gamble the future welfare of our town on them.'

'Hear, hear,' says Joe, heavily.

'Except that they *are* worth the paper they're written on.' It's Pat Doyle, the dairy farmer soon to buy the Flynns' farmland off Nancy. 'Sorry now, Nancy, I've nothing but respect for you but there's no good reason not to think this development is just a once-off. This idea that it's the beginning of the end for Crookedwood sounds far-fetched to me, I'll be honest with you.'

'Rubbish,' shouts a man from somewhere at the back. 'Nancy Flynn was right about that housing development out the Galway road, wasn't she? Built on a fucking swamp. We should have listened to her better then. All this talk' – he gestures at the PowerPoint – 'is nothing but shiny bullshit if you ask me.'

There are a few sniggers at this description. A young man looks around at a friend, grins.

'You may laugh now but you won't be laughing when you're stuck in traffic on the school run this time next year, or you have to close up your business in five years' time. I'll tell you that much.'

He sits down heavily, gruffly waves off the guy with the mike, who has only just reached him.

'I'll ask people to raise their hand first,' says the councillor, 'before speaking.' Then he nods at another hand. It's the principal of the town's primary school. But Nancy stands again.

'Excuse me,' she says. 'I hadn't finished,' and she nods at the guy with the microphone. She has taken courage, Sarah can see, from what's been said.

Everyone watches the young guy walk back to Nancy's row, the microphone being passed along.

'The point I was trying to make earlier,' she says, not even bothering with it, 'before I was interrupted, is that there is significant opposition to this planned development. And that doesn't come from nowhere. Three hundred signatures is ten per cent of the town's population.'

A young girl sitting in front of Sarah puts her hands over her ears, looks up at her mother, who smiles down at her, puts a finger on her lip.

'Ssh,' says the little girl. 'Ssh.'

Again, everyone laughs. Watching Nancy look around defensively, not understanding what's happened, Sarah feels a swell of protectiveness towards her.

'We don't trust this plan,' continues Nancy. 'That is what I'm saying to you. And so far no one has said anything to reassure me anyways.' She glares at Walsh, and Sarah can see that she's really angry now. 'Surely as local councillor,' she says, 'it's your job to present both sides of the argument.'

'Well,' he says.

'Or have you found yourself good reason not to?'

Walsh's expression quickly becomes serious. 'I hope you're not suggesting anything there, Nancy,' he says.

'Well,' says Nancy, 'if it walks like a duck ...'

'My job is to be honest with the people of this town. To support what I think is in its best interests.'

'Like the housing development on a fecking bogland,' she snaps, 'that a friend of yours happens to be responsible for.'

'I'll thank you not to make such serious and unfounded allegations,' he says, his voice hitting a different note. 'I haven't claimed you have a personal stake in this, even though some might argue otherwise.'

The cryptic comment seems to throw Nancy, and she sits back down. Sarah can see her face as she turns to Joe – she looks baffled. Sarah herself can't think what he might possibly have meant by the comment. What personal stake could Nancy conceivably have in opposing Neil's development? It makes no sense. All she can think of is that the politician was flustered after what Nancy had said about him, that he just wanted to throw something back at her, and that was the first thing his mind grabbed hold of.

Now he gestures towards the school principal. 'James,' he says, 'you wanted to say something.' The principal stands, and expresses his support for the plan, before asking about planned transport links from the new development to the town centre, a question Neil answers eagerly. There is one more comment of support before Walsh thanks people for coming, reminds them that Neil will be there for the rest of the afternoon to answer any questions people may have and of the deadline for challenges to the application.

Outside, Sarah waits in the biting wind.

'Mam,' she says, when she spots her mother and Joe.

Nancy's face, when she looks back at her, then walks right up to her. People, Sarah can see, are watching, while pretending they haven't noticed anything.

'What in the name of God was that about, would you mind telling me?'

'Calm down, Mam,' she whispers. She looks to Joe for help but he doesn't say anything. 'People can hear you,' she adds.

'Why did you do that?' asks Nancy.

'I think it's a good development. It's like what I said. Where you're coming from is good but your concerns have no basis.' It's something that this is her sincere view. That at least she doesn't have to lie. But, then, she doesn't think she'd be able to lie like that to her mother.

If Nancy hears the sincerity in her voice, though, it doesn't seem to make any difference. She turns away from Sarah without answering her, walks towards the car park, a grimness about Joe as he follows her.

Someone touches Sarah's arm and she jumps.

Ursula, grinning at her again. 'I'd say that was awkward,' she says.

Sarah nods. She still has the feeling that other people milling around are paying attention. That they are listening.

'No, good for you,' says Ursula, emphatically. 'Your mother has to let you live your own life, sooner or later.'

4

The next morning, Sarah steps out the front door of the cottage. Under a low cloud dissolving into a thin and steady rain, she makes her way, this time by road, back to the woods.

On her way, she texts Neil: *Any chance you can meet me in the woods by our place? I'll be there in about twenty minutes. x*

Doing so feels like breaking an unspoken rule. She certainly had no intention of trying to meet up with him down home. But after the open house, he hadn't been able to speak to her on the phone, Saturday always being a busy night for the pub. And Nancy hasn't spoken to her since. Not a single word, not even over dinner, not even this morning when Sarah said she was walking into town and did she want anything.

Under the canopy of trees, she pauses until her eyes adjust to the deeper darkness, then walks on, as briskly as she can manage without tripping on the woodland floor, its roots hidden by the bracken. She's trying her best to ignore that weird thing trees do – making you feel like they're watching just because you're the one moving while they stand still and quiet. Assuming Neil arrives when she asked him to, she has a good ten minutes or so to herself, which is more than enough time to get down to the hollow, where the guy and his dog were, and look around it in broad daylight.

When she comes upon the small clearing where the canopy of branches thins out enough for raindrops to plunk through, it feels for a moment like she's accidentally walked into her past and she has to stop, as though an invisible wall is preventing her from walking any closer to the circle of rocks that's still in its centre, even a blackened branch inside it. Which surely, she thinks, as she stares, can't be from when they used to meet up here – the girls from her class and towards the end the guys – almost ten years ago now. Others like them must have started coming since then, lighting their own fires, getting away from their own parents, drinking their own cheap cider. Losing their own virginity. But when the feeling of the invisible wall recedes enough that she can go up to it, ease the branch over with her foot, woodlice wriggling away and part of it, sodden, breaking off, she's sees that it has lain there for a very long time. For all she knows, it's been there since the last night they met up in this place, the summer before she did the Leaving Certificate.

She's still standing there when a rustle of footsteps starts up from the road side of the woods. Almost as soon as it's started, it stops, replaced by the distinct sense that she's being watched, not the feeling of the trees this time, but of another person. She can feel it as sharply as her nails digging into her palms, or the wonky hammering of her heart, which has started up again. Beat, beat. Pause. *Thwack*. Beat, beat. Pause. *Thwack*.

Then Neil appears in the clearing, in his hoody and jeans, shadow of stubble, eyes glassy with tiredness. Despite how awful he looks, she is struck by his loveliness, even as the anger that's been there since the open house flares up, the first time she's ever felt anything negative towards him.

It's true that love makes a fool of you, she thinks, as he walks over to her. It makes you into a pure fucking eejit.

'You look like shit,' she tells him.

'Thanks,' he says glumly.

She smiles despite herself. 'Was it hard to get here?'

'No. Though I'd have thought this was the last place you'd want to come, after the other night.'

'No one will see us here.'

He doesn't answer her.

'Are you happy with yesterday?'

'Happy enough. You're not, though.' He rubs his hand down his face. Looks at her in that half-reproachful, half-insolent way of his, as though he's admonishing and being admonished at the same time. Usually, when he looks at her like that, she wants to kiss him. Usually, she does kiss him.

She exhales sharply. It's annoying, the way he won't acknowledge the issue. 'It felt like Nancy was played somehow. Did you not think that?'

He shifts on his feet, folds his arms. There is a trace of archness in his expression now. 'Nancy's a big girl,' he says.

'I know that.' She frowns at the ground. A tiny sprig of green flashes up at her from the brown fern. 'But in Dublin, when you asked me to come down for this, you made it sound like it was nothing.'

'But sure it was nothing. What are you saying?'

'I didn't know that Nancy had started this campaign.'

'No?'

'No. *You* never mentioned it.'

'I assumed your mother had.'

'I've told you, we hardly speak these days.'

'Still.'

'The way Walsh made that joke. It was unnecessary. And what did he mean about her making it personal?'

'Walsh is a bit of a bollocks.'

'He was doing you a favour.'

'Your mother's respected around here. A lot of people won't have liked him doing that. Look, I couldn't do anything about it. He was facilitating the thing.'

'That's true.'

They regard each other.

'There's another thing,' she says.

'Here we go.'

She hesitates, then just says it. 'Ursula said Jane was out our road the other night. Drunk.'

His face changes then, all trace of amusement wiped away.

'There's nothing to it, is there?'

Neil sighs.

'She does know?'

'She doesn't *know*. She suspects, maybe.'

'That you're having an affair? Or that you're having it with me?'

'Just about the affair, I think. Calm down.'

'You think?'

'She doesn't know it's you. I'm nearly sure she doesn't.'

Until this weekend, Sarah has not once felt bad that Neil is married. She hasn't even felt bad about not feeling bad. She has seen enough of Jane over the years to know that she doesn't care about Neil. The reason it's been so easy to vanish her from the picture is because of how she's behaved towards him. Really, she's taken herself out of the picture. She's earned their indifference.

Now, she watches him closely. He looks so worried.

'Why didn't you tell me? Ursula said she's been acting off the rails lately.'

'Oh, look.' Absently he puts a hand to his head. 'I can't do it any more,' he says frankly. Then he adds, 'But don't you worry about Jane.'

'What do you mean, you can't do it any more?'

'I'm going to end it with her. As soon as the planning permission's through.'

For a second, the way he's looking at her, she thinks he's going to say something else. But then she has the impression he's changed his mind, and that what he does say is different from what he'd originally been about to tell her.

'She's angry with the world,' he says.

'You'd tell me,' she says, 'if she might know something about us.'

'Absolutely.'

She takes in his face with dismay. 'She could know.'

'It's unlikely. But I suppose it's not impossible. All the recent trips to Dublin.'

'Oh, Jesus.'

'Look, don't worry.'

'You have to tell me things,' she says. 'I always thought you did tell me.'

'I don't want to be worrying you.' He runs a hand through his hair, rubs his chin.

'When's the last time you had a decent night's sleep?'

He shakes his head, as though it's not worth answering. When she kisses him then, it starts small, almost chaste. She thinks that's all it'll be. But then it changes.

'I really want you,' he murmurs. And she can see it, the sudden desire that has come over him. And as she sees it in him, she feels it rise in herself. He's the first person she's had a real sex life with. With him, to her amazement and delight, it's always been good and it's always been easy. In the handful of times he's been up to her, it's been pretty much all they've done. The second time he'd been up, they'd stayed in her little flat for an entire day and night, only getting up to shower or walk to the takeaway down the road. Falling into a light sleep or chatting until they started kissing again.

For a long time before him, it had never been good, always painful, sometimes her body tightening so much it hadn't even been possible. Vaginismus, the therapist in the women's clinic called it, when she eventually worked up the courage to tell someone about it. Caused by the body automatically reacting to sex as an attack. The muscles in the vagina contract involuntarily, she'd explained, making penetration painful, in some cases impossible. It can happen for different reasons, sometimes none at all. Often, she said, it's caused by a negative sexual encounter, especially a person's first time. She was going to treat it by inserting these weird tubes of increasing sizes into Sarah's vagina. It wouldn't completely solve the problem, she said, but it would help, and once Sarah met someone she trusted, they could have therapy together. But it would also be important for Sarah to work on herself. Figure out why she had developed this. She'd asked Sarah then about the first time she'd had sex, and she had admitted that it had not been a particularly great experience, though it had been consensual. And the therapist had started talking then about how consent can be complicated, how sometimes we can say one thing but our bodies say another. She had said that sometimes she thought the body to be more intelligent than the mind. Sarah had nodded along, pretending to agree with all of this, but instead of going back, she'd bought herself a vibrator, and within a couple of months, she confirmed the problem was resolved with a couple of one-night stands. And then this had started with Neil, desire arising in her so easily and naturally, like it is now, as though there was never a problem to begin with. In seconds, they're on the ground, the cold seeping into her back at the same time as he is entering her, with a warm shock of pleasure. Soon, they are coming together.

'I love you,' she says. It's the first time either of them has said it.

'I love you too,' he says, barely missing a beat.

They regard each other again. He smiles in the ironic way he smiles sometimes. She doesn't know why she's suddenly standing and pulling her clothes back on like this, as quickly as she can.

'You okay?' he asks.

'I'd better get home before Nancy's back from Mass.'

'Through the field?'

'We don't want to risk anyone seeing us on the road.'

'True. Look, I'll try to get up to you this week,' he says. 'It might be tricky but I'll try.'

'Okay.'

She has just turned away when she trips on a hidden root, her body pulled flat onto the ground.

'Jesus,' he says. 'Are you all right?'

'I'm fine. Just a bruised ego.' She manages a smile.

His smile is strained then.

'You go on,' she says.

Back in the cottage, Sarah makes herself look in the small mirror on the coat stand. Takes in her flushed face, the thin bright red line across her forehead, a dab of mud on her left cheek, her hair clinging sleekly to the sides of her face. She's about to go upstairs, have a long, scrubby shower, when the front door opens and Nancy comes in, a bulging shopping bag in her hand. She takes in the sight of Sarah in astonishment, puts the bag on the floor.

'I thought you were at Mass,' says Sarah.

'What in the name of God happened to you?'

'Nothing.'

'There's mud all over you.'

Sarah looks down at her muddy jeans. 'I just tripped, that's all.' Her voice sounds so guilty.

'You're bleeding,' says Nancy, staring at her forehead.

'It's nothing.'

Her mother's eyes widen. Then she shakes her head, as though trying to shake some sense into what she has just heard. Or the nonsense out.

'What happened?' she asks again.

'Nothing, I told you. I went for a walk and fell.'

She can't bear to return Nancy's gaze any longer.

'Look,' she says quickly, staring at the bag of shopping, 'I'm sorry about yesterday. I wouldn't have said anything if I'd known it would go like that.'

Nancy doesn't answer her.

'You were right about that Walsh guy. He gave me the creeps.'

'Go on and take a shower,' says Nancy, lifting her bag and walking past Sarah into the kitchen, her gaze firmly ahead, lips pursed shut.

From the kitchen come the sounds of cupboard doors banging open and shut.

5

Sarah makes a funnel with her fingers and releases the soil from her other hand, so it filters into the small plastic pot. Then she looks up at the semicircle of students on the other side of the table and makes herself smile. None smiles back, unless you count the smirk on one face. The rest look sullen and bored. Contemptuous, even.

They're in the courtyard of the Garden Project. Five minutes in to a ninety-minute class.

'Sage, rosemary, thyme,' she says, holding up the packets of seeds, almost wincing at the jaunty tone that comes out of her. 'They all grow really well in the Irish climate. And they're perennials. You only have to sow them once and you'll have herbs growing in your own garden for years. Way cheaper than those pots in Tesco.'

'Miss.' The girl is pointing almost guiltily at Sarah's forehead. 'Your cut,' she says.

Sarah puts her hand to where she'd stuck on a plaster earlier, and feels the sticky wetness of blood. She was sure it had stopped bleeding when she'd put on the plaster, but had managed to bang her head getting out of the car after arriving late at the Project. It must have started again then, seeping out slowly until it undid the plaster.

'Shit.' She takes her bag to see if she can find a tissue in there, in doing so knocking the stack of pots to the ground.

'Shit,' she says again, as they all stare. The smirking one folds his arms.

But then the girl hands her a tissue. 'You go on and sort that out,' she says. 'We'll get these.'

In the bathroom, Sarah dabs away the blood with tissue, and blots it until it seems to have stopped. When she gets back to the students, all the pots are back in their stack on the table and they're back in their semicircle.

'Will we do the rest the same way?' asks one, nodding at the pots.

'You can,' she says.

In seconds, they're all diligently making their own funnels, letting soil slip through them. When she shows them how to sprinkle in the seeds, covering them with only a thin layer, they pay attention, doing their own just as she did hers. All except the smirking guy who, it strikes her, looks a couple of years older than the others – more early twenties than late teens. But there's always one, she remembers. Many's the student like him she's encountered before – all pointless attitude. The way to deal with them was always to ignore them. And the rest of them. Right now, a couple are even pretending to be interested in the picture of thyme on the packet. Though she hasn't seen their records, she can be sure that each of the six kids before her comes from the Heights and that each of them faced their own particular obstacles to being there on that chill Sunday morning in March. Yet here they are. Some might even be hoping to go on and do a diploma in horticulture. Maybe eventually a degree.

Somehow, they are managing hopefulness.

'What would you *actually* like to grow?' She sounds a bit like herself again. She *feels* a bit like herself, the events of the morning fading from her mind.

'Cannabis?' says someone. They all laugh.

'Preferably something legal,' she says.

They all laugh again.

'Is there any vegetable your parents like?'

'Do chips count?'

'Potatoes are boring,' says Sarah. 'But we could do purple carrots. And black ones. For the weird factor. Will we try that?'

The rest of the class passes without her thinking once again of the time, except when the older guy pulls his hood over his head and starts walking away. It's only twenty to twelve.

'We're not finished yet,' she calls after him.

He doesn't answer and he doesn't stop walking.

'He mustn't like carrots,' she says to the others.

None of them answers. They're all busy sprinkling their seeds.

'How many seeds in each yoke?' asks one.

'Three or four,' she says, a wave of tenderness passing through her.

In the end, Kathy has to come out of her office to tell her they've run over. It's almost quarter past.

'How'd it go?' asks Kathy, when the students have left.

'Bit of a shaky start. But they're a nice bunch.'

'You did something right to hang on to them for longer than the actual class.' Kathy smiles at her. 'You were always good at it.'

Sarah waves this away.

'I wonder sometimes, though, do you mind your mother offering your services to us?'

'Ah, no,' she says, but finds herself smiling sheepishly before she even has the answer out. A flush of heat in her face. Kathy's never been one to lie to. She's always liked her, an American woman who moved to Crookedwood years before, after marrying a local fella. She set up the Garden Project herself and has been running it ever since.

'Just tell her no,' says Kathy. 'We appreciate it but you shouldn't feel obliged. I'd say you need your rest outside the restaurant.'

'Ah.'

'How's it going there anyway?'

'Good.'

'They're not working you too hard?'

'They're not working me too hard.'

'Well, when I was talking to you at Christmas, I could see how much you love it.'

'I do love it,' she replies honestly.

'Good. And you're going to stick at it.'

'That's the plan,' says Sarah.

'How's your mother?'

'Fine.'

'The farm's still to be sold?' she asks, with a subtle, knowing smile.

'Any week now.'

'Great,' she says again. 'I'm glad to hear that.'

'Yeah.'

Kathy cocks her head a little to the side, frowns. 'You look tired. Or something.'

'Do I?'

She'd forgotten about Kathy's tendency to do this – zone in unapologetically any time she picked up the scent of a problem. Instead of pretending she didn't notice anything, like everyone else. It was something about her Sarah used to like and occasionally find irritating.

'Everything's fine,' she says now.

'Well, you know if you ever need an ear ...'

'I do. Know, I mean.'

For a moment then, she feels a longing to tell Kathy everything. About the guy in the woods, and the open house, and Nancy ramping it up with the farm idea again. Even about Neil, and what Ursula had said about Jane. But almost as soon as she feels it, she knows she can't. Everything is so tied up with everything else. She wouldn't be able to tell her one thing without another. And she can't tell anyone about her and Neil, especially anyone down home. Not without asking him first.

'How's the funding application going?' she asks.

Kathy gives her an astute look. But she answers the question. 'Oh, for God's sake,' she says. 'Why they have to put us through this every year I don't know. I think they're secretly trying to give us a nervous breakdown to stop us looking for more money off them. At least I've Lisa to help me now.'

'She's still with you?'

'I made her my assistant last year. Come in and say hello.'

In the office, they find Lisa hunched over a computer screen. She was sixteen years old and the mother of a nine-month-old baby when she first showed up at the Project, already dropped out of school. Yet she had shown up for every one of Sarah's classes and had gone on to do the horticulture diploma, coming top in her class.

'Lisa's been helping me keep this place afloat,' says Kathy.

'No better woman,' says Sarah. 'And the baby? Charlie.'

'Turned three last week.'

'Stop it. I was still thinking of him as a baby.'

Lisa takes her wallet out of her bag, fishes out a photo and proudly holds it up so Sarah can see the grinning boy.

'The little dote,' says Sarah. 'He's gorgeous.'

'Thanks, Miss.'

'Will you stop calling me "Miss"! It makes me feel ancient.'

'Sorry, Miss.'

The three of them laugh. And for the first time since she arrived home this weekend, she can feel it – that the following day, she'll walk from her flat to the restaurant. And, just like that, be back in her world.

'Is that the time?' Lisa's face is all panic. 'Mam's got an appointment with the dentist. She's going to kill me.'

'She's looking after Charlie?'

'I was late yesterday as well. She nearly went through me.'

'I can give you a lift if that's any good,' says Sarah. 'Are you still in the Heights?'

'Still there, yeah. Are you sure?'

'Sure, it's no hassle.'

'You're a lifesaver, Miss.'

They're crossing the car park when Sarah notices the person hunched down at the passenger door of her car. She's immediately sure it's the guy from her class – the one who kept smirking and left early. But no sooner has she clocked him than he's running towards the low wall that separates the car park from the road, and is over it in a deft move, disappearing from view.

She looks at Lisa. 'Who the hell was that?'

'Who was who?'

'Don't tell me you didn't see him. There was a guy right at my car. He literally just ran across the car park and jumped over the wall.'

Lisa stares at the wall.

'He was in my class earlier, I'm sure it's the same guy. You must have seen him.'

Lisa looks puzzled. 'I didn't see him, Miss,' she says. 'I didn't see anyone.'

6

Sarah has never been in Ursula's house before, even though it's only a half-hour walk from the cottage. It's almost as large as the site on which it is built, what Nancy would dismissively refer to as a 'jutty house'. Only a couple of years old, it sticks up incongruously out of the landscape, dwarfing the house next door, where Ursula's parents live, which had always seemed so luxurious to Sarah when she was little. God knows how many rooms Ursula's house has. Even the shed has two storeys, looks to be bigger than Nancy's cottage. All grey and new-looking, an unfinished feeling to the rest of the site too, no gate between the two large pillars, the garden, as far as Sarah can make out in the dark, just rock and soil.

Ursula answers the door with a glass of white wine in her hand, which she promptly hands to Sarah. 'I thought you could use this,' she says.

Sarah takes the drink and follows Ursula into the wide hallway. 'Thanks,' she says. 'It's some place you have here.'

'Still a work in progress. I want to finish it but Paul says we should buy a place in Spain now. Finish the house the following year.' Ursula turns to her. 'Come here to me,' she says, and she wraps her arms around Sarah, squeezes her so tightly she has to hold her arm out stiffly to stop the wine jerking out of the glass. She always hugged too tightly, she remembers. As though unaware of her own strength.

'I'm grand,' says Sarah.

'You're not grand.'

There's nothing for it but to wait until Ursula has decided the hug is over, which she finally does, releasing Sarah and fixing her with an I'm-concerned-about-you gaze. She must have sounded completely unhinged when she phoned Ursula after the Garden Project to say that maybe it would be a good idea to talk to Paul after all.

'It was probably nothing,' she says now. 'I just thought, before I go back tomorrow—'

'You're worried about your mother.'

'Well.' The truth is, it hasn't occurred to her to be worried about Nancy.

'Some fucking weirdo in your woods and then he shows up at the Garden Project.' Ursula looks disgusted. 'I'd be freaking out if I were you.'

'I'm not even sure it was the same person,' she says, following

Ursula into a huge living room, where Paul is sitting on a vast couch, watching a football match, beer in hand.

'There he is,' says Ursula. 'Like something out of a Diet Coke ad, isn't he?'

Paul stands. 'You're hilarious,' he says.

Ursula rolls her eyes at Sarah. 'You two have met.'

'We have indeed.' He's come over to her and as they shake hands, the same instinctive feeling towards him comes over her as she had when they'd met at Christmas, even as she's feeling bad for him after Ursula's comment. There's something insincere about him. A veneer of fake friendliness. She has to remind herself that he's helping her. That she ought to be feeling grateful.

'Sorry for landing on you like this,' she says.

'No biggie,' he says. 'A friend of Ursula's is a friend of mine.'

Ursula rolls her eyes again. 'Give us your coat,' she says. 'And plonk yourself down there.'

She does as she's told, perching at the far end of the couch from Paul.

'How come you ended up being posted down here?' she asks, just to make conversation.

'Drugs scene,' he says seriously.

'Really?'

'I used to be based in north Dublin. Came across a lot of drug cases. I suppose they must have thought my expertise would come in handy down these parts.'

'Is the drugs situation that bad here, then?'

'Heroin's nearly as bad as it is in Dublin.'

'I'd no idea.'

'You need someone from Dublin to help you sort it out.'

'Very funny,' says Sarah.

'Would you listen to him?' says Ursula. 'You'd swear he came from *The Wire*.' She takes the remote control, mutes the television.

'So,' says Paul. 'I hear you were chased up a field by a strange man.'

'I suppose you could put it like that.'

'Great to be in demand.'

'Exactly.'

'This is serious, Paul,' says Ursula. 'She's been scared out of her mind.'

'Sorry, sorry.'

'For God's sake.'

'In fairness, it does sound a bit ridiculous,' says Sarah, 'when you put it like that.'

'What happened, anyway?' he asks. 'You left your house.'

'I left the house to take a walk. You know, before it got dark.' For the third time, she recounts what happened.

'Isn't it weird?' says Ursula to Paul.

Paul frowns. 'No one else down there? Just this guy, like?'

'Just him, I think.'

They're both looking at her closely.

'I'm probably making a mountain out of a molehill.'

'Not at all.' He takes a sip of his beer and she realises with a small surprise that he's nervous. It's almost as though he's trying to guess what he should say next. He flashes a glance at Ursula, who glares at him.

'You know that stuff's carcinogenic?' he says. 'We always wear masks going over it in Wicklow.'

'What are you on about?' says Ursula, her voice all astonishment.

'The bracken,' he says. 'It's grand when it's dead. But new growth starts up this time of year.' His face is growing red as he speaks.

Ursula is still staring at him. 'The fucking bracken,' she says, and looks at Sarah. 'For the second time, I'd like to apologise on behalf of my fiancé.'

'Would you stop,' says Sarah. 'I never knew that about the bracken. All the times we hung out down there.'

Ursula's expression tightens, as though Sarah's comment is inappropriate, even insensitive.

'And you the culchie,' says Paul. 'You should be telling me stuff like that.'

'Oh, don't be such an idiot, Paul.'

Sarah looks at her glass, as though its cut fascinates her. She tries to think of something to say.

'Drink up,' says Ursula to her. 'You're making me look bad.'

Sarah takes a swig.

'Good girl.'

'So,' says Sarah, 'I'm guessing there haven't been any reports of, you know—'

'People being murdered in their beds,' finishes Ursula.

'That kind of thing.'

'Eh, no,' he says. 'You'd probably have seen something in the paper if there was.'

'Thought as much.'

'Have you been down there since?' he says.

She doesn't answer straight away, even as she knows this small hesitation won't go unnoticed. They are both watching her in that close way again.

'I did go down there this morning, actually. Just for a quick look.'

'Well?'

'I didn't see anything. I mean, I didn't expect to see anything, obviously.'

'No,' he says. He taps his fingers on the arm of the couch.

'For God's sake, Paul,' says Ursula. 'What do you *think*?'

'What do I think?'

Ursula makes an exasperated sound – half snort, half sigh.

'I actually went down myself yesterday,' he says, 'after Ursula mentioned it to me. I hope you don't mind.'

'Of course not.'

'Did you?' says Ursula. 'Well, that's something.'

'The sports shop was broken into last week, a load of jerseys and football boots nicked. I thought it might have something to do with that. But there was no sign of anything down there. Then again, if they were stashing the gear there, they'd have moved it by now.'

'Now,' says Ursula. She looks at Sarah, hopeful. 'I wonder was that it?'

'It would make sense.'

'The dog. Chasing you off so you don't see anything.'

'And then moving the stuff in case I reported him.'

'He probably moved it that night. I bet he was raging.'

Sarah nods slowly.

'But then,' says Ursula, 'why would he bother showing up at that garden place?' As she speaks, she takes Sarah's glass, goes out, returning with the two glasses refilled.

'Well,' says Sarah, 'I didn't actually see him in the woods, so. It might not have been him. Going on Paul's theory about the sports shop, I actually wonder now if that guy *did* have anything to do with it.'

'Just some scumbag from the Heights,' says Ursula.

'Or it could have been fly-tipping,' says Paul.

'Fly-tipping?'

'It's a massive problem around here. Did you not know that? People don't give a shit. Leave their crap anywhere. It's you rednecks. Pure animals, like.'

'Ha.'

'Only kidding you.'

'You don't think it was dealing?' Ursula asks him.

'I wouldn't rule it out.' He turns to Sarah. 'But if it was, it's nothing to do with you. You know?'

'I know.'

'I hear your mother's selling the place,' he says. 'Moving into town.'

'Best thing for her,' says Ursula. 'Your mother, I mean.'

'It is,' says Paul.

'Once that happens, it won't be your problem if something dodgy went on,' says Ursula.

They're handling her so carefully, like she's a child.

'No,' she admits.

'No one's going to go near Nancy,' he adds. 'If I were you, I'd just give this place a wide berth until the sale is through.'

'Still.' She pauses. They're both looking at her, patiently waiting for her to finish whatever she's started to say. Except Sarah doesn't know what she's started to say. 'I suppose,' she tries uncertainly, 'it would feel better to hand it over to someone else as a ... you know ... a clean slate.'

That is not the thing at all. She's not even sure it makes sense. From their expressions, she guesses it doesn't.

She laughs. 'What am I trying to say?' She tries to put her

finger on it. 'If I could understand it,' she says. That's closer to the mark, coming with a ring of truth that surprises her. 'But I think I do understand it now. Anyway, I feel better after telling you. I think I was getting a bit paranoid. Putting two and two together and ending up with ten.'

'Unless, of course, you weren't.' Ursula grins into her glass before draining it.

'What do you mean by that?' asks Sarah.

'Well, maybe there is some crazy bastard out to get you.'

Paul stares at Ursula. He looks shocked. But Sarah's glad she's making light of it now. It makes her feel less embarrassed.

'I was actually feeling better before you said that,' she says drily.

Ursula laughs gleefully. 'Right,' she says. 'We'd better get going or we'll miss the team arriving.'

Sarah looks at her. 'Are you talking to me?'

'I'm hardly talking to him. I've said it to the others, Geraldine and Marie. They can't wait to see you.'

'But I can't go out tonight. I'm on in the restaurant tomorrow. Remember, I said.'

Ursula stares at her, as though not understanding. Then her expression changes to disappointment. 'Oh. Sorry. I just thought when you called back ...'

'Sorry. I just couldn't risk it.'

'No, you're fine. My fault.'

'Oh, I suppose I could go for one. But look at the state of me.'

Ursula's face lights up. 'Stick a bit of my make-up on. And I have a sparkly halterneck that would look completely sexy on you.'

7

In the hotel, the others are already there, their faces and names as familiar to Sarah as her own but, besides that, strangers to her. They've had at least a couple of rounds, if the sharp laughter and glasses on the table are anything to go by. She says hello, then goes to the bar to get in another.

There, to her surprise, she finds Joe, sitting on a stool on his own. She comes up beside him, nudges his arm.

'How come you're not in Hart's?' she says.

He looks around in surprise and her heart sinks when she takes in how bleary his eyes are.

'Sarah Flynn,' he says. But as quickly as his face lights up, it darkens again.

'Oh for God's sake,' she says. 'You're not annoyed with me as well.'

His mouth tightens into a thin line. 'I don't drink there any more.'

'Because of this planning application?'

'What?' Then he nods.

'Right. Well, besides all that, how are you?'

'The same. Why wouldn't I be?'

As long as she has known him, which is as long as she's known anyone, he's been like this – prickly and over-sensitive, liable to take things the wrong way or to see a slight where there is none. She has always put it down to his living alone all that time on his farm. The drinking and the isolation. Especially when in Joe's case, at least as far as she knows, there's no reason to think things may change. But now, standing at the bar beside him, Sarah has the uncharitable thought that maybe this is just what Joe is like anyway. Maybe if he was in a happy relationship and didn't have a drinking problem and all was good in his life he would still be a cranky old bastard.

'How's the farm going?' she asks him.

'I don't know why I bother with the damn thing.' He looks at her. 'You're out for a night on the tiles,' he says.

'No, I'm not. I got dragged out. I'm going to have one drink and then I'm making my excuses. I'm on in the restaurant tomorrow.'

'I saw that article in the *Chronicle*. I have it stuck on the wall.'

'You don't.'

'Very proud of you.' He takes a sip of his pint.

'Ah, Joe.' She puts a hand on his arm. 'I haven't been in to you in ages,' she says.

'Sure, what would you be calling in to me for?' he says, all annoyance again.

'Because I like you,' she says to him. 'Because you're my uncle. Jesus Christ.'

She was fifteen when she came upon the stash of magazines under his bed, after Nancy had dragged her up there to help clean his house on a rare occasion he was away. Probably on a bender. It was when he'd had that kind of breakdown you weren't allowed to call a breakdown. She'd sat there on his floor, blushing as she leafed through them, staring in amazement at the graphic images of naked men. She'd never seen anything like it and, at first, she couldn't comprehend how they'd got to be under Joe's bed. She even wondered how he hadn't noticed them, before the penny dropped that he must have bought them himself. That they belonged to him. As soon as she realised, she quickly pushed them back under the bed. Then she took off the clean sheets she'd just put on and returned the dirty ones, refolded the clean ones and returned them to the hot press. Through the shock, the understanding came to her – that it would be unbearable for him to know she'd found them. That he could never know.

'It's a pity you didn't think of that yesterday,' he says now.

She sighs. 'It's a good development, Joe. With a Lidl. Crookedwood could do with a bloody Lidl.'

'If that's all it was, I would agree with you.'

'But it is all it is. Honestly, you and Nancy are a pair of conspiracy theorists in your old age.'

He doesn't answer this.

'It's not like Neil Hart is some evil developer,' she adds.

'Neil Hart's not the worst,' he concedes grudgingly.

'So why are you expecting the worst?'

'Because what follows doesn't have to come from him. Why did you have to say anything? That's what I'd like to know.'

'Well,' she says, 'it's my town too, you know.'

'I don't know that I do know that.'

She sighs again.

'You're hardly thinking of moving home?' he asks her.

'No. Why?'

'Just with your mother's idea, you know, of you keeping on the farm together, going organic, all that.'

'No,' she says again.

He looks at her sharply. 'She doesn't want to let go of the place because then it'll seem like there was never a point to any of it. All your father's hard work. All those years.'

'I know.'

'I know you know. Nothing but a pipe dream,' he adds.

'I'm glad you say that.'

'But the last thing you need to be doing is getting involved in local affairs. Even if you're disagreeing with her, she'll think you're putting down roots here.'

'All I said was that it sounds like a good thing for the town. Which it does. What difference did it make anyway?'

But he's looking into his drink, his face closed to her again.

When she gets back to the others, someone has already gotten another round in – now bright pink cocktails that they're all drinking through straws.

'At last,' says Ursula, as Sarah puts the tray of pints on the table. She hands Sarah the only cocktail with an umbrella in it. 'You get the special one. Because you're special.' She's grinning, a sheen of bitchiness coming from her, and something about her feels all turned up, like the way she was outside the garda station. The way she could sometimes be at school. Her eyes are burning.

'Go on,' she says now to Sarah. 'Drink up.'

Sarah takes a sip of the cocktail, which is horribly sweet with a nasty tinge of cheap vodka. As she does, music starts up – horrible shite music coming out of speakers – so that now everyone has to yell across the table at each other in order to be heard. They throw back their drinks all the faster for this, every now and then erupting into laughter. When Sarah tries to make her excuses, she is literally held onto by Geraldine Claffey, who insists that she at least let her get one round in.

'What was the name of that nun in school who hated you?' Ursula shouts over at Sarah.

'Camillus,' says Sarah.

'Sister Camillus. Remember she went at you with a yard brush that time?' She does Camillus's high-pitched voice. '"Drone bees should know their place."'

'What a fucking bitch,' says Marie Donlon.

'Do you remember the time she found a condom in Laura Feeney's homework notebook?'

Shrieks of laughter.

'"I will not stand for this,"' says Ursula. 'Do you remember she just kept repeating that? Like she was malfunctioning. "I will not stand for this."'

They are all laughing helplessly at the memory.

'What about that time Nancy found a pregnancy test in your bedroom?' says Ursula to Sarah.

'Jesus,' says Sarah. 'I'd forgotten about that.'

'*Were* you pregnant?' asks someone.

'No. But my period stopped for months. For no reason. I've never been so scared in my life.'

'But had you slept with someone?'

'Remember she shagged David Fitzpatrick down in the woods that time?' says Ursula.

'Was he your first?' asks Geraldine.

'For my sins.'

'That's right,' says Marie.

'And then he dumped you,' cackles Ursula. 'And he went around telling everyone it was like having sex with a plank of wood.'

'And we all called you a slut afterwards,' says Geraldine. 'Weren't we awful when you think about it?'

'The only time that ever happened to me,' says Marie, 'was after my granny died.'

'What – you slept with David Fitzpatrick?'

'No, smart-arse. I mean my period stopped like that.'

'Nancy completely freaked,' says Ursula. 'Didn't she?'

'Her hands were literally shaking when she was holding out the test. I can see it like it happened yesterday. She was just dangling it there, like it was something she'd picked up off the street.'

'Christ,' says Geraldine.

'Well,' says Ursula, 'you can't really blame Nancy in a way. You always were a dark horse.'

'What do you mean by that?' asks Sarah.

Ursula smiles at her.

'Is she still like that?' says Geraldine. 'Like, funny about sex?'

'Dunno. I've managed to avoid the subject with her since then.'

'What if a sex scene comes on the telly?'

Sarah mimics her mother grabbing the remote, blindly pressing buttons. The others roar with laughter. Another round of the awful cocktails arrives, just as the football team shows up with their cup to cheers and applause. The night continues long past that but when Sarah wakes the next morning to the evaporating tail-end of a nightmare, something to do with water, all she can bring back of the rest of the night is flashes. More rounds of the awful sweet cocktails. Talking to Joe again, though she has no idea what she said to him. People staring at her. Ursula holding her hair back as she gets sick into a toilet. A security guy leading her to the exit. She cannot remember how she got home. Which means she probably walked, drunk out of her mind, along that skinny twisty road.

This hangover is like no other she has had before. For a long while, all she can do is lie there, her mouth parched, unable to move her head in case her headache worsens. She can barely bring herself to reach for her phone to check the time. When she does and sees it's seven in the morning, she feels a mild panic. The meeting with the solicitor is at ten and she's on in the restaurant at two. If she doesn't get back to sleep now, that leaves very little time to nap before she starts work.

She closes her eyes, is miraculously drifting away when the quiet is punctured by Nancy shrieking her name.

'Sarah! Sarah!'

It's coming from outside the front of the house, which makes no sense. But when Sarah manages to sit up and make it to the window, she sees Nancy is indeed standing there, out on the road, her face all fury as she stares up at her.

She opens it. 'Mam? What's wrong?'

'What's wrong?' she splutters up at her. 'You come down here right now and tell me what's wrong.'

Outside, shivering in her dressing-gown, Sarah fights an urge to get into her car and drive away, as she walks down the path and out onto the road, where Nancy is still standing. She's pointing at the wall, in a way that brings back that time with the pregnancy test.

'What is it?'

'You tell me,' says Nancy, thrusting her finger at the wall. 'You tell me what it is.'

Sarah looks at the wall, where a single word has been scrawled in bright red paint.

Slut.

8

Olive bustles them into a small, dismal room at the back of Cormac Hart's office, its only furniture a battered table and three plastic chairs. Light from a fluorescent strip on the ceiling, complete with dead flies, reflects dully off pale green walls. Boxes filled sloppily with files are piled up against the wall, an old furniture catalogue lying on top of one. The air smells slightly damp, and there are black mould marks on the edges of the window frame. Condensation on the glass reduces the outside world to a grey blur.

'He'll be in any minute.' She goes out and returns directly with an oil heater, waving off Nancy's offer to help as she deposits it heavily on the floor, plugs it in. 'I'm putting you back here,' she says, 'because the meeting room takes an age to heat up. But the damp is something shocking. He needs to get the walls dry-lined in this place.'

'It's grand,' says Nancy.

'He's a pure skinflint, to be honest with you. Now, will ye have tea or coffee? Probably tea because the coffee is only instant.' She goes out to the hall. 'He got some cheap espresso machine and the thing broke,' she calls back to them.

Sarah stands by the heater and presses her calves against the iron bars. It feels like the cold has gotten into her bones, that she'll never be able to warm up, or get rid of this nausea from breathing in the paint fumes, after two hours spent painting the garden wall. The headache has been banished with paracetamol but she still feels shaky and tired, her mind anxiously flitting from one thought to the next.

'Sit down, will you,' Nancy says, without looking at her, as from the kitchenette come the sounds of Olive filling the kettle, taking down cups. Nancy is sitting primly at the table, her bag neatly under her chair, her stiff skirt and jacket far too formal for the occasion.

'It's just Cormac Hart,' says Sarah. 'A small-town solicitor.'

It's the first time they've spoken to each other since she'd finally managed to cover over the word so that no trace remained. Sarah had gone into the kitchen where Nancy was and told her, voice tight and querulous, that there'd been a lot of very drunk people in the hotel the night before, that one young guy she didn't know had asked her to dance and she had turned him down. All she could think was that he had done it. Nancy had sat there at the table silently taking this in without looking at her.

Now Olive comes back into the room, a piece of unfinished knitting in her hands, complete with needles, a ball of bright yellow yarn, and what looks like a magazine about knitting.

'This is the pattern I was telling you about,' she says to Nancy, taking the seat beside her. 'Are you frozen?' she says to Sarah, looking at her.

'I'm grand,' says Sarah.

'An Easter bunny,' she says to Nancy.

'Isn't that good?' says Nancy.

'For the grandkids, you know.'

'Will you have it done in time?'

'Easily. I get a lot done here, you know. I'm doing little covers for chocolate eggs as well.'

'Very nice,' says Nancy. She looks up at Sarah. 'Will you please sit down,' she says again.

If Olive notices the tension between them, she says nothing.

'What's the difference if I'm sitting or standing?'

'It's bad manners,' says Nancy.

'It isn't,' says Sarah, but she takes the seat beside her mother, just as the front door opens and snaps shut. Sharp footsteps, coming towards them, then another door opening and closing. Silence.

'He has ye forgot,' says Olive. 'I'll go and get him.'

But before she even stands, the footsteps start up again and the door opens. And he is standing right there in the doorway: Cormac Hart, older brother of Neil, in a smart suit, eyes just like his brother's. 'Ladies,' he says. 'Don't get up. I'm so sorry I'm late.' He shakes hands with Nancy first, then Sarah. Then he turns to Olive. 'Why are we down here?'

'The meeting room, as you well know, is like an ice box.' Olive stands, making no attempt to hide or explain the yarn and needles she is holding.

'Well,' he says, and for a moment, despite everything, Sarah has to stifle the urge to laugh, 'have you offered Nancy and Sarah tea or coffee?'

'I offered them tea,' says Olive, 'because that coffee is undrinkable. The kettle takes for ever, as you well know. Will you have one yourself?'

'If it's not too much trouble.'

She bustles out of the room.

Cormac smiles tightly at Sarah and her mother. 'Would you believe I was here earlier?' he says, taking a seat opposite them. 'Hadn't I left your file at home? I'd brought it home to give it a final run-through.'

'Aren't you very good,' says Nancy.

He waves this away, takes some papers out of his briefcase.

'God, it's absolutely freezing in here,' he says. 'You might put the heating on, Olive,' he calls.

'It's been on this past fifteen minutes!' Olive shouts back.

'Nice fresh day,' says Nancy.

'Lovely,' he says. 'Mind you, it could be a blizzard this afternoon, the way the weather is going.'

'You said it,' says Nancy.

'Are you home for long?' The question, which is clearly directed at Sarah, throws her for a second.

'I got down Friday. Heading back up straight after this.' She closes her eyes briefly. Even speaking makes the nausea worse.

'A very dutiful daughter you have there, Nancy. Coming down to help you with this.'

'Oh,' says Nancy. 'That's it.'

'Fortunately, there's very little help you'll be needing. All looks in hand.'

Nancy nods at him tersely.

He opens the file, leafs through a few pages. 'You got a good price,' he says, to Nancy.

'Do you think so?'

'Very good. You wouldn't get better than that.'

'He'd asked me enough times to sell it to him.'

'He'd been renting off you, what? Five years?'

'Four. The plan had been for Sarah to come home and run it with me, after she did her agricultural-science degree. But she's adamant she doesn't want to do that now.'

'Things change,' he says diplomatically.

'I was running it there myself for a while but I couldn't do that for long on my own. He offered to rent it and I thought, Let him have it a few years. Maybe by then ...' she looks at Sarah '... but no.'

'Young people,' he says. 'They get their own ideas of what to do with themselves.'

'Oh, they do. Even after four years of studying agricultural science. Gutting fish in a kitchen makes for a better career, I'm told.'

He laughs awkwardly, glances at Sarah. 'She might be on to something, believe it or not, Nancy,' he says. 'Small farms like yours, well, you know better than myself, I won't call it a fool's errand but you're on a hiding to nothing with them these days.'

Sarah can feel Nancy stiffen beside her. 'Dad,' she says, 'managed to keep it going okay.'

'Oh, of course he did. I had nothing but respect for poor Liam.

No, I only mean to say the small farmer isn't being protected by the government. It's all going the way of big farmers, dairy farmers especially.'

'I know,' says Nancy.

'It isn't the small farmer's fault,' he adds, flustered, 'that it's no longer viable. No, no, I didn't mean anything like that at all.'

'Some farms manage it though, don't they?' says Sarah. 'There's that place outside Dunlone. They make porridge oats and cookies.'

'Places that go organic,' adds Nancy, throwing a grateful glance at Sarah. 'There's a growing market there.'

'Well, yes, you'll find the odd exception, where a place diversifies. Of course, there's a lot of expense involved in such things. I understand it's very competitive too, trying to get a footing in the organic market. Look, I suppose it's always a wrench, isn't it, to leave a place but there's nothing like a new start.'

Nancy's smile is more like a grimace.

'Now,' he continues, 'we have almost everything we need before we sign. Title deeds, mortgage approved by the bank, price agreed. Sale agreed on what will be your new home, Nancy.' He pauses, frowns, as he looks back at his papers. 'A decommissioned septic tank on the property.' He looks at Nancy. 'Would that be right?'

'Oh,' she says. 'I'd forgotten about that thing.'

'It got overlooked unfortunately,' he says curtly, looking towards the door, through which they can hear Olive humming. Sarah gets the impression that, whatever's causing the delay, Olive may have had something to do with it.

'What's the problem?' asks Sarah.

'I wouldn't call it a problem. We just need the planning permission for it, before you can sign the place over.'

'I didn't even know we had to get planning permission for that,' says Nancy.

'Well, back then people didn't bother a lot of the time.'

'Where is it?' says Sarah. 'Do you have it?'

Nancy looks bewildered. 'I don't know,' she says. 'I don't know where that would be.'

'If it's anywhere, it'll be with the county council,' says Cormac. 'Now Liam, God rest him, was a man to abide by the rules, so I'd be surprised if it wasn't there.'

'That's right,' says Nancy.

'The trouble is getting civil servants to do anything in a hurry. It's a damned nuisance because if it wasn't for that, we could sign this week. And your house is ready and waiting for you in town. I've been on to them since last Monday about it but you'd swear it was the Holy Grail I was after. If it had come to my attention sooner ...' He seems genuinely frustrated. 'I wouldn't mind,' he says, 'but there's been all the talking of putting this stuff up online for the past couple of years. Have they done it? No.'

'Would it make any difference if we chased it?' asks Sarah.

He looks at her. 'If the owner goes down in person, makes a nuisance of themselves, that can make a difference.'

'I could go,' says Sarah.

Nancy turns to her. 'I thought you were anxious to get back to Dublin.'

'I'm not on until two.'

She could still have time for a quick nap, she tells herself, if she goes straight into the council now and then continues on to Dublin.

'Well, sure,' says Nancy, 'there's no great rush.'

Cormac looks awkwardly at Sarah. 'You could probably just phone them.'

'Going in won't make a difference?'

'Well, the thing is, it might. If you make a nuisance of yourself, as I say.'

'I'll go in now. Might they even give it to me there and then?'

'Unlikely, but you never know.'

'And if we had it, the sale could literally go through next week?' The idea is dizzying.

'No reason for it not to,' he says. 'You know, the beginning of the week is a good time to ask, just thinking about it. And it'll save you having to come down again.'

'Oh, she'll be down again, all right,' says Nancy.

Sarah and the solicitor look at her.

'What do you mean, Mam?'

'Sure, amn't I going to need help clearing out the place? All that. It'll take a long time. I don't know why the big rush on all this.'

'Still,' says Sarah, carefully, 'I may as well run in now.'

They're making their way back to the car when Cormac Hart calls Sarah from his door, telling Nancy he just wants to run through what to ask for at the council and that she should wait in the car, out of the cold.

As soon as Nancy is out of earshot, he fixes an uncomfortable gaze on Sarah. She waits.

'This is awkward.'

'What is?'

'He didn't want you worried unnecessarily.'

A feeling of dread creeps in her gut. 'About what?' she says.

'Look,' he says. 'I know about you and Neil.'

'I didn't know Neil told you.'

'Well, he hadn't,' he says, 'until last night.'

'Right.'

'I'm not the only one who knows.'

She looks at him helplessly. 'Jane.'

'She figured it out last week.'

'He said she hadn't. He said he was nearly sure.'

'He doesn't want you worried, you see. And he's right because, once you're back in Dublin, you've nothing to worry about. I wouldn't have said anything if it wasn't for your mother saying you'd be coming down more often.'

'What am I going to do?'

'Nancy will be grand with the move. I'll see to it. You need to look after yourself now. Stay up there until this all blows over.'

After he's gone back inside she phones Neil, walking up the road, away from where Nancy is sitting in the car, watching her.

He answers straight away.

'She knows,' she says to him.

Silence.

'Your brother told me. I thought you two hated each other. But he knows before me.'

'Sarah.'

'You told me she didn't know.'

'I said I was nearly sure.'

'Someone wrote "slut" on our garden wall last night,' she tells him.

'What?'

'Nancy went insane, she made me paint over it.'

He doesn't say anything.

'Who do you think wrote it?' she says.

Again, silence.

'Neil. What are you thinking?'

A heavy sigh.

'Answer me.'

'Look,' he says, finally, reluctantly, 'I don't want to worry you.'

'Worry me about what?'

Silence again, as though he's trying to weigh up whether or not he should say something to her.

'Just say it.'

'Jane,' he begins. 'She has – mental-health problems.'

'What kind of mental-health problems?'

It's nothing for you to be concerned with. It's just sometimes when she's drinking a lot, it affects her medication. Sometimes it's hard to get her to take her medication.'

'You never told me.'

'There was no need to tell you. Up to now.'

'What happens,' she asks quietly, 'when she forgets to take her medication?'

'Then ...' he says. 'Then, it can get messy.'

'And lately,' she says, 'she's been drinking a lot.'

'She has.'

'You think she wrote it, don't you?'

'She might *not* have written it.'

'It was her.'

'It's not impossible.'

'Jesus Christ.'

'I'm sorry, Sarah. I think, for the next few weeks—'

'How, though?'

'How what?'

'I just – I can't see it.'

He doesn't answer.

'*You* can,' she says. 'You can see it.'

'There's not much I wouldn't put past her,' he says, 'when she gets like this.'

'What should I do?'

'You should do what you were going to do anyway. Just stay in Dublin for the next few weeks.'

Still, when she's back in the car with Nancy, driving towards Dunlone, telling her it was the restaurant on the phone, and trying to imagine it again – Jane Hart on their road, spray-paint can in hand – well, it's ludicrous, no matter how crazy the woman might be, or angry. If Neil thinks her capable, surely it's because he's so worried, so burned-out with everything, he can't think straight. That's the truth she heard in his voice. His exhaustion.

But if it wasn't Jane, who was it?

And then she thinks of him. The student in the Project, who'd kept smirking at her and who, she is now certain, *was* waiting for her at her car. Who, she's now certain, is the person she encountered in the woods. And the thought occurs to her coldly. Maybe Jane paid him to do it.

She takes a left off the main road, onto the old, pothole-ridden boreen that goes through the woods and past the cottage.

'Why are you taking this road?' asks Nancy.

'Just a second.'

'You're not dropping me home now,' says Nancy. 'I'm coming in with you.'

Sarah keeps driving until they've reached the point in the road where the wood is on either side. Then she pulls over.

'What in the name of God?' says Nancy.

'Just a second.'

Sarah gets out of the car and stands at the edge of the road. She peers into the quiet dark of the conifers, the carpet of bracken below. There is a light wind in the branches, some desultory birdsong.

Nancy gets out of the car, stands beside her.

'What is it?' she says, an edge of panic in her voice.

'Nothing. Nothing.'

A black car whooshes past, clipping the side mirror on Sarah's car, not even slowing down afterwards.

'Madman,' shouts Nancy, after it. 'Sarah, would you get back in the car for the love of God. It's not safe standing here.'

9

In Dunlone, Sarah parks by the castle, and she and her mother make their way across the bridge. She registers at a remove how the wind has picked up, spitting its sharp cold drops of rain, how the vast river churns darkly beneath the bridge, even how modern and impressive the council offices are, behind the Protestant church off the narrow Main Street, the sleek building also housing the new library, spacious and warmly lit. And when the woman behind the reception desk comes over and Sarah tells her their request, and the woman answers her, she has to ask her to say it again.

She passes Sarah a pen and paper. 'The best thing is to give me the folio number, and your contact details, and I can put the request in.'

'But we were hoping,' she says, 'we might be able to get it off you now.'

'The thing is,' says the woman, 'it's not like pulling something out of a filing cabinet. It's archived. I don't mean digitally, I mean actual, physical archives. Someone has to go in there and rummage around. They won't exactly be prioritising it either.'

The phone starts to ring.

'But our solicitor was under the impression,' says Sarah, 'that if we came down ourselves, you'd be able to get it for us now.'

'Never mind,' says Nancy. She smiles at the woman.

'It's no harm to come in. Emails can slip between the cracks when they've a backlog. I'll make sure this lands on someone's desk but that's the most I can do for you now. All right?'

She answers the phone.

'Well, that was a pile of rubbish,' says Sarah, when they're back in the car.

'Sure, what harm?' says Nancy. She glances nervously at Sarah. 'I meant to say earlier, I appreciated you speaking up for the place to Cormac Hart.'

'What does he know about it?'

'You're not going to tell me what that stop at the woods was about.'

'I lost my scarf in there yesterday,' she lies. 'I was half thinking of going in and trying to find it.'

'Fair enough,' says Nancy.

Neither of them speaks again until they're back at the cottage.

'When will you be down again?'

'Let me check the schedule at work,' says Sarah. 'I'll give you a ring during the week.'

'Well. Travel safely.'

'I will.'

Nancy opens her door.

'You know what?' says Sarah. 'I'm going to run down and look for that scarf. If I don't do it now I'll never get it back.'

'All right,' says Nancy, uncertainly.

This time, Sarah runs all the way down the field, not pausing until she reaches the gully, and then only to judge her footing before stepping over it and into the woods. Once among the trees, she heads straight for the hollow, wades through the rust-coloured bracken, here and there punctured by a green shoot, until she's standing in its centre.

Just as Paul said, there is nothing to suggest anyone has been there recently. Everything is as it always used to be at this time of year – the brown bracken coating the floor, here and there a green shoot. She only notices the bracelet when it happens to catch and reflect the sunlight, drawing Sarah's eye.

It's such a distinctive thing – the way the snake coils, wrapping itself around the arm. She's only ever seen one person wearing it.

Back in her car, she calls Neil again.

'She was down here,' she says, when he answers. 'She was down here in the woods. With that man and his dog.'

'Calm down,' he says, but like that time on the phone, his voice echoes her panic. 'I can't make out what you're saying.'

'Jane,' she says. 'She was here in the woods.'

'I thought you were going straight back to Dublin.'

'Why would she have been down here? She wouldn't even have known I was home. What was she doing here?'

'Calm down, Sarah, for Christ's sake.' But he is shouting now. 'You're hysterical. What makes you think she was down there?'

'I found her bracelet,' she says.

There's a pause.

'Mightn't have been hers.'

'Of course it's hers. It's the one with the snake.'

'Well, look,' he says, and she can tell he's scrambling around, wanting to find something to reassure her. That really he's as frightened as she is. 'Maybe she lost it another time. Maybe your man got hold of it.'

'What would he be doing with it?'

He sighs. 'I don't know, Sarah. I don't know what was going on. I'll tell you one thing, though. You need to stay away from here for a while.'

'You're right.'

'I thought that was what you wanted to do anyway. To keep Nancy off your case until the sale is through.'

'Yeah.'

'You get into your car and go back to Dublin. The next time you're home, everything will be very different.'

'I love you, Neil.'

'I love you too.'

Of course he's right. None of it matters at all, because right now she's going to drive away from Crookedwood. In Dublin, she's going to shower and change, and somehow she's going to get through the evening shift without making a single mistake and then she'll get back to her flat where sleep will be waiting for her. And in the morning everything will seem, if not quite like a bad dream, at least no longer her concern. She has fulfilled her promise as regards Neil's development. Nancy can't force her to come home, no matter how much she might want to. She can chase that paperwork for the farm by phone. What else would bring her back here, with everything that's going on? If she never understands exactly why Jane was in their woods, or that man and his awful dog, it doesn't matter. Soon it won't be their woods any more. She doesn't need to understand any of it, if she doesn't want to.

10

It was almost dusk when Sarah walked down the road towards the woods on that last Friday of the summer before their final year of school. Still warm, the air was fragrant with the scent of the cream, red-hearted flowers of the wild honeysuckle that twined itself into the length of the hedgerow. Halfway down she stopped walking and took off her jacket. She would need to put it back on once she reached the trees but for now the sun felt good on her skin.

Her mind was still buzzing from her meeting with the guidance counsellor that morning. She'd managed to work up the courage to tell her she didn't really know what she wanted to do after school and that she liked the idea of working for a year, maybe even two, before she had to think about what she wanted to study. The woman had fixed her in a serious gaze. She thought, she'd said, Sarah was to do a degree in agricultural science. That she was going to keep on the family farm. Now, she'd said then, if Sarah was having second thoughts about that, there was no reason why she couldn't aim higher. If she applied herself a bit more, there was no reason not to think she might get enough points to train as a primary-school teacher. Or there was nursing: had she considered that? There'd be a lot more security in either of those professions than there was in farming, that was for sure. But Sarah had persisted, asking again in a just-out-of-interest way, until the counsellor had begrudgingly handed her some leaflets. One was about a work-abroad programme in the States. The idea that she could go to live somewhere like New York was too preposterous to imagine properly, but there was a thrill in knowing that it was even theoretically possible. A couple were about post-Leaving Certificate courses in Dublin. Part-time ones, she could work alongside. That idea felt almost possible and thinking about it made her almost light-headed. That she could just choose something that interested her, and do that.

Of course, she hadn't told Nancy anything about this conversation. As far as Nancy was concerned, Sarah was doing the agricultural-science degree. Her plan for the two of them to keep on the farm and somehow make it viable might as well have been set in stone. She would as soon tell Nancy about her doubts as she'd tell her that, rather than going to Ursula's for a chemistry study session, they were all meeting up in the woods. She'd had to put on her make-up and earrings outside, using a torch and a pocket mirror. She'd even worn jeans leaving the house, stashing them in a hedge as soon as she was out of sight.

Now she wonders if maybe she should have worn jeans and a top after all. She definitely should have worn leggings under the dress.

The voices of the others reached her before she could see them – Geraldine exclaiming about something, followed by laughter from Marie and Ursula. Sarah checked the time. Only ten to eight, and they had arranged to meet at eight, but it sounded as though the girls had been there a while and there was the odd flicker from a campfire. This had happened the weekend before as well, when she'd turned up for a sleepover at Geraldine's and found they'd been hanging out all afternoon. No one had acted as though anything was wrong so she hadn't commented. In fairness, she and the others had done it to Geraldine that time she, Ursula and Marie had gone to the pub in Dunlone that served underage drinkers. But remembering that didn't help as she made her way carefully. In this part of the wood, bracken hid roots that you could easily trip on. At least, she told herself, she couldn't hear any male voices. It would be worse somehow to arrive after *they* did.

As soon as she reached the edge of the clearing, she paused. Marie and Geraldine were cross-legged by the fire, looking across at Ursula, who was standing on the other side, a can of cider in her hand. They were all wearing jeans.

'I mean, who says something like that?' she was saying. Then she looked in Sarah's direction. Squinted.

'What?' said Marie.

'Someone's there.'

'It's me,' said Sarah, stepping quickly into the light of the fire.

'Jesus,' said Ursula. 'What were you doing standing there?'

'I'd just arrived, honestly.' She sat beside Geraldine and Marie and put her hands out towards the flames. Pretended not to notice Geraldine's stare.

'I'm not surprised you're feeling the cold,' said Geraldine.

'What a slut!' said Ursula.

Sarah adjusted her sitting position.

'I'm *kidding*. Jesus, the face on you.'

'She's been thinking over what you said, Urs,' said Marie. 'She's going to do the deed with David after all.'

'I never said any such thing.'

Ursula hunched down beside her.

'Our little girl is becoming a woman,' said Marie, in a bored voice. Sarah was pretty sure she hadn't slept with anyone yet herself.

'Look, make-up and everything.' Ursula pulled out Sarah's bra strap, let it snap back. 'About time, my lovely.'

'You're all getting ahead of yourselves.'

As far as Sarah had been able to make out, sex was something that had to happen sooner rather than later if she was to avoid being labelled frigid. For all of them, and before finishing school. Frigid meant cold. It meant being stiff, like a corpse. No one wanted to be that. The tricky bit was to avoid being called that while simultaneously managing to sidestep being called a slut. That was worse than being frigid. Being a slut meant having sex too freely, giving too much of what was wanted, like that girl in the year ahead, who they said would talk dirty and give blow-jobs. It meant enjoying the thing – like that other girl who, everyone said, made loud noises when she had sex with her ex, or the girl who was caught by her brother and his friends masturbating in her bedroom. Sarah could think of nothing worse than that. Most of the time, she could half convince herself she never masturbated, and she was pretty sure none of the girls ever did it. Not that they'd ever spoken about it. No one would dream of bringing that up.

You should only sleep with someone after you've been going out with them for a while. That was the right thing to do. A couple of months, maybe, which happened to be how long she'd been seeing David Fitzpatrick. Not like that girl who slept with someone she'd met at the same disco just a week later and got herself promptly dumped. That was so embarrassing. First you let them kiss you and then you let them touch your breasts, and then maybe finger you. She'd already let David do the first two. The last one she decided was optional. And then you went the whole way, like everyone expected you to. Like you were supposed to. When you thought about it, like really thought about it, it was clear that there weren't any actual decisions to make. You just had to figure out the rules and follow them.

'Have you met his parents yet?' asked Ursula.

'Nope.'

'I wouldn't give it a second thought.'

'His mother's a stuck-up bitch.'

'We hardly mind him sticking anything up, though.'

'Don't be saying things like that in front of Sarah. Her mother will have her saying fifty decades of the rosary if she hears about it.'

'Washing her ears out with soap and water.'

'You're all hilarious,' said Sarah.

'Remember,' said Ursula, 'she gave you that book instead of the talk about the birds and the bees. What was it called again?'

'*Ready, Steady, Grow*,' said Sarah, taking care to keep her voice dry.

Ursula put her hand to her chest as she laughed. 'Did she really never tell you about periods?'

'I thought I was dying when I got my first one.'

'Didn't you ask her once why nuns don't have babies?'

'I ended up answering the question myself. I said it must be because they're too busy praying, and she said, yes, that was it. End of conversation.'

'What age were you?'

'About twelve. No, older. Maybe fourteen.'

The girls laughed so much that Marie lay on the ground and tears shone on Geraldine's face. Only Sarah kept her face straight. It was funnier that way.

'Oh, you're a ticket,' said Ursula, when she could finally talk. 'Poor Nancy. Does she still do the Stations of the Cross in your house?'

'She's not that unusual,' said Geraldine. 'I was given that book too.' She affected a warbling tone. '"Sexual intercourse between man and woman should only take place within the sanctity of marriage."'

'"Intercourse outside the sanctity of marriage is sinful,"' added Sarah.

'Remember Father Roache,' said Marie, 'at that Mass before our Confirmation.' She affected his lisping voice. '"Don't ever underestimate the sin of sex."'

'I wonder, though,' said Ursula, when they'd stopped laughing, 'would your father have been as bad.'

Sarah picked up a twig. She tried to break it in two but it bent over on itself, instead of snapping like she had thought it would. 'Should we get more firewood?' she said.

'Like, he might have balanced her out a bit.' Ursula regarded her pityingly.

'Joe made a stab once,' she said, the memory suddenly returning.

'Joe? What in the name of God would he know about sex?'

'Once he handed me a copy of the *National Geographic*,' said Sarah. 'Open at an article about AIDS and contraception.'

'Ah, God love him,' said Marie.

'I was mortified.'

Marie and Geraldine laughed.

'You wouldn't want it rubbing off on you, is all I mean,' said Ursula, ignoring this comment about Joe.

'Rubbing off,' repeated Geraldine, but her smile disappeared as Ursula ignored her.

'On the bright side,' said Sarah, and she looked at Geraldine, 'at least I'm not a lesbian like her.'

Ursula stared at Geraldine, her face all faux-amazement. 'I never thought of that. This one's all butter wouldn't melt and maybe the whole time she's been salivating over the sight of us changing after PE.'

'I'm not a fucking lesbian,' said Geraldine, her cheeks suddenly red.

'Are you sure?'

'Of course I'm sure.'

'We're only messing you,' said Ursula. 'Jesus Christ.'

'At least,' said Sarah, 'I know what a blow-job is.'

This was a reference to Geraldine once having admitted she thought it involved actually blowing on the guy's cock.

'She has you there, Geraldine,' said Ursula. 'In fairness, like.'

'That was a million years ago,' said Geraldine, who looked like she might start crying.

'I think I hear the guys coming,' said Ursula. 'Maybe we could ask them to explain it to you.'

'Yeah, Geraldine,' said Sarah. 'We could ask them to give you a tutorial.'

'It's them all right,' said Marie. 'Morons. They're going the wrong way.' She put two fingers into her mouth and whistled loudly.

'Over here,' called Ursula.

'Don't get yourselves lost now,' said Sarah.

The rustling paused for a moment, and then it started up again, quickly growing louder until three figures appeared at the edge of the clearing.

'Girls.' It was Marie's brother. He stepped into the clearing, grinned at them.

'You're late,' said Marie.

'Did ye get lost?' asked Ursula.

'We got detained, shall we say.' He sat cross-legged beside Geraldine, started rolling a joint.

'Where'd you get that?' asked Marie.

'Ask me no questions,' he said. 'I have my contacts.'

Marie rolled her eyes. 'Contacts. Some knacker from the Heights, you mean.'

David, who had already sat beside Sarah, stretched an arm across her shoulders and planted his dark eyes on her. It still surprised her that he was her boyfriend. He was so good-looking. When he'd asked her to dance at the disco, she'd actually looked behind her, thinking he was talking to someone else. If they didn't have a lot to talk about, she figured that was probably normal. The main thing was he was such a catch and he liked her and they'd done everything the right way so far – the proof of this was that no one had said she was frigid *or* a slut, except the girls but that was just slagging. When he asked her suddenly if she wanted to go for a little walk, she knew what he meant and she said yes, why not? And when they were down in the hollow, away from the others, and they'd been kissing for a while and he said, 'Will we do it?' she nodded and said yes. She hadn't felt any worry or doubt or anything like that at all. She hadn't really felt *anything*.

It was only when he suddenly started yanking up her top that she knew she didn't want to. She didn't want to at all. But instead of pushing him away or telling him to stop, she stayed where she was, as though, if she didn't move at all, she would become a thing rather than a person, and then it wouldn't be happening. It wouldn't be happening to her. He broke away from their kiss, which had been going on for ever, and looked angrily at her. That was when he'd started pulling violently at his belt until it was off, and then, in a sudden sharp move, at her pants until they were around her knees. When he did that, her legs clenched together, and when he tried to prise them apart he couldn't. Her legs stayed glued together, surprising even herself at the strength. Again, he looked angrily at her.

'For fuck's sake,' he said, and then he was digging a knee between her thighs until he'd forced them apart and then he was between them, and the whole weight and smell of him on her, a root or stone pressing sharply into her back.

She still didn't say anything or try to get away, even as he was painfully – so painfully, like a knife – pushing himself inside her and then he was doing it while she stared at the branches above her, so heavy and grave with their dark green leaves.

PART II

11

The view from Sarah's bedroom hasn't changed since she was a child: scrap of lawn, low wall, grey scrawl of road, then hedgerow and trees, the church spire beyond – all that's visible of the town. Another overcast day, the sky low and heavy-looking. From downstairs come the sounds of Nancy clanking plates and dragging chairs.

I need to ask a favour, her mother had said on the phone, all the anger from the weekend clean wiped out of her voice. *Come down for my committee meeting. Just to show everyone you're on my side.*

Afterwards, Sarah had called Neil, only mentioning this after they'd been chatting for a while. She would just stay down the one night, she told him. First thing the following morning, she'd get into her car and drive back to Dublin.

'You're wavering,' he'd said flatly. 'You're wavering with your mother.'

He was the only person in the world she'd ever talked to about Nancy. Like, really talked to. The way when down home she sometimes felt herself dangerously close to capitulating. Especially lately. That longing for the undeniable relief there would be in giving Nancy what she wanted so much. The strange sensation, not quite unpleasant, she felt when she imagined succumbing.

'I'm not,' she'd said, even though she'd been surprised herself at how quickly she'd agreed to Nancy's request.

He'd not softened. 'Getting you down twice in as many weeks. Helping out with her campaign now. She'll be getting strength from this.'

'Wrong.'

'And what about the other reason for you to stay away?'

'Jane.'

'Of course Jane.'

'I've been thinking about all that,' she'd explained. 'I know you're saying she's capable of anything, and it's not that I don't *believe* you ...'

'Right,' he said guardedly.

'Of course I *believe* you. It's just – I can't see her doing any of it. I mean, can you really see her painting that on our wall?'

He doesn't answer.

'Or being down our woods with that guy. I mean, what would she have been doing there? I think now she must have lost her bracelet before, on a walk or something.'

'I thought I explained it to you,' he said. 'I thought I explained to you that Jane—'

'That Jane what?'

'Well,' he said. 'That she's dangerous.'

'Dangerous.'

'Maybe I wasn't clear enough. I didn't want to scare you. But maybe I should have scared you.'

'What's the worst she can do? I'm only down the one night. She won't even know I'm home.'

'Let's hope not. And let's hope you're not relenting to your mother.'

'I'm not,' she'd insisted.

But he'd rung off angry with her and even though he'd sent her flowers the next day, they hadn't spoken since then. Then again, she didn't seem able to please anyone lately. The evening before in the restaurant, she'd managed to confuse two types of fish, frying the one that was supposed to be poached, ruining two of the menu's dishes in the process. That was after being sent home on the Monday evening halfway through the shift, after Jack found her sitting on the back-door step, asleep.

Yelled at twice in the one week. It was a new record, since her promotion.

Now, the doorbell rings downstairs, followed by Olive's voice, in the hallway. Almost immediately, it rings again. More voices, people making their way into the living room. Nancy calls up the stairs.

'Sarah. Come on down, would you?'

She recognises everyone in the sitting room – Olive and the two other women crammed together on the sofa, the couple of men sitting on chairs brought in from the kitchen. But, besides Olive, she'd be hard-pressed to put a name on any of them.

'There she is,' says one of the women, in a bright voice, smiling up at her. 'The image of her father, God rest him.'

'How are you?' says Sarah.

'Not a bother.'

Down home, this always happens – not knowing who someone is, while they know exactly who she is. As the men resume their quiet conversation, it occurs to Sarah for the first time that they might know about the message scrawled on the garden wall. They wouldn't have to have seen it themselves. It had been a Monday morning. All it would take was one person with an early start, driving past after it grew light but before Nancy saw it.

And if they didn't know about that, they might well have heard about her behaviour in the hotel. All the gaps in her memory have since been thoroughly filled in by Ursula when she'd called Sarah only the day before. Sarah had gotten into an argument with someone on the dance-floor. Sarah had tried to get off with one of the football players in front of his girlfriend. Sarah had thrown up in the beer garden. Sarah had eventually been kicked out – practically dragged, she'd said, by one of the bouncers.

'Who's for tea and who's for coffee?' asks Nancy, just as the doorbell rings again. 'That'll be Joe,' she says to Sarah, disappearing back into the kitchen.

It's Joe, all right. Red-rimmed eyes, slightly swaying, stinking with alcohol Joe.

'Sarah.'

'You're drunk.'

'I had a small couple.'

'Tell me you didn't drive.'

'Will you stop nagging me.' He goes past her into the hallway.

'Where's your mother?' He goes on into the living room, Sarah following.

'Well,' he says.

They all look up at him.

'Joe,' says Olive. 'You're drunk.'

'What of it,' he says.

'Sit down,' Sarah says to him, just as Nancy comes in.

She takes one look at Joe, who has sat himself down on the armchair in the corner of the room. 'For God's sake, Joe,' she says.

'What?'

'Give him a cup of tea,' she says to Sarah. She turns back to Joe. 'One peep out of you and you may take yourself home.' She sits herself down. Everyone watches as Sarah gives Joe his tea.

'These custard creams are the business, Nancy,' says one of the women.

'I'm partial to the Hobnob myself,' says one of the men. 'Nancy always looks after us on the biscuit front,' he adds, taking a lanky step forward to help himself to a couple.

'A humble offering, Bill,' says Nancy.

Bill dunks his biscuit. 'He has the application in anyway,' he says, still holding it half-submerged in the tea.

'He does.'

'And we have our challenge in.'

'Not yet,' says Nancy.

They all look at her.

'We have another week to the deadline. I thought I'd wait and see if we got a few more signatures.'

'I suppose,' says Bill, 'it wouldn't weaken our case to delay.'

'No, you see,' says Nancy. 'It can only stay the same or strengthen.'

'It's strong as it is,' says Olive. 'There isn't a person in this town who doesn't regret not signing our petition against that housing estate. There's no way he's getting his planning permission.'

The woman who likes the custard creams clears her throat. 'It could have gone a *little* bit better at the open house. Maybe.' She takes a delicate bite of her biscuit.

In the awkward silence that follows, Sarah expects Nancy to throw her a sharp look or agree with what has been said, but she just sips her tea and smiles politely at the woman.

'What I still don't understand,' says Bill, 'is how they even think they're going to get past those spatial planning guidelines.' His voice is full of indignation. 'They couldn't be clearer. No retail development by a motorway.'

'No *significant* retail development by a motorway,' says Nancy. 'The devil's in the detail.'

'As far as I can make out,' says Olive, 'guidelines don't make a damn bit of difference in this country anyway.'

'Not a damn,' says Joe.

Everyone looks over at him. Two of the women raise their eyebrows at each other.

'Not with Paul Walsh on Hart's side,' Joe adds.

'You have a point there, Joe,' says Bill, solemnly. 'Getting enough votes in the next election is all he gives a damn about. And Neil is in a good place to help him with that, him being what they call a pillar of the community and with the pub and all. Isn't that it?'

'All that talk about bringing employment and more business

to the town,' adds one of the women, the one who'd said Sarah looked like her father. 'You might have said he had a point, if you could trust him.'

'Those lads go back years,' says Olive. 'They'll have it all planned out. In a couple of years' time, in will come an application for a residential development. Maybe a small shopping centre. You mark my words.'

This is met with a murmur of agreement. It's as though, Sarah thinks, on some level they're enjoying all this. The venting. The dark speculations. The little bit of drama in their lives.

'I can't see why you've all decided you *can't* trust Neil Hart,' she says, careful to keep her voice light, as though she's really just wondering.

'I'll take another drop of milk, Nancy,' says Olive. 'Where's the jug gone?'

They all watch Bill pass it to her, and Olive pouring more milk into her tea.

'I know he was good to you when you worked in the pub,' says Nancy, looking at Sarah, 'but what benefits his pocket is bad for the town.'

'Even if what benefits his pocket also happens to adhere to really good standards and includes social housing, all of that?'

'It's like the song goes,' says Bill, looking around at the others.

'Who's that, Bill?'

'I can't remember it now. Something about a greedy man not knowing what he's at.'

'Why don't you just ask one of the other councillors to weigh in?' asks Sarah. She doesn't care now if they catch the shimmer of anger in her voice. 'If Walsh is so biased.'

'Doesn't work like that,' says the other man, who has said nothing up to now.

'Anytime there's a vote about a development,' explains Olive, 'all the other councillors defer to the one representing the area concerned.'

'That's ridiculous,' says Sarah.

'It is ridiculous,' agrees Nancy.

'What do *you* think, Joe?' says the woman who likes custard creams.

'Is it ridiculous, or is it some kind of conspiracy?' asks the man sitting beside Bill. As he says this, he winks across at the women.

They're egging him on, thinks Sarah, for their own amusement. They want the gossip. They are always hungry for gossip. Even if it's just that Joe Flynn was drunk at the campaign meeting at six in the evening. No doubt they will justify it to themselves later that evening. Joe Flynn will drink himself to death, they'll say. If he was a sandwich short of a picnic before, he's out of sandwiches completely now. And Nancy's young one isn't much better. The way she was carrying on the other night in the hotel. Did you hear what someone wrote on the wall about her?

'This whole damn country is a fucking conspiracy,' barks Joe.

'I do think it's a fair point,' says Nancy, reaching back and pressing Joe's arm, 'that the open house could have gone better from our point of view.'

The woman who had made this point nods.

'We could do with one more string to our bow, along with the petition,' adds Nancy. 'To seal the deal, if you like.'

'We can't go to the county manager if that's what you're

thinking,' says Bill. 'We'll get short shrift there. Anyway, they're probably on our side.'

'That's not what I have in mind,' says Nancy. And then, she looks at Sarah, whose stomach clenches, even before Nancy continues.

'As you all know, we happen to have a local TD who is also a junior minister. Not any old junior minister either. Minister of state for local government and planning, no less.'

'I'd say we can give up getting a meeting with him, Nancy. When's the deadline? A week? How many times have we asked for one now? The Dáil sits Monday to Wednesday and he'll hardly be down at the end of the week. Anyway, that'd be cutting it too fine if you ask me.'

'Well, that's what I thought myself. Until I discovered we have a secret weapon.' And she turns again to Sarah and smiles. 'You all know my daughter,' says Nancy.

They all look at Sarah. Like they're watching a tennis match, she thinks. Olive giggles.

'Who do you think came into the restaurant Sarah works in up in Dublin but this very same minister's son ... who happens to be an old flame of Sarah's.'

Sarah stares at Nancy, as though if she stares hard enough, Nancy will have to answer why she didn't tell her she was going to do this before everyone showed up. But she already knows the answer. Nancy didn't tell her because if Sarah knew what she'd been planning she wouldn't have come home.

Hoodwinked by her mother.

'Ten years ago,' she manages. 'And he's hardly an old flame.'

'Why else was he there, if he doesn't carry a torch for you?' Nancy looks around at the others.

For a moment, Sarah is tempted to ask the women on the sofa if maybe they would like some popcorn.

'Hadn't he read that article in the *Chronicle*?' continues Nancy. 'And he remembered her. He even gave her his card.'

One of the women lets out a snort, which she unconvincingly tries to turn into a cough.

'Now,' says Olive.

'I don't even know if I still have his bloody card.'

Nancy looks briefly worried, but she quickly recovers. 'Well, if you don't, you know where he works and you can get him that way.'

'I don't think so.'

'Look. I'm not saying you weren't speaking in good faith at the open house last week, but by God if it didn't make things harder for us.'

'It would have made zero difference.'

'It's too good a contact not to use.'

'He's hardly a contact.'

'Just give him a call today, and ask if he wants to meet for coffee during the week. What have we to lose? Now.' Nancy folds her arms.

'Ah, Jesus, Nancy,' says Olive. 'You have the poor girl mortified.'

'That's some stroke to pull, Nancy,' agrees Bill.

'I'll give him the wrong idea,' says Sarah.

'Just say we were hoping for a meeting with his father. Tell him the deadline. Pass on a letter for him. We've already sent it, but if he gets it again from you, he might act on it. He might not even have gotten round to reading the one we sent. Now. That's it.'

'What if he doesn't want to meet me for coffee?'

'Then you'll have done your best. You owe us that much. Anyway, he will.'

I owe you nothing, she wants to say. Instead she says, 'You have it all figured out.'

'You'll do it.'

'I'm not coming down again for this meeting. If it even happens.'

'She'll do it,' says Olive. She's smiling at her.

'Oh, for Christ's sake.'

They're all smiling at her now.

Everyone except Joe, who is staring out the window even though the lace curtains make it hard to see much of anything beyond.

12

She comes upon Joe in the fridge section of the Spar when she goes down later to get something for dinner. He's holding one of the doors open, staring in at tubs of yogurt and ready-made desserts as though he's never seen the like before. As she watches him, he closes that door and opens another, stares in at cream and litres of milk with the same perplexed expression, before closing that door. Then he looks around him, as though he has no idea how he got to be standing there, in the fridge section of the Spar in Crookedwood in the first place.

'Joe,' she says, coming down the aisle to him. 'Are you all right?'

His face, when he turns to her. All wounded bafflement.

'What's wrong with you?'

'What do you mean, what's wrong with me?'

'You're vexed about something.'

'Well,' he says, 'it makes no sense.'

'What makes no sense?'

He looks back at the fridge. 'The butter.'

'The butter.'

'The butter,' he says, his voice rising angrily, 'has been here every day since this shop opened. Here.' He points at the first door he'd opened, the one containing the yogurt, as though the fact the butter is not where he expected it to be amounts to a personal insult. An attack.

'Oh,' she says, casting her gaze around for the butter. 'I think they moved things in here.'

'Moved things,' he repeats, in an outraged voice.

'There it is.' She grabs a pound of Kerrygold, which is displayed only a couple of doors up, and drops it into his basket. There's Pot Noodles in there, a sliced pan. Packet of rashers, sausages.

'I thought you always bought your meat from the butcher. You haven't fallen out with them as well,' she says, smiling.

He looks at her defensively.

'Ah, Joe, come on, I'm only joking.'

He doesn't say anything, yet he doesn't walk away either.

'What's wrong with you?' she says.

'Nothing is wrong with me.'

Suddenly, as though from nowhere, the sad pile of magazines she'd found under his bed that time comes back to her. The time he had his breakdown that no one ever called a breakdown, when he stopped looking after the farm and Nancy found him one morning asleep and half frozen in the barn. Still drunk from all he'd put away the night before.

She'll leave him be. He's probably still drunk. There's no point in trying to talk to him when he's like this.

This is what she tells herself.

'What are you up to this evening?' she asks him.

He doesn't answer her.

'Come up to the house,' she says, 'and I'll make a bit of dinner for the two of us.'

'I won't inconvenience you.' Still, he doesn't move, his expression cagey and raw, chin set hard.

'Nancy's up with Olive going over the challenge,' she says. 'You'd be doing me a favour. I could do with some company.'

They take Joe's car the short drive back to the cottage, Sarah driving. He doesn't speak and neither does she, not even when she notices a black car pulling out quickly behind them and, despite her slow speed, only passing when she turns off for the road to the cottage. A Peugeot, it looks just like the car that had driven so fast past her and Nancy that time when she'd pulled over. The last thing Joe needs is to be fed a new line of paranoia.

The silence continues inside the cottage as she gets the oven on, slices up the potatoes and then the onions. Steak and chips, French beans on the side. Quick and comforting and not without nourishment. In minutes, she has the chips in the oven, the onions frying softly in butter, beans washed and ready for blanching. When everything is done, she makes them tea, then takes the chair opposite him at the table. Ignoring the urge to turn on the radio, she blows on her tea, takes a sip. 'Hot,' she says.

He gestures with his head, not quite a nod, but a communication of sorts. They sit in the non-talking a while longer, the smell of onions filling the room, their quiet hissing.

'I'd a funny one last week,' she says. She keeps her eyes on the window as she speaks, even as he glances warily at her. Square of grey sky. 'A friend of mine, one of the waiters in the restaurant, lovely guy. He and his boyfriend had a party in their house. Didn't I turn up at the wrong place. Not even the wrong house but the wrong part of town entirely.'

'Hm,' he says.

'It was funny.'

For a second, she thinks she hears Nancy at the door. But it's nothing. Just the wind clattering something on the path outside.

'I saw your magazines.' She blurts the words out.

When he turns to her, his expression is all confusion, behind this, a kind of dawning horror.

'Don't be mad,' she says.

'What are you talking about?'

'Oh God. It was years ago. Nancy dragged me up to clean your house that time you went off the rails. She asked me to change the sheets on your bed. Now.'

She goes back to the hob, where she stirs the onions, sprinkles in more salt, tastes a slice. They're turning translucent. It's almost time to spoon them onto a plate, then return the pan to the heat, add the oil and turn up the heat until it's spitting. Instead, she turns the heat off, sits back down.

'I always thought you'd hate me to know,' she says, her voice coming out all agitated. 'But now I don't know. You're drinking yourself into an early grave.'

There is a kind of rage in his expression when he looks at her. 'Who else knows this?' he asks.

'No one.'

He stares at her.

'You can trust me, Joe, for God's sake. On Daddy's grave, I haven't told a soul.'

Something in him relaxes when she says that. He looks back out the window.

'There's nothing to feel bad about,' she says.

'Is that right.'

'Of course it is.'

The silence that follows seems to last for ever. She's about to return to the hob when he speaks.

'So you know. All these years.'

'Yes.'

She waits as this sinks in. Another long silence, but this time he shifts in his seat, even glances her way. Still, when he finally speaks, the words come out so quiet she barely catches what he's said.

'Jim Byrne.' His gaze is now on the window. 'Out the Dublin road there.'

'Jim Byrne,' she says slowly, because she doesn't understand, though the name is familiar. 'Byrne's. The seed suppliers?'

'I used to buy off him.' He throws her a wary glance.

'Jim Byrne,' she says again, still not understanding. 'He used to drink in the pub. Oh.' She looks at him, quickly looks away.

'He did,' he says. 'He did drink in the pub.'

Though his gaze is still stiffly on the window, she can tell from the side of his face that she has understood right.

She can also tell that if the penny hadn't dropped, or if it had but she had started talking about something else or doing something else, that would have been it. They would never have spoken of it again.

'Him and myself,' he says. 'It's over now.' He clears his throat.

'How long?'

'The guts of fifteen years.'

'Fifteen years,' she echoes. 'How?'

'You find a way.'

'Joe.'

'Now you know.'

'Now I know.'

She still can't quite believe what he's just told her. Jim Byrne is married with two daughters. Back when she worked in the pub, he and Joe were often there at the bar at the same time. It occurs to her then that she never once saw them sit side by side.

'When did it end?' she asks him, after another long pause.

He closes his eyes. 'Christmas.'

'Christmas.' A memory is coming to her. 'He came round the bar one night at Christmas,' she says. 'Stephen's Night. I was out with the girls. Neil had to go out, he asked me to cover for him.' She doesn't add that afterwards, the two of them had stayed chatting until the early hours of the morning. That that was the night it began between them. 'He had to go do something for Jim but he wouldn't tell me what.'

'Stop me from telling his wife,' says Joe. 'That's what he did for him.'

'Oh God.' She searches for the thing to say. 'I'm sorry.'

He waves this away.

'Is this why you're back drinking?'

'I suppose it is.'

'That time years ago,' she says, 'when you were drinking a lot as well.'

He nods. 'The same. It's different this time, though. It's for good.'

'And does his wife—'

'Are you joking me?'

'She doesn't know.'

'Doesn't know a thing. Though she must know something's not right.'

'Jim Byrne. He always seemed nice.'

The gesture with his head again. The not-quite-a-nod. She reaches across the small table and for a second he lets her squeeze his hand before pulling away.

'Does anyone else know?' she asks him.

'Only your friend.'

'Who's that? Ursula?'

'Neil.'

'Why did you call him that?'

He looks surprised at her reaction. 'Didn't you speak up on behalf of his thing?'

'Oh. Yeah. How long has he known?'

'Oh, since years. One night, it was just myself and Jim inside in the pub. Neil had nipped out for a minute. He never said a word but he only needed to clock the faces on us when he came back in. We'd been arguing, you see.'

'And he knew.'

'Never breathed a word of it to anyone.'

'I told you he was nice.'

'I never disagreed with you.'

'So how can you support the campaign against this development?'

'That's different,' he says. 'That's business.'

'Business,' she repeats indignantly.

'Anyway,' he says, 'that's it.' He looks at her sharply then. 'You won't say anything about this to your mother.'

'Of course I'm not going to tell her.'

'Not that she'd judge the way some around here would. But just the same.'

'She wouldn't judge? Are we talking about the same person?'

'You shouldn't blame your mother if she has hang-ups, as they say. The country she and I grew up in was a different place from the one you grew up in.'

'Still.'

He grimaces. 'I remember a young man from Dunlone. A story went around about him and some other lad on the building site he was working on. Beat him to a pulp on his way home from the pub one night. He never walked right after it.'

'Fucking hell.'

'That was only three short decades ago. It could still happen now.'

There's another pause.

'You're right, though,' she begins. 'Ireland *has* changed.'

'Oh, I know all that. What good is it to me?' He shifts angrily in his chair. 'None of that,' he says, 'has a thing to do with me.'

'All right, all right. But you can't keep living like this, Joe.'

'Sure, what other way am I going to live?'

'Well. Did you ever think of ...' She can't finish the sentence. But when she looks back at Joe, she sees, to her surprise, that he's smiling.

'Coming out?' he says. 'Isn't that what they call it?'

'Well–'

'Can you imagine it? Your mother turning on the news and seeing me on one of those Gay Pride marches up in Dublin.'

They laugh together at the thought of this.

'Still, Joe,' she says. 'It must be terrible, having to keep so much of yourself a secret.' She looks at him.

'It is,' he acknowledges. 'You're better off without secrets, if you can help it. They eat you up, is what they do.'

'Yeah.'

'Now, I thought you were going to feed me. Nothing like the smell of onions to put an appetite on someone.'

13

The following morning, fog has turned the landscape of fields and road into a pale sketch of itself, all the way from the cottage to the Garden Project. If anything, it has grown thicker by the time Sarah stops off there on her way back to Dublin; she can barely see the rest of the car park, or the wall surrounding it, or even the Project building, and walking to it, she has the feeling of being watched. When Lisa opens the door, she all but pushes past her to get inside.

'Are you all right?' asks Lisa. She looks alarmed.

'Sorry.' She tries to smile at her. 'My mind's playing tricks on me. This fog.'

Lisa nods but she still looks uneasy. 'You don't have a class today, Miss?'

'No, no. I just wanted a quick word with Kathy. Is she in?'

'Out in the courtyard,' says Lisa.

From the back door, Sarah can see Kathy, whacking a bin against the side of the composter to empty its contents. Her face scrunched against the unpleasantness of the task, she shows no sign of having heard anything. There are maggots in there, the harsh smell of decay.

Sarah walks into the courtyard. 'Hey.'

'Jesus Christ.' Kathy drops the bin. The lid of the composter clangs noisily shut.

'Did I frighten you?'

'Oh my God.' Kathy laughs at the shock.

'Sorry.'

'You're grand.' Kathy takes Sarah in. 'You look like you've seen a ghost yourself,' she says.

Sarah picks up the bin, which has rolled towards her, hands it back to Kathy. Nods at the composter. 'I always hated that job.'

'Everyone hates this job,' says Kathy, lifting the lid and shaking in the last of the contents of the bin. Then she turns back to Sarah. 'Down home again.'

'I'm going straight back to Dublin after this.'

'Cup of tea?'

'No, thanks.'

'You look like you could do with one.'

'I just wanted to ask you something. It won't take a minute.'

'Okay, shoot.'

'It's probably nothing.'

'Spit it out.'

'Well, there was this guy in my class last week. He seemed a bit – off.'

'Off.'

'Yeah. Hard to, you know, put my finger on it.'

'Are you sure you're okay?'

'Fine. He left early. The class, I mean. But afterwards he was waiting beside my car.'

'Beside your car?'

'He took off when he saw me and Lisa.'

'That's odd. Lisa didn't know who he was?'

'She didn't notice him.'

'Oh.'

'But he was definitely there.'

'Okay.'

'It's just ... It's probably nothing, but when I was down last weekend, this guy followed me home. From the woods behind our house.'

Kathy's eyes widen.

'It was really fucking scary, actually. He had this awful dog.'

'Jesus. That *is* scary.'

She hadn't expected to feel this relief, telling Kathy.

'Right?'

'Right.'

'Then someone painted a not very nice message on our garden wall.'

'A not very nice message.'

'"Slut", it said. I was out with some of the girls from school and there it was the next morning. So that was nice.'

'Jesus, Sarah.'

'Mam went nuts.'

'I can imagine. You've no idea who did it?'

'That's what I'm trying to figure out.'

Kathy seems to start to say something then, but stops herself, and it occurs to Sarah, suddenly and out of nowhere, that Kathy would be about the same age as Jane Hart. That it's not impossible the two women might know each other. Might even be friends.

'But you think it might be this guy? Or he might have something to do with it.'

'Maybe,' says Sarah. 'I don't really know what's going on.'

'Let's check the records for that group. See what we find there.'

In the office, they find Lisa frowning at a computer screen, her distracted hello faint and far-away sounding, as Kathy pulls open a drawer of the filing cabinet and takes out a file, from which she pulls a sheet. 'Here we are,' she says. 'There are five in that group. The oldest is, let's see ... nineteen.'

'He was definitely older than that. I'd say early to mid-twenties. And there were six of them.'

'Definitely five.' She narrows her eyes. 'Some of them look older than their years.'

'He was definitely older.'

Kathy looks at Lisa. 'You didn't see this guy?'

'Who's that?' Lisa doesn't look up from her screen.

'An older guy in Sarah's group last week.'

Lisa shakes her head, her slightly frowning gaze still on the screen.

'Well, they're due in to us any minute now. Why don't we wait for them outside and you can nab them when they come in?'

'It's bizarre really,' says Sarah, when they're back out in the courtyard, 'that neither of you saw him.'

'I guess.' Kathy looks at her apprehensively. 'Sarah?'

'Yeah?'

'Remember when you were in school? You had an awful time with some of your classmates, didn't you?'

'Not particularly.'

'You did. I remember you coming in to me and crying because they were all calling you ... Well.'

'A slut.'

'Yeah.'

'We all called each other "slut". I wasn't special.'

'Right.'

Sarah looks at her. 'You don't think one of my old school friends wrote that message?'

'Well, no. No.'

'One of them went home after the hotel, got a can of red paint and a paintbrush, checked on the kids, if it was Geraldine, and then walked all the way to our house?'

'Obviously not. No. I was just thinking out loud.'

'That's just what teenagers are like. It's not like I didn't give as good as I got back then.'

'All right.' Kathy puts her hands up, just as the doorbell blares, followed by the knocker rapping loudly. 'That must be them.'

They listen to Lisa opening the door, the students trudging in. When they make their way into the courtyard, Sarah is both relieved and disappointed to see he's not among them.

'Hi, folks,' says Kathy. 'You remember Sarah from last week?'

They nod mutely at her. Back to the sullenness at the start of her class.

'Hey,' she says. None returns her smile. 'There was a guy with you last week. A bit older? Skinny, wearing a dark hoody?'

No one replies.

'He left about halfway through when we were taking out the carrot seeds. You must know who I'm talking about.'

A couple of them exchange a look, everyone else keeping their gaze on the ground.

'I just want his name,' she says. 'That's all.'

Finally, one of the girls gives her a meek, 'No, Miss.'

'No? Not a single one of you registered this guy. Then I guess I must be going crazy.'

'Why don't you lot take out the seed trays?' says Kathy. 'And I'll be with you in a second.'

Kathy turns to Sarah as the students file off. 'Go on into the kitchen and make yourself a cup of tea. I'll just get this lot started and I'll be in with you.'

'I really should get going.'

'What time do you start?'

'Not until four. But I have to meet someone for coffee first.'

To her surprise, when she'd texted David Fitzpatrick after Nancy's campaign meeting, he had replied straight away. They were going to meet in town, before Sarah started her evening shift.

'Five minutes,' says Kathy. 'Just a quick chat.' It's a statement rather than a question.

In the kitchen, Sarah fills the kettle, flicks it on, stares at it for a moment, then presses the palms of her hands hard against her eyes.

'You okay, Miss?'

It's Lisa. At the table.

'Jesus. I didn't notice you there.'

'You're all right. Why don't you sit down?' But there's an edge to her voice. As though she's hoping Sarah won't sit down.

'You must remember him, Lisa.'

Lisa shakes her head, her expression blank.

'You really didn't see him?'

'Can't say I did, Miss.'

'Then I must be losing it.'

'I doubt it,' says Lisa, awkwardly. 'I wouldn't worry about it,' she adds.

'I'm not worried, it's just weird.'

'He was probably just sussing the place out, trying to decide whether or not to sign up.'

'You think?'

'We get lads like that showing up here all the time.'

'Maybe,' she says. 'Look, would you mind telling Kathy I had to go?'

'Back to Dublin?' says Lisa.

'To Dublin.'

'You're better off, Miss.' Lisa smiles weakly.

'Yeah.'

Back outside, the fog has not lifted. When the sound of footsteps rings out cleanly as she walks towards her car, like a sharp echo of her own, she can't make out anyone.

'Hello?' she calls, her voice crisp in the cold air.

There's no answer. But when she starts walking again, more quickly now, the footsteps start again too.

And when she stops, they stop.

'Who is that?'

Again, there's no answer but now the footsteps start again on their own, coming towards Sarah from the other side of the car park, until the bare outline of a person emerges. Not Kathy or Lisa – she'd recognise them. But it is a woman.

'Can I help you?'

Silence again. The woman stops walking. Sarah can just about make out the door ahead. If she ran, she would be there in seconds. She's about to do this when the woman takes another step, and Sarah sees who it is.

'Sarah Flynn?' she says. 'I heard you were back working here. I was looking for you.'

Jane Hart speaks so softly, Sarah's not sure she didn't imagine it, her face and hair pale as the fog. As though she's made of the fog.

The way she's staring at Sarah, as though *she*'s frightened of *her*.

Or of what's going to happen next.

'It'll just take a moment,' says Jane Hart, walking towards her again.

'I'm sorry,' says Sarah, and she walks the last few steps to her car as quickly as she can without breaking into a run. Gets into it and slams her door. Only then does she notice the man standing right there, on the other side of the car, by the passenger door.

He must have been crouched, waiting for her.

And now he's opening the door, before she even has a chance to start the engine. He's sitting in beside her, snapping the door shut behind him.

'You couldn't give us a lift home?' he says, and he smirks, just like he'd smirked in her class. 'I was freezing my balls off out there.'

14

Her fingers have barely touched the door handle when his hand is on her wrist, squeezing it painfully. His face is so close now, she can smell his breath. Smoke and something sweet.

'I wouldn't go back in there if I were you, Sarah,' he says.

Even though he would have learnt her name in the Project, it makes her flinch to hear him say it. She looks through the rear-view mirror, but can barely make out the building, let alone the door.

'Not unless you want the whole town to know about you and Neil Hart. It's always the quiet ones, isn't that what they say?' He tuts slowly. 'What would your mother say? That's what I want to know.'

'Get out.'

'No need to be like that.'

'Get out of my car.'

'Do ya *want* everyone knowing about you and him? No, didn't think so.'

She can see a faint trace of stubble over his lip and, when he smiles at her, the way one of his front teeth is slightly yellower than the others.

'Sarah,' he says again, his voice sliding playfully over the syllables, his eyes on her.

'How could you know?'

'Well, you haven't exactly been careful, have you, Sarah? Meeting him in those woods like that.'

He watches her closely, his face breaking into a smile as she realises what he means.

'What do you want?' she asks.

'I'll tell you what I want, Sarah. I want the two of us to take a short drive. Have a little chat. I've been feeling bad about that night. I only want to explain myself. You'll be back in Dublin in plenty of time for the restaurant, don't worry.'

She stares into the fog, all she can see beyond the car bonnet.

'Unless you just want to sit here all day,' he says.

She lets go of the door handle.

'Attagirl,' he says, and he loosens his grip on her wrist. Lights himself a cigarette.

'Where?'

'Where. Where, where, where. Back towards town, where do you think?'

If there are any people about on Church Street, she can't see them. She can barely make out the buildings – the church, the post office, Neil's pub, the garda station. She almost misses the turn for Carrigy Heights, slowing down just in time.

'You think I live in that shithole estate? That's prejudice, you know that?' He opens the window, flicks out his cigarette butt. 'Take the left up here for the motorway,' he says. 'We're not actually *going* on the motorway. Did you think I wanted to come with you all the way to Dublin?'

There is something hard as concrete about his gaze, which bears down now on her as she keeps hers on the road.

'You can run, I'll give you that. You fairly legged it up that field, didn't you? You were shitting yourself.'

'What were you doing there?'

'Sure, amn't I after saying that's the whole point of me being here in your car, Sarah? To explain. You're not thick, are you, Sarah? Earth to Sarah.'

'I don't suppose you have a name.'

'A name? Johnny. How's that? Ah, no. I'll tell you what it was. It's a bit embarrassing, really.' He brings his face in close to hers again. Lowers his voice into a mock whisper. 'It was what they call a personal matter,' he says. 'I'd been dumped, Sarah. Can you believe that? Someone wanting to dump a catch like me? Wasn't she having it off with someone else the whole time? What do you make of that?'

She doesn't say anything.

'Broke my heart, she did. Basically, I went down to those woods to cry my little heart out. Isn't that terrible?'

'Terrible.'

'I knew you'd show some – whaddaya call it? Sympathy. You're a sympathetic person, Sarah, I can tell. Now, you're probably wondering, why our woods? Why not his fucking bedroom? Well, let's just say those woods have a certain significance to us. Sure, you know all about it.'

They are on a bridge over the motorway now and he nods at the hard shoulder ahead. 'You can pull in here. This'll do nicely.'

The fog hides the motorway below but she can hear the cars when she turns off the engine.

'It's peaceful here in a way,' he says. 'Don't you think, Sarah? Nice place to get away from it all. Know what I mean?'

When she doesn't answer, he taps the side of her head, his fingernails meeting her skin.

'I just said it's peaceful here. Isn't it?'

'I suppose.'

'Did you hear about that guy last year, though?'

'What guy?'

'Awful. Parked right here, got out, jumped off those railings there. You didn't hear about that?'

'No.'

'No? It was on the news. I suppose that's one way of getting away from it all. Ah, no, I shouldn't joke about it. He didn't even die straight away. It was the next day in hospital. Hard to imagine that kind of pain. It was night time too. This'd be kind of a spooky place at night. No one about, no lights or nothing. All the CCTV picked up was him hitting the road. Sad, isn't it? For the family, like. But no, I knew you'd understand. It's the kind of place I like to come and have a think. A bit like your woods.'

'They're not my woods.'

'I thought ye owned them.'

'My mother's selling the farm,' she says flatly.

'And here, your father's dead, is it?'

She gives a bare nod.

'Awful sad. But at least your mother has you. Isn't that it?'

'Why did you follow me home?'

'I never followed you home.'

'Yes, you did. You shone your torch on me.'

'Did I? I was chasing the *dog*, not you.'

He is clearly enjoying how implausible his story is. How she has no way of challenging it.

'I was a bit embarrassed,' he continues. 'Sure, you probably heard me crying and everything.'

'No.'

'No? What did you hear?'

'Hardly anything.' She glances at him. 'You said I wouldn't want him on me. Something like that.'

'Want him on you?' He laughs, then abruptly the hard brazen stare is back. 'That was it?'

'That was it.'

'It was just me there.'

'I know that,' she says, surprised by the comment. And then she's remembering – the rustling sound she'd taken to be a frightened animal.

'It's a bit creepy though when you think about it,' he continues. 'You standing there, eavesdropping on me.'

'I wasn't eavesdropping.'

'No? What would you call it?'

'Trying not to be maimed to death by that animal.'

'Wolf? Sure, he's harmless.'

'He's dangerous.'

He puts his hand on her wrist again. This time he squeezes even tighter.

'You're hurting me.'

'He's harmless. What did you hear?'

'Hardly anything. Just what I said. And then you calling your dog.'

'What else?'

She keeps her eyes on the windscreen but his gaze bears down on her, his face close now to hers.

'That's it?'

'That's it.'

'You're not bullshitting me?'

'I'm not bullshitting you. That hurts.'

'So why'd you go to the cops?'

She looks at him. 'I didn't. I just— How did you know about that?'

'You wouldn't want to be wasting their time,' he says, ignoring her question. 'Would you?'

'No. It's like I said. I thought you'd followed me home.'

'Wrong.'

'Okay, okay. I believe you.'

Finally, he lets go. 'I think we'll be grand, Sarah. You just get back to your fancy restaurant and we won't have to bother each other again.'

She doesn't know where the courage comes from, but suddenly she's saying it. 'You weren't really on your own, though, were you?'

He looks startled.

'I guess it was your girlfriend who was with you.'

'Have you not heard a word I said?' he says. But his tone has changed, as well as the expression on his face, all the cockiness wiped out of him.

'I have,' she says, her voice calm. 'It's just I was sure I heard someone else down there as well.'

'I just told you,' he says, 'I was on my own.'

'She said something,' she continues, knowing somehow that he won't detect she's now lying. 'Didn't catch what exactly but she definitely said something.'

He looks at her, confused or startled.

Frightened. He looks frightened.

'The weird thing is,' she continues, because even though she is also frightened, something else is rising inside her. It's the same feeling she had when she reached the cottage that night, and he shone his stupid damn torchlight right in her eyes. 'I could have sworn I recognised it. The voice, I mean.'

'Is that right?'

'It is, yeah.' She looks at him and now it's as though the hardness that was in his gaze has shifted to her own. 'Weird, isn't it?'

He doesn't answer.

'But I can't imagine Jane Hart is your girlfriend. She's far too old for you, isn't she?'

He stares. And now she knows. Jane Hart *was* with him that night when she came upon him in the woods.

'Or your ex, I should say,' she continues. 'Sorry. That was insensitive of me.'

Now, he takes her wrist again. Except this time, he twists her arm back until a yelp of pain escapes her. 'I'll give you one more chance to tell me everything you heard.'

She wants more than anything to tell him to go to hell. To call him a stupid wanker. But he's twisting her arm tighter now, the pain becoming so sharp she feels nauseous and instead she says, 'Please. Please stop.'

'You're taking the piss now, you know that. You're taking the fucking piss.'

He twists her arm tighter.

'I might have imagined it.'

'What's that?'

'I couldn't even see her.' Her eyes are closed against the pain. 'I think I did imagine it.'

At last he releases her arm. 'Of course you fucking imagined it. And now you're going to stay away from them woods. And stay away from the fucking cops. You're going to stay away from Crookedwood for a while. Until your mother is nice and settled in her new place in the town.'

'Okay.'

'I didn't hear you.'

'I'll stay away.'

He appraises her. 'Anyone can see this is starting to take a toll on you. You're like someone having a breakdown.' His voice is regaining its composure as he speaks. 'Spouting fucking crap like that. I doubt anyone would be surprised if you followed your man over that bridge some night.' He laughs. 'Can you imagine it? Splat. Ah, no. Only joking. So, are we good, Sarah? Hey. I asked you a question. Jesus, I'm beginning to think you *are* thick.'

'We're good.'

'I couldn't hear you there.'

'We're good.'

'You're staying away for a while.'

'I'm staying away.'

'That's all I wanted to hear.'

He gets out of the car, snaps the door behind him, raps his knuckles on the roof, the way a friend might.

15

When Sarah first moved into her flat – a single room in a Victorian red-brick – almost five years ago now, the first thing she did was paint, turning dirty-beige walls to powdery lilac, laminated kitchen cupboards to bright mustard. Then she'd asked the landlord to take away the sad single bed, which she'd replaced with the futon that now sits folded beneath the large sash window. Old, discoloured curtains she'd stuffed into a cupboard under the stairs of the building, replacing them with this single cotton drape, white and stained with a blue flower that does nothing to keep out the draught but makes the room airy and light. She even paid someone to sweep the chimney so that she could light a fire, and bought the round wooden table in a second-hand market down the road, which she'd sanded and oiled until its loveliness emerged.

Now, in its centre, sit the flowers Neil sent to her the week before. Lilies and pale pink roses, they fill the room with their heavy fragrance. When she'd left for home, they were still fresh, but now the heads of the roses hang heavily over the vase, and some of their petals lie on the table. The lilies have all opened, the table smeared here and there with their yellow pollen.

She picks up the card, reads it again: *I'll be up soon, darling. I love you so much. Neil xx.*

They'd arrived the day after their stupid argument about her coming home for Nancy's campaign meeting. When she'd answered the door to find the courier there, holding the bouquet, she'd been so surprised by the gesture it hadn't occurred to her then that the note doesn't sound like him at all. She'd even forgotten her dislike of being sent florist flowers – the way they come with all that hedge, the thousands of air miles usually involved, the chore of pruning and arranging, then finding somewhere to put them – and had taken down her only vase, deciding to place them on the table so that they'd be the first thing she saw when she came through the door after work. Ringing him then to gush her thanks.

When her phone buzzes suddenly now, she's sure it's him, calling back so that they can talk properly. On the drive up, it had been so hard to hear him against the noise of the motorway, his efforts to calm and reassure her coming through so far away and tinny. As though he wasn't fully grasping what she was saying.

Now they can have a real conversation.

Except it's not him. It's Nancy.

'Mam? Are you okay?'

'You're probably about to head out the door,' says Nancy. 'I won't keep you. We'll just run through it one more time.'

David Fitzpatrick. She had completely forgotten.

'Don't get annoyed, now. The first thing is, you have the letter?'

'The letter.'

'For his father.' A note of panic rises in Nancy's voice. 'I left it on the coat stand this morning.'

'I have it.'

'Thank God.'

'But – I'm not meeting him now.'

'What?'

'He had to take a rain check.'

'A rain check?' Nancy's voice is sharp with incredulity.

'Something came up, he said. I'll get him again.'

'He didn't give a reason?'

'He was very apologetic.'

'Well, damn him anyway.'

'He promised we'll meet up this week,' she says. She'd say anything to get off the phone.

'You'll set another date with him? A lot depends on it.'

'Of course I will.'

She's about to hang up and then she's asking, 'Mam, you don't know Jane Hart, do you?'

There's a pause.

'You mean Neil Hart's wife?'

'Yes.'

'A bit, to say hello to, not much more than that. Why are you asking about her?'

'Ursula mentioned her the other day. It just seemed a bit sad or something. I was just wondering, never mind.'

'A sister in Dublin,' says Nancy, 'and I think both her parents dead.'

'The stories about her. They're all true, aren't they?'

'Oh, I wouldn't have time for that kind of gossip.'

'No.'

'And neither should you.'

'No.'

'She does have a bit of a drinking problem,' Nancy acknowledges. 'And Olive said to me once she'd heard she has some kind of mental-health condition. She has to take medication for it.'

'What is it?'

'I don't know what it's called. What's wrong with you?'

'Nothing.'

'You sound – jumpy. I've always found her grand,' says Nancy. 'If you believed half of what people around here said, you'd swear the woman was a witch.'

'Did I imagine it or was she friends with Tom Fitzpatrick's wife when they lived in Crookedwood?'

She has what she thinks is a memory of the two women chatting outside the church after Mass.

'Really?' says Nancy. 'I can't see it.'

It's reassuring, that she should struggle with the idea. But then Nancy speaks on.

'Jane Hart used to play golf when she moved here first, now that I think of it. So I suppose she could have known her that way.'

'Jane Hart played golf.'

'She did and she was good at it. I don't think she had a drinking problem in those days.'

'But I remember her coming down to the bar one night and taking a bottle of gin. She didn't even say anything to me. That was back then, when they still lived upstairs.'

'Well, I don't know. I only mean to say, she played golf. So she can't have been that bad.'

'What's the story with the sister? Didn't they have a falling-out?'

'As far as I know, there was something like that.'

'That's what Ursula said.'

'But why the sudden interest in the woman?'

'Just, like I said, Ursula was talking about her.'

'Idle gossip is all that is.'

'I was just curious.'

'I wonder thinking about it now should I find out her views on her husband's development.'

'Hardly.'

'You never know, she mightn't agree with him. And if she doesn't, you'll be doing her a favour too.'

'I'd better run, Mam.'

'Another thing about Jane Hart is that she used to live in Dublin, didn't she? Like her sister. But then she moved down here. So people do it. Didn't she work in a hotel, now that I think about it? You never know, she might have an interest in the organic beef idea. She might have contacts herself.'

'I really have to go.'

'What's wrong with you?'

'Nothing.'

'One minute you're asking me about the woman, the next you're annoyed with me.'

'I'm not annoyed. I'll call you soon.'

After she's hung up, she sends a quick text to David Fitzpatrick, apologising for the late notice but that she has to cancel, something's come up at work, she says. She'll be in touch during the week. So sorry again.

Then she calls Neil, but it rings out. A text comes through seconds later: *Miss you so much. Busy here for a Monday but text me when you're finished, might be able to chat then. Jane is going crazy. But all this will be over soon. Love you xxx.*

Her laptop is a heavy old thing she bought second hand before she dropped out of college. It takes an age to turn on and another age to connect to the internet. When she's finally logged on, she doesn't know what to search for. After staring at the screen for a moment, she tries 'crime Crookedwood'. But all that comes up is a couple of articles on a robbery of a petrol station outside town that happened a few years ago and a piece on an old story she's heard many times before, about a farmer who murdered his brother after a dispute over land, way back in the 1940s. Nothing to suggest there's been any recent robberies. Nothing even on the supposed increase in drug-dealing in the Heights. When she types in 'Jane Hart', nothing comes up either, at least nothing connected to Neil's wife. Only when she types in her maiden name – Jane Flaherty – does she come upon something that might be about her. It's an article from a local Galway-based newspaper, dated 1985, about a twelve-year-old Jane Flaherty who had won a local piano-playing competition. At the top of the narrow column, there is a photo of a girl. The quality is poor, but the thin face and straight blonde hair fit. Sarah stares hard. Tries to recall the woman taking the bottle of gin from the bar that night, years ago. The ghostlike woman outside the Garden Project. She thinks it's the same person. And the timing is right. But she can't be sure.

The last time she used a phone box was in her second year of college, before everyone suddenly had a mobile. She's not even sure if the one across the road works and, even if it does, she doesn't have any change. It seems very unlikely it has a directory in there, like they used to do. But it does, one for Dublin residential listings and a *Golden Pages*, both of them heavy and damp, covers ripped off, on a shelf by the phone, the smell in there sweet like rot. In the residential one, she finds seven Christine Flahertys listed.

She tears out the page and crosses the road back to her flat. The first number's engaged, both times she tries. The second rings out. For the third, the woman who answers has a frail voice that announces someone much older than Jane Hart's sister would be. The fourth number, a child answers. When Sarah asks to speak to Christine Flaherty, she calls for her mother. Waiting, Sarah can hear a woman's assured footsteps clip-clopping closer.

'Hello?' It's a confident voice, of someone who's used to being listened to.

'I'm sorry to bother you,' says Sarah. She hesitates, then just asks, 'Do you have a sister called Jane?'

Silence. Then, a sigh. 'What's happened?'

'Nothing. Nothing's happened.'

'Is she all right?'

'She's fine, I think.'

'I didn't catch your name.'

'I'm just a friend of hers. I was calling because, well, I'm a bit worried about her.'

'Why is that?' Christine Hart's voice is wary.

'Because she's just learned her husband's having an affair.'

Silence again.

It's a wild card, and Sarah can't quite believe what she's saying. But she finds it's not that difficult either, to say something like that to a stranger on the phone. And it's not like that she'll ever meet the woman.

'She's out of her mind about it,' she continues. 'And, well, I haven't seen her in a few days.'

'I can't imagine Jane caring less if that husband of hers was having an affair. Look, you're really going to have to tell me who you are.'

'Have you seen her recently?'

'As it happens, she was here,' she admits, 'just a few days ago. She never said anything about that.'

'How did you find her?'

'Oh, raving about some nonsense. Look, I can't continue this conversation unless you tell me who you are. Are you from Crookedwood?'

'Yes,' says Sarah.

'Well, if you won't tell me who you are, let me give you a small piece of advice. An addict is an addict. If she won't help herself, there's no point in trying to help her. That is a lesson I've learned the hard way.'

For a long while after talking to Jane's sister, Sarah sits at her table, taking in the yellow streaks still on its surface. Dabs a finger in the powder, and rubs it between finger and thumb, staining her skin. It must be the flowers' heavy scent, mixed with the cigarette smoke that still comes from her clothes and hair that's brought back her headache. And only now does she notice that it's almost four, and even if she hurries, she'll be late for the restaurant.

16

Friday afternoon, Sarah is sitting on a bench by the cricket pitch on the campus of Trinity College. It's a clear sky, the first day of the year with real warmth in the sunlight. Blossom buds gauze the branches of the trees lining the pitch. People are taking off their coats, as they wait for the game to start. There is even a couple sitting on the grass. Sarah has cake and coffee from The Runner Bean, the lovely deli on Nassau Street.

And this headache, like something is trying to break out of there. Thin and sharp, it's been humming off and on all week, ever since she drove back to the city in the lingering smell of the guy's cigarette smoke.

Alongside the headache, her wonky heartbeat is coming and going more than ever, even right now as she waits for David Fitzpatrick. Especially right now. She took a beta-blocker on that Monday before work, after her phone conversation with Christine Flaherty, but that had made her feel weirdly flat and tired all evening, on top of being late. Five plates had been sent back, each one her fault. It hadn't been much different on any of the other nights that followed. After David, she's going to the restaurant. Not because she's on but because Jack has said he wants a chat.

All week, the events of Monday have been playing and replaying in her mind, and she is still no closer to understanding anything. Unlike the week before, she no longer has the option of deciding there was nothing to any of it, that there was no connection between the guy in the woods and Jane Hart after all – a case of putting two and two together and coming up with five hundred. That ended, if not outside the Garden Project, certainly when she'd said to him that she thought she'd heard Jane Hart that night in the woods. His face, when she'd said that. Jane Hart was with him that evening, there's no doubt about it. The fact that it makes no sense is neither here nor there.

Because she can't have been there with the intention of hurting Sarah. Even if she did know she was down that night, which is unlikely, she can't have known Sarah was going to take a walk to the woods, given that she herself didn't know until seconds beforehand. Now, in the clear light of day, she even feels embarrassed when she recalls how she'd acted when Jane had approached her in the car park of the Garden Project, practically running back to her car like that, when Jane had been so – cautious. Polite even, almost apologetic. What did it all mean? It seems too much of a coincidence that she and the guy from the woods had been there at the same time, but maybe that's all it had been. It *feels* like that's all it had been. But maybe she's wrong. Surely she's wrong, now she knows they were both there that night in the woods. The one time she and Neil had been able to talk since Monday, she'd come away from that conversation just as confused. Maybe even more so. He seemed to think that Jane had intended to threaten Sarah at the Project. Tell her to stay away. He'd even seemed to imply it wasn't impossible that there *was* a connection between the two of them. That Jane was somehow involving that guy in a plan to hurt Sarah. He'd said she'd been acting increasingly erratically. That he was thinking of talking to her psychiatrist about the possibility of having her admitted to hospital, for her own safety, as well as anyone else's.

He'd been annoyed with her then for not telling Paul. That guy ought to be reported, he'd said. If Jane's doing something that could endanger Sarah.

But his arm hadn't been twisted like that. He hadn't been threatened on that overpass, in the fog. Anyway, she'd said, all she needs to do is stay in Dublin until Nancy has moved, which should be just a matter of weeks. Which was what she'd planned to do anyway.

She opens the last text message he sent her, just the night before: *Miss you. I might get up for a night next week. Stay strong. Xxx.*

And her reply: *Great xx.*

She's still looking at it when David Fitzpatrick sits down beside her, so close their coats touch.

'Oh.' She puts her phone into her bag.

'If it isn't Ms Flynn,' he says.

'Hi there,' she says, making herself return his smile. As in that time he showed up in the restaurant, she's struck by how different he is from the person she encountered when they were in school. It's not just the physical changes either – dull gleam of the beginnings of a bald patch, or the way his face has filled out, robbing him somehow of his looks. More than that, it's the change in his demeanour. Whereas before he was so confident, now there's this neediness.

'Good to see you again,' she says, handing him his coffee. 'Thanks for meeting up.'

She takes the slices of lemon cake from the paper bag, using the opportunity to move a couple of inches, so their coats are no longer touching.

'What's this? Humble pie?'

'You could say that. Sorry again about Monday.'

'Crisis averted?'

'What?'

'At work.' He watches her closely, the hint of a smile on his face.

'Oh. Yeah.'

She busies herself with napkins. 'Someone had to go home early. I wasn't sure if you take sugar.' She tries her coat pockets.

'No sugar.'

'Oh. Good.'

'Sweet enough and all that.'

'You're barely late at all,' she says brightly. When she'd called him to apologise and re-arrange, he'd made it sound as though he might not show up at all, he was so busy with work.

'No?' He looks at his watch.

'So, how are you?'

'Busy,' he says, shaking his head, as though to say he'll spare her the details. 'You?'

'Same.'

'You dropped out of the ag science.'

'I did. For my sins.'

'That always seemed weird to me.'

'What? A girl doing it?'

'You doing it,' he says.

'Oh.'

'You like working in that place anyway?'

'The restaurant? You wouldn't last long in there if you didn't.'

'Suppose not. Down home much these days?'

'A bit,' she says. 'When I can.'

'Helping out on the homestead?'

'Not really. Mam's been renting the land out for years now. She's selling the place actually.'

'Right, right,' he says. She has a flashback of how awkward it used to be trying to make conversation with him all those years ago.

'Do you ever go back to those woods?' he says then, with a smile.

'No.'

'Some messing that went on there.'

'Do you ever go back home yourself?'

'To Crookedwood?'

She nods.

'The odd time. Not much.'

'Your parents still have connections down there?'

'Not really.'

'No? They must have had friends there.'

He shrugs. 'I suppose. I dunno.'

'They were in the golf club, weren't they?'

'That's right.'

'I seem to remember your mother and Jane Hart being friends.'

He looks at her curiously.

'Well, anyway,' she says, 'speaking of mothers, I think I said to you already my mother wants to ask a favour.' As quickly as she can, she takes him through the whole thing – Neil's planned development, the committee's opposition, their concern it will be to the detriment of the town, how the deadline for challenges is very close and they understand how busy David's father must be, but if there was any chance he could fit them in for a quick meeting in his constituency office in Dunlone, given his Crookedwood roots ... A short meeting was all they were looking for, whenever suited him best.

'Right,' he says, when she finally stops talking.

'It's all in there,' she says, pulling the letter from Nancy out of her bag and handing it to him. 'If you could pass that on to your father, they'd be very grateful.'

He takes the envelope, looks at his father's name written across it in Nancy's careful script, like he's faintly amused by the whole thing.

Amused, and something else. 'You're not convinced,' he says.

'It's a Lidl,' she says. 'A few decent houses, which the town needs.'

'I'll pass it on,' he says, putting the letter into an inside pocket of his coat.

'I appreciate it.'

'I can't promise anything beyond that.'

'Of course not.'

'So,' he says. 'You're off to work now.'

'I am.'

'No rest for the wicked.'

'That's it.'

'What time do you knock off? I might be out – maybe I could catch you for a drink.'

'Oh, it'll be way too late. Mam says it's too antisocial working there. I never get to go out.'

'They must give you a night off now and then.'

'Normally they do,' she says, 'but we're short-staffed at the moment.'

'Fair enough.'

'Thanks again for your help with Nancy's thing.' She goes to stand.

'It's funny,' he says, 'you asking me about Jane Hart.'

'It is?'

'She's married to Neil Hart, isn't she? The guy behind this development?'

'That's right.'

'You worked in his pub, if I remember correctly.'

She looks at him.

'I could have sworn I saw him in your restaurant that evening.'

She takes her phone out of her bag, squints at the screen, as though she just got a text message. All the while, he's watching her. It never occurred to her that he might have noticed her talking to Neil that night. He'd been careful to take a table on the other side of the room, and she hadn't come out of the kitchen again until David and his friends were gone.

'Was he?' she says, dropping her phone back into her bag. 'I can't remember. People come up from home all the time.'

'You were talking to him, actually.'

'I was?'

'I had to go back for my scarf,' he explains. 'And there you were, standing at his table.'

'Maybe. I honestly can't remember.' She zips her bag shut. 'Well, thanks again,' she says.

'My mother always said Jane was the one who had the raw deal in that relationship. Everyone in the town feeling sorry for him.'

'I think they had good reason to feel sorry for him.'

'You know what they say. There's always two sides to a story.' He's all but leering at her. 'You must have a thing for local boys.'

'What do you mean?'

'Ah, nothing. In this day and age, there's no shame in it, I suppose.'

She's walking away from him and then she's turning back. 'I wonder,' she says, 'what your side of the story is.'

He looks at her, thrown, taken aback by not so much the words but the tone in which they were spoken.

She's surprised herself by this sudden swell of anger. 'In those woods,' she adds. 'That night.' She waits. 'What would you call what happened between us?'

He's either confused or pretending to be.

'You must have known I didn't want – to do that.'

It's satisfying, the way his face changes. To leave him standing there like that. But her mind is racing now and she walks to the restaurant without registering much of what she passes – the people, the streets, the traffic. She only realises she's passed the place when red lights at a pedestrian crossing tell her she's gone too far.

17

When the waitress, a new girl, starts setting the table beside the one where she and Jack sit waiting, Sarah almost asks her to stop. Stop moving, stop clanking cutlery and glasses, stop carefully acting as though we're not here. It's making her headache and her wonky heart worse.

And then she's gone, the steel doors to the kitchen swinging behind her, and it's just Sarah and Jack in the pale, high-ceilinged dining room. She watches him run his hand through his hair in that distracted way of his. Doesn't say anything, even as he looks at her, all tired and fed-up looking. He's the one who said he needed to speak to her. Let him start.

'So,' he says. 'What's going on with you?'

Sarah tries to look as though she doesn't understand the question.

'Don't pretend you don't know what I mean.'

'I'm sorry about yesterday,' she says.

'If it was just yesterday, we wouldn't be having this conversation, Sarah. I'd say you've made more mistakes in that kitchen over the past month than you did in the year before. No?'

In only a couple of hours, this room will be full of people talking and eating. She wonders about the couple who will be sitting where she and Jack are, their reason for going out – a birthday or an anniversary. Or maybe, she thinks, they're just very rich and are eating out in a place like this for the hell of it.

'I'll ask you again. What's going on with you?'

Sarah shifts in her seat. Reluctantly she returns Jack's gaze. 'There's been some stuff at home,' she says.

'Okay. Do you want to tell me about it?'

'My mother's got a lot on,' she says. Because this at least is true. This might be something.

'Right.'

'She's started this campaign opposing a housing development.'

Jack is looking at her, waiting for more.

'I think she might be going through the menopause.' This is also true, even if it's the first time she's actually acknowledged it to herself. As soon as she's said it, though, she can hear how it sounds.

Jack raises his eyebrows. 'Your *mother* is going through the menopause. You're going to have to do better than that.'

Sarah looks at him blankly. 'I don't know what to tell you.'

'Well, Sarah, *I* don't know what to tell *you*. When you decided not to move home but stay on here full time, I'll be honest with you, fewer things have given me greater pleasure since I started here.'

'Thanks.'

'Once you made that decision.' He sighs. 'Your appetite for the job, you inhaled the fucking thing. Everything. You just kept taking it all in.'

She looks across at the huge blue painting that takes up most of the wall opposite. An abstract work, for the first time, it strikes her as being of something lying at the bottom of the sea. A board from a ship that sank, maybe. All this time it's been holding itself against the weight of heavy miles of water.

'In the last couple of months, though.' He pauses. 'How many dishes were sent back this week?'

'A lot.'

'Damn right a lot. And you forgot to put that order in with the butcher. Again. They're in demand. We can't lose our account with them or we're screwed.'

'I know. I'm sorry about that. I'm sorry about all of it.'

'You know as well as I do that a place like this can't rest on its reputation. Not for a single night.'

'I'm sorry,' she says again. 'I – I'm tired.'

She stares at the painting as his gaze bears down on her.

'Maybe you *are* overworked,' he says quietly, 'if you have this stuff going on at home.'

But his saying it out loud just reveals its weakness. She's about to apologise again, when something about him has her stiffen in her seat.

'I know this isn't any of my business,' he begins. 'And you know me, whatever people here do in their private lives is their business. Life gets messy. God knows, I get that.'

'Right.'

'It's just. All this started in the past month or so. Not long after that guy started coming here. You know who I mean,' he says kindly. 'The one who always turns up some random night of the week, always when you're on, about an hour before we close up. Sits at that table over there and orders a dessert.'

'He pays. I'm not giving him freebies, if that's what you're worried about.'

Jack looks at her sharply when she says that and Sarah is surprised at the tone that has shown up in her voice.

'I know that,' he says.

'I keep working when he comes.'

'I didn't say you didn't.' Now Jack looks at the painting, keeping his gaze on it when he speaks again. 'You being off your game started around the time he began showing up, though. I just wondered ...'

'What?'

'Oh, Sarah. We've all been there.'

'Been where?'

'In a relationship that isn't any good for us.'

'His name's Neil,' she says. 'And he is good for me.'

He looks at her awkwardly. 'Is he from down home?'

She nods.

'Look, I'm trying to help you, believe it or not.'

'I know. I appreciate it.'

'I've told you, you're next in line to be sous-chef.'

'Maybe I shouldn't be.'

'What do you mean by that?'

'You once said to me that if something feels constantly like a struggle, maybe that's a sign you shouldn't be doing it.'

'That was after you failed your final year in ag science. Which you told me you had no interest in.'

'Yeah, well, maybe I should have sat out that one.'

He sits back. 'You're telling me you're now regretting not moving home and being a farmer.'

'I don't mean regretting. Well, maybe. Maybe I am regretting it.' She looks at him. 'You just said it yourself. I don't seem to be exactly up to the task any more. That's as station chef.'

'You used to be up to the task. I wouldn't be trying to talk to you now if I didn't think you could be up to it again.' Jack glances at the kitchen doors. 'You're the most talented person I've seen come through here, Sarah. You have a perfect sense of balance. Perfect. That can't be taught. You've got passion. You're not afraid to try changing things. You work really hard. You can handle the stress. I've told you this before. I have no doubt that if you really set your mind to it, you could become a top-class chef.'

'Okay.'

'You sound like you don't believe me,' he says. He looks exasperated.

'I don't know,' she says.

'I never said you weren't up to scratch,' says Jack again, his voice hardening. 'I wouldn't have spent all that time and effort training you this past couple of years if I wasn't pretty damn sure you're up to scratch.'

She's just so tired, she thinks. She's just so tired.

'Maybe,' she says, 'if I could take a break.'

He looks at her in astonishment. 'A break? What – from here?'

'Just a week. Or two maybe. Two weeks.'

'Do you want your job, Sarah? Because there are a lot of good sous-chefs in this city that I could easily poach if I set my mind to it.'

'I do want it,' she says. 'I don't know.'

'Okay,' says Jack. There's a new quality in the way he's talking now, the way he's looking at her. 'Maybe we did move a bit fast over the past while.'

'I'll take time off?'

He nods. 'Take your couple of weeks. We'll check in then.'

'Okay. Thanks.'

Soon it will be time to open, welcome the evening customers. Soon the first orders will get shouted out back in the kitchen. There'll be the sound of oil sputtering in a pan, the smell of things frying. But Sarah's in the lobby, with its ornate sofa and fancy light fixture. She's pushing open the glass door, walking down the curved path with its potted trees, back out onto the street.

18

She'd almost passed the place without noticing it. A quiet doorway on a Georgian street that led into a small courtyard, where a trail of immaculately trimmed potted trees hemmed a narrow path to a glass entrance on the side of a townhouse. Beside the doorway, a wooden plaque with the words 'Number Seven' imprinted on it. She would have passed it too, had a guy not walked through the doorway and into the courtyard, just as she was standing there, carrying on his shoulder a large wooden box, which, as far as she could see, contained raspberries and only raspberries. She'd never seen so many raspberries all together like that before. Perfect-looking, all fat and cool-red, begging to be picked up, massaged between finger and thumb, crammed into the mouth.

After he'd disappeared through the glass door, she had followed him up the pathway. Peered through, to find already he'd disappeared through a further door. All she could see was what looked like a small lobby with a standing desk, a maroon velvet sofa, and a light fixture that looked more like a sculpture hanging from the high ceiling.

By then, it was almost four and she'd been walking the city streets for the best part of the day, dropping her CV into each bar, café and restaurant she passed along the way. Not wasting any of the precious last couple of notes or loose change in her wallet on public transport. One bar had pretty much guaranteed her a job clearing tables, telling her to call back once she knew her college timetable for the year. A grotty place that smelt of stale beer. And another place had asked her to call again at the end of the week, telling her they'd probably take her on for a trial run the following weekend. She had done what she'd set out to do. She didn't need to keep going. Her shirt was clinging to her back, her knickers sticky from discharge, it being around the time of her ovulation. She was so skint that when she'd done that week's shopping, she hadn't been able to afford the luxury of panty liners. All she'd had to eat was Weetabix for breakfast and a slice of pizza for lunch, which she had devoured on the street. It was time to return to the house share she'd moved into only a couple of days before. Shower and get some food into her. The following day she was to start the third of a four-year degree in agricultural science.

She had been about to turn away when the guy from earlier, now minus his box, pushed open the glass door, walked past her, back towards the street.

And then he stopped, and turned to face her. 'You looking for a job?'

'Yes.'

He took her in. 'Student?'

'Yes.'

'Their dishwasher just quit. They're all in a tizzy about it. Interested?'

'Yes.'

He walked back up to the door. 'Follow me.'

She did follow him, through the small lobby and into a sleek, wood-panelled bar, and on into a dining room, all its space stopping her in her tracks. So much space – between the tables, with their elegant, weighty-looking chairs, between the deep-carpeted floor and the high, ornamented ceiling. On a vast wall, a massive blue abstract painting.

'It's huge,' she said.

'Two Georgian ground floors knocked into one. Come on.'

She followed him across the room, through swinging doors and into a kitchen, all stainless steel and pale, tiled walls. At one long island, a man was chopping onions with alarming speed. Sarah stared, entranced. She had never seen vegetables being chopped like that before, so quickly, his hands all but disappearing into a blur. At another island behind him, an older man in a chef's hat. He was tapping a pencil on a notebook, in front of him the box of raspberries and, beside it, a massive white bowl filled with a salad leaf. Sarah had never before seen those spidery leaves. She had never seen salad look so – salady, even when they'd grown it in the Garden Project. This stuff was such a sharp shade of green, as though it had just been pulled from the earth. She found herself with a sudden desire to put her face right into it. Suck in its smell.

'Don't tell me I don't solve your problems.'

The chef looked up at the man she'd been following. Then he looked at Sarah.

'May I present your new dishwasher?' the man said. 'Jack – what did you say your name is?'

'Sarah.'

'Jack, Sarah, Sarah, Jack. Found her outside with her nose pressed up against the window,' he added, as he walked back towards the still-swinging doors. 'See you all tomorrow.'

Jack took in Sarah. She put him in his mid-fifties maybe, handsome with grey hair and a paunch. He scratched his head as he glanced down her CV.

'I'm looking for part-time work,' she said.

'Agricultural science?' He looked at her quizzically.

'We have a farm at home. My mother and I.'

'So the plan is, to go home and – farm?'

Sarah nods.

'And, what, your mother's been running the place while you study?'

'I've been going home when I can, helping. I work on and off in a pub at home when I'm down as well.'

'Hart's,' he said, reading it off her CV.

'That's it. Just for my final year, I need to be in Dublin more for exams and assignments, stuff like that.'

'And then you move home for good?'

'That's right.'

'It's unusual.'

She didn't say anything to this. There didn't seem to be anything to say. Nothing she could think of, anyway.

Jack looked back at her CV. 'What was this place Hart's like?'

'Really busy. Especially at weekends.'

'Okay. Well, our dishwasher just quit after three nights. That must be a record, Jean?'

The man chopping vegetables nodded without pausing in his work. 'No great loss, I do not think.'

'This is Jean. He was our dishwasher. Now he's a kitchen porter. Prepares the veg, stuff like that.'

Jean turned, looked at Sarah. 'Tall,' he said.

'He means all the stooping. Your back will probably ache. But that'll wear off after a day or two.' He glared at Jean. 'Are you trying to put her off? You want two jobs for yourself this evening?'

Jean spread his hands, grinning at Sarah. 'Very welcome,' he said.

Jack smiled at Sarah. 'Basically, all you do is load and empty the two dishwashers here. It sounds straightforward. It *is* straightforward. But it gets intense. Not many chances for a break. You could be going flat out for six hours.'

'Hard work isn't a problem.'

'I don't imagine it is. Well, nine euro an hour, and you get your share of the tips. They can be decent enough.'

'That sounds good to me.'

'And you can start this evening?' He looked at his watch, made a face. 'We'd need you to start within the hour. You probably wouldn't even get a chance to go home and change.'

Sarah's gaze fell on the fruit, the salad as she took in what he'd said.

'I'm making a raspberry soufflé with those,' said Jack. 'The rocket's for a courgette and capers salad.'

'Oh.'

'You can pick up a thing or two about cooking if you're interested, working in a place like this.'

'I'm no cook,' she said.

'Well, it's not mandatory. Probably better for the dishwashing if you're not interested in what's happening on the hob.'

'Definitely,' said Jean.

'Jean agrees. So what do you think?

'Why not?'

Jean filled her in on her duties. Showed her where the dishwashers were and how they worked. Explained how her one and only job was to keep them going, all night long. That, and empty the bins, which, he said, she could expect to do about ten times in the course of one evening. She was to make sure to remember to line them each time. He showed her where the waiting staff left the dirty dishes. How if the bins ever overflowed, they wouldn't bother scraping the leftover food into them, and then she'd be in trouble. And when a dishwasher load was done, how she was to dry off everything before putting it all away. Making sure everything – pots, pans, knives, plates – were exactly where they should be for the chefs. By the time he'd finished, the place had filled with more staff and bustle.

'You got all that?'

'I think so.'

He returned to his vegetables. 'So you can wash your hands now. Always wash your hands as soon as you arrive. And find a hairnet in that back cupboard I showed you.'

She got snapped at a few times that first evening. For leaving the dishwasher door open, so that one of the junior chefs had almost tripped over it. For not cleaning up sauce someone spilled on the floor. For getting locked outside the first time she put out the bins. For forgetting the rinse aid with one load. For putting the cutlery in the wrong places the first time she'd to do that. For letting the bins overflow towards the end of the evening during a particularly busy spell, so that, just as Jean had warned, the waiters left the scraps on the plates instead of cleaning them off, and everything built up messily.

By the time the dishes eventually stopped coming, her back ached horribly, she felt light-headed with hunger and was certain Jack was going to tell her she needn't come back. But instead he stopped on his way out to ask her how she'd found it. Told her he'd seen worse. And then, when they were divvying out the tips, Jean gave her a twenty-euro note.

'Are you sure?'

'You hungry?' He went to the fridge, cut her a slice of cake.

'Moroccan orange,' he said, handing her a fork. 'Eat.'

'Oh, my God,' she said, when she had taken the first bite.

'Good?'

'I've never tasted anything like it.'

It was weeks later that she asked him to give her a lesson in chopping vegetables, promising to turn up an hour early if he'd do so. He showed her first how to sharpen a knife – thumb always behind the guard on the sharpener, fingers kept away from the blade – and then how to use the knife, thumb and little finger for stability gripping its base, how she was to imagine the handle was on a wheel, keeping the tip of the blade always on the board.

All her life, food had been nothing more than a necessity, neither good nor bad, something to be consumed so that a person could function. Her housemates, on learning she'd grown up on a farm, had all assumed she'd had a childhood full of homemade soda bread and comforting stews, whereas the reality had been chicken nuggets and spaghetti from a tin. Which, as far as Sarah had been concerned, was all that could reasonably be expected of food.

That was up to now. In the restaurant, cooking, she learned, was something that she loved. Really, actually loved. She loved the ingredients. She loved how, in the right hands, they could be used to make something new and good. She loved the idea of a dish being placed in front of someone, and that person enjoying it. Their day made that bit better. Around the time of that first lesson, she developed a tendency to gravitate towards the hob whenever she could, snatch glimpses in the chaos of new things coming into being. Accepted in exchange for this occasionally being yelled at for letting the dishes pile up now and then, the bins fill to overflowing. She seemed to get away with it too because she always stayed late to finish cleaning up, regardless of when her lectures started the following morning. Sometimes when she stayed late, she tried to do something she'd seen done that evening in the kitchen. Always something small. But one night all the ingredients had been still there for a particular dish – seared duck breast, with a beetroot purée, decorated with blackberries and chicory – and, without thinking, she started making it, lightly scoring the pale skin with a sharp knife, grinding the seasoning ingredients and rubbing them all over the cool, burgundy flesh. Oiling and baking the beetroot, then blitzing it with oil, salt and lemon juice. Deciding in a sudden flurry to add some of the blackberries to the purée, dipping her finger in to taste, adding a little sugar, tasting again. She didn't notice Jack was standing behind her, watching, until she turned to grab the salt cellar.

'Fuck.' The word was out before she'd a chance to think.

Not that swearing was exactly frowned on in there, but still. She was the dishwasher and Jack was the head chef. Not to mention that, technically, Sarah was stealing.

'Sorry,' she began.

'You may as well finish.'

'Really?'

A nod.

Under Jack's poker gaze, Sarah fried the breasts, gradually increasing the heat as she'd seen the other chefs do, until the skin had gone from milk to gold. Turned them over, pressing down with the spatula. Sliced the chicory. She would go for it, she thought. Get it on the plate as though Jack was a customer.

'I mixed some blackberries into the purée.'

Jack frowned at this news, but it was not an angry frown. Dipped a finger into the purée and tasted it, his expression changing as he did so, as though his gaze had settled on a far horizon. Then, briskly, he cut a slice of the duck, sloshing up some purée before putting it all into his mouth.

It took all of Sarah's willpower to wait until he'd finished before asking, 'Well?'

He nodded slowly. 'There's balance all right.'

'Really?'

'You need a little more sugar with the blackberries in the purée. But that's not bad, actually.'

'Thanks.'

'I don't need to ask if you enjoyed that.'

'I did,' she admitted.

'You know,' he said, 'the Sarah standing in front of me is a completely different person from the Sarah who showed up here looking for a job.'

'I thought you were going to tell me not to come back after that first night.'

'You managed the pressure okay. Better than most on their first night.' He fixed her with a serious stare. 'You know you don't need to study culinary arts to get a career in cooking?'

'I didn't.'

'I mean, it helps, but you can work your way up in a kitchen. Plenty of really good chefs started out as kitchen porters.'

'Really?'

'I don't say this often, but I think you could have a career as a chef. If you wanted one.'

'Nah,' she said. 'I do my finals this year.'

'In ag science.'

'Yep.'

He looked at her, as though debating whether he should say something or not.

'You think I'm mad to go home to the farm,' she said.

'I don't think you're mad,' he said. 'I just wonder is your heart in it.'

She'd been there for more than half a year and it was the first time they'd had any kind of real conversation. She hadn't even known he'd considered her at all, beyond her duties as dishwasher.

She tried to summon her mother's enthusiasm. 'We're going to make a go of it.'

'Right.'

'My dad put everything into the place,' she added.

'So it's for his memory.'

'I suppose,' she said, 'in a way.'

'Maybe, though,' he said then gently, 'if someone isn't here any more, what was important to them doesn't matter.'

She thought about this. Its shocking truth.

'My mother's still here.'

'Well, I don't know your mother. I do know that you hardly seem to go to college any more. You do every shift we ask you to do.'

PART III

19

'You see what I mean?' says Nancy, her eyes hard on Sarah. 'They've already started.'

They are standing on Neil's thin stretch of land down by the motorway, which once comprised a couple of fields and is now a building site. On each side of the worked-on earth stands a digger, arms coiled patiently, each like a mirror image of the other. Across from where Sarah and Nancy are standing lies a mound of earth and stones. Beside it, one sign declares the wearing of a hard hat mandatory, another that only authorised personnel are allowed. All the effort it seems is in removing the slope – the one that starts at their field behind the cottage and runs all the way down to the motorway.

'He's been planning this a while, of course.'

'Really?' says Sarah, though she knows all about it. Neil had told her every detail of how his plan began, one evening in Dublin on a drive out to Howth.

'Didn't he have an architect do up the plans a couple of years ago,' continues Nancy, 'before they'd even started building the motorway. He'd been looking for investment funding but couldn't get enough, Olive said. And then when it came out last year about that development on the bad land, no one would go near it. They knew it wouldn't get the permission then.'

'He had to wait.'

'He must have rummaged the investment out of somewhere in the meantime.'

You can't see the cottage from here, or even the big field – all that is hidden by the thick hedgerow marking the boundary between the site and the field beyond – but you can see the thin peninsula of woodland, or its end, the dense huddle of trees not ending neatly at the hedgerow but leaking beyond it, so a trickle of trees dot that corner of Neil's site, as though the wood is growing, slowly encroaching on his space. She remembers then the game she used to play when she came down to these fields as a kid, sometimes with friends but more often alone. Pretending a monster lived among the trees, she would dare herself to go closer and closer, until the sound of anything in there – the wind in branches, a bird rustling leaves – would have her turning and running back down the field screaming, half in delight, half in terror.

Then, of course, there was no building site. There wasn't even the motorway, with its car drone so frighteningly close now. A mere five-minute walk, through a single field, where cows stare at Nancy and Sarah as though amazed by their nerve. It's been there almost a year but it still astonishes her, the way it slices through the landscape so close to their cottage, cars zooming past at 120 kph, the same all the way to the city.

'It speaks of a certain confidence, wouldn't you say?' says Nancy. 'That he'd start before the permission comes through.'

Reluctantly, Sarah returns her gaze to the site. As far as she can remember, Neil hasn't mentioned this to her – that they've already started on the foundation. But, then, she hasn't told him about her coming home this time. In fact, she hasn't told him anything this week. Especially about what's happened with the restaurant. If she's to be honest with herself, that's the reason she hasn't called him. And he hasn't called her, well, because he's particularly busy; the week of St Patrick's Day is always a crazy one for the pub. For the first time since they started seeing each other, there's only been a couple of stray texts between them.

I'll get up as soon as I can. Pub is insane! Miss you xx.

The restaurant is crazy this week as well. Miss you too xxx.

Then Nancy had called her on the Tuesday, practically talking over herself in her excitement as she told Sarah that they'd been given a meeting on the Thursday morning with Tom Fitzpatrick, in his constituency office in Dunlone. And would Sarah please come down to it, as a huge favour to her mother?

She'd spent the previous days watching TV until the early hours and then sleeping in late. Going on grim walks along the litter-strewn canal near where she lives. Eating takeaway food.

'Well?' says Nancy now.

'He probably had to let someone start while they were available,' she manages.

'Rubbish.'

'You know what it's like trying to get builders these days. It most likely made sense to start before the permission came through. Take the risk of the cost.'

'Well, what do you make of this, then?'

Nancy walks over to what looks to be a small roundabout on the Dunlone edge of the site, away from the woods, not far from where they've parked their car. Climbs up onto it and stares triumphantly down at Sarah. Like a child, thinks Sarah, playing King of the Castle.

'Car park?'

'Wrong. The car park is meant to be right outside the building.'

'Then I don't know.'

'You already have an exit onto the motorway over there. And that roundabout's supposed to link back up to the town. So what's this thing for?'

Sarah tries to think of something that will serve as a reasonable explanation for the mystery roundabout. Anything that will draw an end to this conversation, so that they can return to the car, out of sight of those woods.

'Maybe,' she says, 'there's to be two car parks.'

'I'll tell you what it's for,' says Nancy, coming back down to her. 'It's for another development.'

'Oh, Mam.'

You mark my words, if he gets his planning permission, before this year is out we'll hear all about another little plan for down here. A hotel, maybe. Or a fast-food place. Something small and grubby.'

'They hardly want to build a hotel down here.'

'An hour's drive from the airport? A stone's throw from where that new motorway will join this one? You're kidding me, aren't you?'

The expression *bone tired* presents itself to Sarah. As if tiredness has seeped down inside her skeleton to become a permanent part of her.

'Bit by bit,' continues Nancy, 'getting their planning permission, one here, another one there. On and on, until we have a lovely ugly mess that has grown under our eyes and everyone will say, "How did that happen?"'

'Even if that's true, it's not as if anyone will be able to see it from the town. Unless they want to come down and, you know, actually buy something.'

Nancy narrows her eyes at Sarah. 'You're not going to take that line at this meeting.'

'No,' she admits.

'No. Good.' Her expression softens then. 'You pulled it off, anyway.'

'I still don't believe it worked.'

'Well,' she says, 'I suppose when he saw the petition ... He only gets to be TD if people down here keep voting for him.'

Sarah looks at her watch. 'We'd better go,' she says. 'We don't want to be late.'

'And you coming down for it too,' says Nancy. 'I appreciate it.'

Sarah shrugs.

'They didn't mind giving you the day off at short notice like that?'

'Hardly.'

'I thought the place was run off its feet.'

There is a dandelion at Sarah's feet. Somehow it survived the diggers but its head is squished against the earth.

'Well?' says Nancy.

Sarah picks the dandelion, starts pulling the thin petals from the seedhead. 'I'm taking a break,' she says.

Nancy stares at her. 'What do you mean?'

'A couple of weeks.'

'A holiday, like.'

'Maybe.'

'When did you—'

'Last week.'

'But – why?'

'Dunno.' She looks back at her mother. 'I felt like I needed a break.'

'Well, I'm not surprised,' says Nancy. She looks nervously at Sarah. 'Are you all right?'

'I'm grand.'

She keeps looking at her, as though afraid to look away. 'You're still getting that promotion? When it comes up?'

'Who knows?' Sarah says. 'We really will be late.'

'You're right,' says Nancy. 'You're right. I don't like the look of that either.' She nods at the darkness gathering in the sky beyond the woods. If Sarah hadn't followed her gaze then, she might not have caught a glimpse of the wire, caught in that instant by the sun, which almost immediately disappears behind the looming cloud, the wire disappearing with it. She's not sure she didn't imagine it.

'Did you see that?'

'See what?'

Sarah squints, shields her eyes. 'There's something up at the woods there.'

'I can't see anything. Where are you going? We really will be late if we don't go now.'

But Sarah keeps walking, around the dug-up soil, past the mound, and up through the wet grass to where the woods wait. 'Look,' she says, pointing for Nancy's sake. Her mother has come behind her. It looks like a series of wooden posts, tracing an uneven line between the hedges on either side of the woods.

'A fence,' says Nancy in surprise.

'There never used to be one here before, did there?'

'No.'

They go up to it. It's taller than they are and it goes all the way from the end of one hedgerow to the other, severing most of the woodland from the site. The posts at each end have been driven so deep inside the hedge that they're only visible when they get right up to it. The others look like they were rammed in at speed, a couple of them crooked, the wire mesh nailed to them clanging tinnily from a couple of the nails not having been driven in fully.

'Someone's put a sign up,' says Nancy. 'Look, there.'

It's nailed to one of the posts. Sarah goes up to it. Inscribed roughly on it, in red paint, are the words, 'Private property. Entry forbidden by law.'

Sarah traces her finger against the red paint, dry but fresh-looking, as though it's only been done in the past week or so. 'It looks new.'

'Doesn't it?'

What she doesn't say is that it's the exact shade of paint as the message someone had left on their garden wall. That same bright orange red.

'I suppose,' says Nancy, 'he had to put it there for insurance reasons.'

'Who?'

'Neil Hart, of course. Isn't it his site?'

'It is his site.'

'He probably didn't want any of the builders wandering off it, onto our land.'

'You think he put this here?'

'Sure, who else would have?'

Sarah stares at it, then beyond, into the gloom of the trees. Absently, she takes hold of a thin branch of a young sycamore at its edge, bends it with her fingers.

'Would you look now it's starting to rain. Come on, Sarah. We'll be drenched as well as late.'

Rain is suddenly sleeting across the trees. The downy branches shudder.

20

Tom Fitzpatrick sits on one side of his desk, Nancy, Joe and Olive on the other, Sarah just behind them, by the window. Leaning towards them, he says how glad he is they shared their concerns with him, and that on a personal level he agrees with their campaign. It's developments like this, he says, that have ruined the country's landscape over the decades. As you know so well, he adds, referencing the doomed housing estate they had campaigned against. And, what's more, he doesn't share the view of some that this development is guaranteed to be a standalone one, that it won't be followed by others, thereby posing a threat to the fabric of the town. As they have pointed out, the precise phrase from the guidelines is 'a general presumption against *large* retail centres being located adjacent to motorways'. It seems to him that that phrasing allows for some wriggle room, and even if this particular developer doesn't intend to exploit it, there's nothing to say that others won't be emboldened to do so if this gets the green light.

Nancy looks around at Sarah when he says this and raises her eyebrows. *What did I tell you?* Sarah gives the reaction she's looking for – a nod, a half-smile. *Yes, you were right.* Nancy turns back. The conversation drones on.

Jane Hart knows about her and Neil. Fact. She is an alcoholic and has a mental-health condition that requires medication. Fact. She was definitely there that night in the woods. Fact. Sarah knows this was not welcome news to the man who threatened to kill her. Also fact. According to Neil, Jane's furious about the affair. He thinks it may have been her who wrote 'slut' on the Flynns' garden wall. And whoever wrote it did it with paint that probably belongs to him.

Jane Hart can play the piano. She used to play golf. Nancy has always found her to be okay. David Fitzpatrick's mother thought she wasn't the only one in her marriage who was at fault. When Jane approached Sarah at the Garden Project that time, she had seemed frightened. Her sister thinks she wouldn't care less that Neil was having an affair.

'Can you do anything for us, Tom?' asks Nancy.

Sarah forces herself to pay attention.

Unfortunately, he says, his hands are fairly tied. His responsibility begins and ends with planning policy. If the councillors resolve to re-zone the land concerned from agricultural to mixed-use, as per the application, they would be adhering to the 2000 Planning Act and there's not a thing anyone can do about that. The only person who could overturn such a decision would be the county manager, whose job is to consider all the concerns laid out in challenges like their own, as well as the arguments in its favour, which will be laid out in the planning application. If he concluded that the development ran counter to the Act, or to the council's strategic plan, says the politician, then that would be reason for him to overturn the decision. But other than that, the county manager won't be able to do a thing either. Neither will either of them have an iota of influence if the case goes to An Bord Pleanála. Now a big flaw, of course, with the system, which this case highlights, and which they'll know well themselves from their last campaign, is that a local councillor might not represent the interests of some of his community if they run contrary to the interests of those other members of the same community whom he *has* chosen to represent. And on that basis, given how divided the community is on this, he can request that special consideration is made of their challenge.

'Right,' says Nancy. 'Well, that's something.'

He might, he says, flag a couple of potential sticking points. The first one is that the natural landscape has already been disrupted by the motorway, which might undermine the aesthetic argument. 'I wouldn't play that up as much,' he says. 'The other is that speculation about future developments won't be entertained. So ye might want to revisit those aspects of it.'

Outside, a starling is trying to pull a crust from a paper bag that lies discarded by the kerb. Over and over, he keeps almost having it, before a car passes and he flaps away, coming back to try again. And then he gets it, and just as he does, another starling arrives and tries to pull it from him.

'Now having said all that,' adds the politician, 'you have a particularly strong case.'

'Do you really think so?' says Nancy.

'Oh, there's no question. And I'll tell you why. It's your petition. Over three hundred signatures. That's ten per cent of the town, isn't it?'

'It is.'

'The county manager won't be ignoring that in a hurry. Mark my words, the petition is what will make all the difference. The deadline's when again?'

'Tomorrow,' says Nancy.

'We cut it tight,' says Olive.

'I think he's in there with them today,' says Tom Fitzpatrick.

Nancy looks alarmed. 'What for?'

'Another pre-planning meeting.'

'Another pre-planning meeting. We should get those as well. How do we know he's not lobbying them while he's at it?'

'Neil Hart?' asks Sarah.

They all turn around, as though they'd forgotten she was there.

'Who else?' says Nancy.

'He won't be lobbying them,' says Tom Fitzpatrick. 'They'd be strict on that kind of thing, in fairness. It's probably something he had to clarify.' He stands, extends a hand.

'You'll say it now to the county manager?' asks Nancy.

'I'll do it today,' he says, shaking her hand.

Back on the street, it's even colder than it was when they arrived, a sharp wind cutting into them as they button coats, pull hats out of pockets.

'It's worse now than it was in January,' says Olive, looking accusingly at the sky.

'It's coming from the Arctic,' says Nancy. 'Now. What do we think?'

'Encouraging,' says Joe.

'Wasn't it? Even though he can't do much.'

'He sees the way the wind's blowing.'

'Do you reckon?' says Nancy, eagerly. 'That's what I was thinking. If he thought we were a lost cause, he'd hardly give us the time of day.'

'I might run up to the council while I'm here,' Sarah says. 'See if that paperwork is through.'

'Oh,' says Nancy. She looks surprised. 'Is there any need?'

'No harm,' says Sarah. 'While I'm here.'

'Myself and Olive are meeting Bill and the others in a couple of hours,' says Nancy. 'To fill them in.'

'I wondered if Joe or Olive could give you a lift home? I thought I might do a bit of shopping while I'm here.'

'And she living in Dublin.'

'They don't have everything, Nancy,' says Olive.

Joe looks at Sarah. 'Are you all right?'

'Grand.'

'Sure, I can give you a lift, Nance,' he says.

'Thanks,' says Sarah.

'Oh, now,' says Nancy, peering behind Sarah. 'It looks like you've company anyway.'

Sarah looks around to see David Fitzpatrick on the steps of his father's constituency office. He's looking at her.

'Now the secrecy makes sense,' says Olive, winking at Nancy.

'I need to talk to you,' he says, when the others have started walking down towards where their cars are parked.

'I was about to go to the council.'

'I'll walk with you.'

'Okay.'

Once they're up the street, he looks around him, then leans in towards her. 'What you said last week,' he says, 'about that night, in the woods. You know what I mean.'

'What about it?' she asks.

'You said you wanted to do it. I explicitly remember you saying that. You can't deny it.'

Bone tired.

'Well?'

'I know I did,' she says.

'Right. Good. So then what were you saying?'

'I'm not sure.'

'You're not sure? You don't want to be slinging shit like that around about someone. It's a criminal offence, doing that.'

'You've nothing to worry about,' she says.

'I know I've nothing to worry about. You said yes. You can't just twist it like that because you want to. For whatever screwed-up reason.'

'I didn't mean to twist anything.' Finally, she returns his gaze. Stops walking. 'You really couldn't tell?' she asks him. 'The way I – acted. You couldn't tell I didn't want it?'

For a second, he looks flustered. 'You lay down on the fucking ground,' he says. 'You can't agree to have sex with someone and do that, then claim you didn't want it.'

She starts to walk again.

'Huh? How does that work? What – was I supposed to be psychic?'

'No.'

'Sure, we were the same age. I didn't know what I was doing.'

His face reminds her of a spoiled child's.

'Everyone goes on about how hard it is to be a girl,' he continues. 'No one ever talks about how hard it is being a guy. You have to play football if you're any good at it. Doesn't matter whether or not you want to. Do well at school because your parents are so-and-so. You know? Be one of the lads or else you're not one of the lads.'

'What did you want to do?' she asks. 'Be a ballet dancer, maybe.'

'That's typical,' he says. 'You're allowed to have a hard time but I'm not. That's fucking typical.'

'Or a poet.'

He looks at her. 'Why do you say that?' he asks.

They've reached the council.

'I was just kidding,' she says. 'Anyway, I have to go.'

'You weren't exactly Little Miss Perfect yourself, if I remember correctly,' he blusters.

The comment makes no sense. 'What do you mean by that?'

'Didn't you fuck over one of your friends? Something like that.'

'No, I didn't. Who said that?'

'It was a story going round.'

'A lot of stories went around.' She walks through the door.

'Like butter wouldn't melt,' he calls after her.

21

Sarah puts her face right up against the glass of Neil's car window, until she can see the dashboard and steering wheel, new-car clean, then two takeaway cups, coffee dried into stains around the rim of one, and croissant crumbs dusting the driver's seat, a crumpled paper bag on the floor by the pedals.

Like he cleaned the car thoroughly, then decided he wasn't bothered what state it was in after all. His grey scarf, flecked with tiny glints of dandruff, is all twisted and flat against the passenger seat, somehow making her think of a dead animal.

Sarah sits on the ground, by the passenger door, wrapping her arms around her knees for the warmth. The paperwork wasn't there. Someone will be sure to email you when it's ready, the woman had said. The same woman who had been there when she and Nancy had first asked for it. There really is no point in coming in, she'd even added. The backlog is terrible at the moment. God knows when they'll have it dug out for you.

She's not waiting long before she hears the sharp clack of Neil's footsteps coming towards her. Carefully, she checks to see he's alone and then she stands up.

Straight away he stops walking, his face a hive of worry as he takes her in. Without saying anything, he beeps his car open, looking around him as he does so, then gestures for her to get in.

'What are you doing here?' he says, when they're both sitting inside the car. 'No one saw me,' she says.

She has placed his scarf on her lap, and now when he takes off his coat, she takes that too. It smells of him. The woody aftershave he uses.

'I didn't know you were home,' he says.

'Nancy got that meeting with Tom Fitzpatrick.'

'Oh.'

'She asked me to go.'

'Right.'

'He mentioned you'd a meeting in the council, so ...'

He looks at her sharply. 'Who did?'

'Tom Fitzpatrick. I had a reason to come here anyway, for that paperwork.'

'Did you get it?'

'No.'

He tuts. 'You'd swear it was the Holy Grail.'

'Yeah.'

'Look,' he says. 'We can't hang around here.'

'Do you think we could drive for a bit? It feels like ages since we've actually been together.'

'It's difficult for me to get up, these days, I told you.'

'I'm not having a go at you.'

'I should get up next week.'

'I understand.'

He starts the engine, eases them out of the car park onto the road.

'How'd it go?' he says, after a few minutes have passed with neither of them speaking.

'With Fitzpatrick? It went well, I think. For Nancy, I mean. Not that there's much he can do for her,' she adds quickly. 'I doubt it'll make any difference. He said he agreed with her but that there's very little he can do beyond request special consideration by the county manager.'

'Feck-all is what he can do for her.'

'Yeah. I mean, I think she was pleased he saw the merits of her case.'

He throws her a look.

'At least, he said he did. He's a politician, though.' She glances at him. 'Did you mind?'

'Mind what?'

'Me waiting at your car?'

'Of course not,' he says.

She closes her eyes and tries to pretend it's that time in Dublin when they drove out to Howth, the lights of the city against the sea. A rare elation coming over both of them on the way, as she told him about her dream of one day owning her own restaurant, and he told her about his dreams for the development. During that drive, she had felt as though her life was a thing that belonged to her, and her alone.

Now, she opens her eyes to find they are crossing the vast bridge that divides the town into two provinces, so that one side belongs to the west of the country, the other to the east.

'I've been given a couple of weeks off,' she says.

He looks at her. 'Off what?'

'The restaurant.'

If she hadn't yelled, 'Brake!' right then, he would have driven through pedestrian lights. Even as it is, the car shrieks and its nose juts into the crossing. A man who had just stepped off the kerb gives them the finger, his face all raw fury.

'For fuck's sake,' snarls Neil, his expression for a moment reflecting that of the man on the street.

'Sorry,' she says. 'Sorry.'

His hand goes to his forehead. He stares bleakly at the people crossing.

'No,' he says eventually. 'I'm sorry. That wasn't your fault.' He clears his throat. 'I'm the one driving,' he adds. 'Hang on until I find somewhere to park.'

He continues on down Main Street, then turns right onto a narrow medieval street that leads them to the water, where the milky-brown river fattens itself acres-wide, flat but for one choppy line betraying the weir, beyond that a dim horizon of low scrubby trees on ancient islets. Opposite, the cheap-yellow apartments thrown up the year before, already with a dingy look to them.

'A holiday,' says Neil. 'Is that it?'

'Sort of.'

'Sort of.'

She bites her knuckle. 'I haven't exactly been at my best in there recently.'

'Jesus, Sarah.'

'I know.'

'You haven't told Nancy, I hope.'

'I have.'

'For Christ's sake.'

'One thing she's said about the farm makes sense.'

'What was that?'

'Well, if we did do it, I'd still be part of the industry. I'd just have moved into the supply of quality ingredients.' She chances a glance at him. He's staring at her in incomprehension. 'When you think about it,' she continues.

'Don't think about it. It's fucking bullshit. Jesus Christ. What's stopping her getting a job or just living off her miserable widow's pension?'

'It's not about the money.'

'Don't start all that again. She's a bully.'

'You've always done what your father wanted you to do.'

'And don't I regret it?'

'Don't be mad.'

'I'm not mad. It's just – frustrating. To hear you talk like this.'

She looks at him, looking out now at the water. 'She dragged me down to your site earlier,' she says.

His eyes widen but he keeps his gaze on the water.

'She thought it would help get me onside, I think.'

Now he looks at her. Warily, she thinks.

'Did it?' he asks.

'Of course not.'

'Good.'

'I saw that fence you put up at the woods. And the sign.'

He doesn't answer.

'The paint,' she says. 'It was the same paint as on our wall that time.'

Now he frowns, as though confused.

'So you must have been right,' she says. 'Jane must have used your paint. It must have been her.'

'What did I tell you?' he replies, almost straightaway. 'Have you told Paul yet about that guy getting into your car that time?'

'I can't tell him that without telling him about us.'

He seems to think about this. 'I suppose.'

'Did you ever ask Jane?'

'Ask Jane what?'

'*If* she wrote that thing on our wall?'

'Did I ever *ask* her? Is that a joke?'

'You didn't.'

'I wouldn't dare,' he says, touchily.

'Well, I've decided something,' she says.

'What's that?'

'I want to talk to her. I want to talk to Jane.'

'Are you insane?'

'I had the idea during that meeting with Tom Fitzpatrick and it's the only thing that's made me feel better since all this started. I think it's a good idea.'

'Believe me,' he says, smiling bitterly, 'you do not want to talk to Jane.'

'It's literally the only thing I want to do right now. I mean, she's a human being, isn't she? At the end of the day.'

He stares at her.

'You won't help me.'

'Trust me, Sarah. It's an awful idea.'

'All right.'

'Tell me you're heading back to Dublin now.'

'Straight back,' she says.

'Good.' He looks at his watch. 'I need to get to the pub.'

A boat is pulling slowly away from the town, towards where the river widens.

'Are you really ending it with Jane?'

'Hand on my heart. As soon as this thing with the development is through.'

She puts her hand on his arm. It's so tense. '*You* need a holiday,' she says.

'I'll try to get up soon.'

'We could drive out to Howth again.'

'Definitely,' he says. But his smile is so strained. 'Where's your car?' he asks. 'I'll drop you back.'

'No need. I could do with the fresh air.'

Her voice comes out so strange. Like someone testing how they sound in a new altitude.

22

As soon as Sarah has walked far enough up the street that Neil's car is out of view, she takes her phone out of her bag and taps in the number she's been holding in her mind since she managed to slide his phone out of his coat pocket and hold it between the door and her body. But she waits until she's back in her own car, outside the minister's office by the castle, before hitting call.

It goes to voicemail, Jane's low, hesitant voice telling her to leave a short message and her number. Like she can barely be bothered to say it. Or she finds it a pointless exercise, as though she doesn't expect anyone to call. Sarah says who she is and that she'd like to meet. She leaves her number. Then she walks along the full stretch of the main street and through the park bordering the river at the east side, before turning back towards the town, past the friary and the row of small terraced houses, making sure to approach the place where Neil had parked earlier carefully, until she's sure he's gone. Then up across the bridge, and around the castle. By then, there's still no reply from Jane. She goes into a small, brightly lit café, from where she can see her car. Gets herself a coffee and waits. She waits a whole hour, then drives back to Crookedwood slowly, taking the old road instead of the motorway. When a tractor has her down to sixty, she stays behind it, instead of passing it out, even when it moves halfway into the hard shoulder for her. Let the other drivers overtake them both if they're in such a hurry. When one stays behind her longer than the others, and she recognises the black Peugeot again, she slows down even more, until it finally overtakes, going too fast for her to make out the driver. She stays behind the tractor until she's on Church Street.

A Monday afternoon, the town is busy, the street bordered on each side by a hem of parked cars. Beside the Spar, a lorry is slowly backing out onto the road, emitting its loud, slow beeps as it moves. People are crossing at the lights, others chatting outside the post office. A man coming out of the newsagent on the corner of the lane to Neil's house, eyes on his lottery ticket, doesn't seem to notice Sarah as she sidles past.

Neil and Jane moved out of the flat above the pub and into this place the year before Sarah left for college. A year after they had married. A large, detached two-storey built by someone else in the eighties, it had always seemed impressively mansion-like to Sarah when she was younger but now strikes her as dated – by its pillars either side of the front door, its bay windows. It also looks uncared-for, a house no one lives in any more – the way the curtains are drawn, the black streaks of water stains on the front wall, the dark wet leaves that lie in a slimy clump under a young chestnut tree.

She finally gets out of her car, walks up to it and rings the doorbell, but no one answers. When she follows up with a couple of firm thuds of the knocker, and rings the bell again, this time keeping her finger on it for a good few seconds, she's met by more silence. It's the same when she goes round to the back, where she finds that door locked too and all the curtains drawn. When she worked in the pub, Neil used to sometimes send her or whoever else was on up here to borrow the vacuum cleaner, the one in the pub often breaking. He even used to keep a spare key in the back room of the pub for that very purpose. Then the curtains were never drawn. And even if no one was at home, there was never this empty feeling.

She walks around to the newsagent's, which she finds empty of customers when she pushes open the door, the bell above jingling her arrival. Just Mary, the woman who has been behind that counter any time Sarah has dropped in for a newspaper over the years or, before she had her car, a pile of junk food to eat on the bus to Dublin. Always with a word or two to say to her about the weather or any local news – a wedding worth mentioning or someone who had died.

Sarah takes a copy of the *Chronicle*, puts it on the counter with what she hopes passes for a smile. 'Hi, Mary.'

Mary looks at her with what seems to be surprise. 'Sarah.'

'Long time, no see.'

'Indeed.'

'It's brisk out today. They're saying it might snow.'

Mary nods. 'Two fifteen, please.'

There's a definite coolness off her. She's not imagining it.

'I was just calling on Jane Hart there,' says Sarah, handing over a five-euro note. 'No sign of her. You haven't seen her today, by any chance?'

Mary places the note slowly into the till, takes out the change, all the while frowning slightly, as though the task is difficult. And when she does answer, the words come out slowly. 'I haven't seen that woman all week,' she says.

'I thought she always bought her fags here.'

'That's right.'

'Is she away or something?'

Mary puts Sarah's change on the counter. 'I didn't know you were friends with her.'

'I'm not, really. Mam asked me to drop something up to her.'

The door swings open behind her then, the bell jingling again as it clanks shut. Sarah turns to see Bill from Nancy's committee.

'Bill,' says Mary.

'Mary. Bitter day,' he says.

'What can I do you for?'

Bill ambles up to the counter. 'Sarah Flynn,' he says.

'Bill.'

'How'd it go?'

'Grand. Good. He was very supportive.'

Bill looks at her, waiting for more.

'He can't do much but he thinks it's a strong case.'

Mary is watching her so closely.

'Mam has this campaign going,' Sarah continues.

'I know all about it,' says Mary, curtly, looking away.

'Well,' says Bill, looking awkwardly at Sarah and then at Mary. 'That's it.'

'Did you sign the petition?' Sarah asks her.

'I did,' she says icily. It feels like she's about to say something else. But then Sarah's phone pings inside her bag. It's a text message, from Jane: *Under the bridge by the castle at five.*

Sarah checks the time. It's just gone half past four. 'I have to run,' she says.

'Right you are,' says Bill. 'I'm just heading around to your mother's. She's giving us the full story.'

Sarah gets to the bridge at five to, walks down the slope that leads to the water's edge, where a few boats are moored. Under the archway, its stones black, those boats are no longer visible, only a couple of other ones further down, and the backs of a couple of cars parked nearby.

Her heart starts up its wonky hammering but it's another moment or two before she becomes aware of there being someone else in there with her, when a gloved hand presses sudden and hard against her mouth, and then an arm is painfully holding onto her body, across her ribs. Before she has a chance to react, she's being pushed up against the damp stones of the bridge. Then her head is being yanked back by her hair, the pain shocking. Instinctively, Sarah's hand goes to her face, just as her head is thrust back to the wall.

'Keep away from my husband. Or you'll be fucking sorry.' The voice is strange and hoarse, like and not like the voice on the phone. The words are barely spoken and Sarah is released. There is the sound of quickly receding footsteps and when she looks around, all she catches is a glimpse of a woman in a long black jacket, hood pulled up, before she disappears out of sight.

Sarah stays still for a moment, a wave of nausea threatening. Then she lowers herself to the ground, her back resting against the cold stone, and takes out her phone. When Neil doesn't answer, she tries again, and again. Then she texts him: *Call me*.

In a minute, she'll figure out where to go and what to do. But first, she'll sit here a while longer. Keep her eyes on the cars parked further down, the light that's still in the sky. Let her thoughts turn to that night back at Christmas, when she started to fall in love with him.

23

Sarah had been in the pub less than an hour when Neil came over to the table where she was sitting with Ursula and some of her other old school friends.

'I hate to ask this,' he said, 'but is there any chance in hell you could cover for me? I need to nip out for a bit. Yvonne can't manage on her own.'

It was Stephen's Day, the busiest night of the year. The place was already heaving, and even as he stood there asking the favour, another group doing the Twelve Pubs of Christmas arrived in, all hot-looking jumpers and flushed cheeks.

'Neil,' said Ursula, 'we just got here. You can't do that.'

'I wouldn't ask if I wasn't desperate. I'll be back within the hour. Look, I'll let ye stay in after closing for a bit if you do this for me.'

'All right,' said Sarah. 'An hour tops.'

The truth was she was relieved to be asked. She hadn't been out with those girls in nearly a year and already the conversation was starting to feel strained, that old tension from Ursula rearing its head. And a lock-in later, even if it was just for a little while, would give her a chance to talk to her old boss. She'd rarely seen him since she'd worked for him, back when she was in school, but they'd always gotten on in a quiet kind of way. She'd even had a mild crush on him. She'd almost enjoyed its bitter-sweetness when his whirlwind romance with Jane started, ending with their marriage.

'How come you've to go out?' she asked him, following him into the back room to wash her hands.

'Don't ask,' he said, pulling on his coat.

The back door, she noticed then, was open. Out there, a trail of cigarette smoke was rising thinly in the cold night air. Then the person smoking coughed and she knew who it was: Jim Byrne, a regular at the pub.

'I'll be back as soon as I can. Don't mention this fella. I'm going to send him in to you for a pint now.'

Back in the bar, she served Jim Byrne his pint, tried not to look at him, take in his quick gulps, the way every minute or so he'd look around the bar, once catching her eye and betraying a fear that made her immediately look away again. She tried to avoid the gaze of Neil's father too, who was sitting at the bar among the regulars. He'd retired a couple of years before Sarah used to work there, and even though he only came in behind the bar now and then, and tended to keep his barbed comments to his son at a minimum when people were drinking there, she'd seen enough to develop a strong dislike of him. Stephen's

Day was the only time he ever sat on the other side of the bar, like he was then, to all appearances getting himself slowly and thoroughly drunk. But if he wanted to say something to her, it was too busy. She and Yvonne worked in a blur, notes and cards passing overhead, orders shouted and passed out, and even then people were getting irate. By the time Neil appeared, closer to two hours later than one, even she was angry with him, especially when, instead of going straight behind the bar, he'd stood chatting to Jim Byrne, until Jim visibly relaxed as he took in whatever Neil was saying into his ear.

'Pour him another pint,' he said to Sarah, as he finally returned to work.

There was no question of her leaving then – it was too busy. Until suddenly a couple of buses came to take people to a nightclub in Dunlone and the place almost emptied completely, half an hour to closing time. By then, Jim Byrne had long taken his leave. The only people left were the girls still at their table, and a couple of men sitting at the bar.

'A fine way to run the place.' It was Neil's father, the words coming out heavy and slurred. 'Leaving this poor one in charge on the busiest night of the year while you swan off.'

The other men at the bar stared studiously at their drinks. One made a comment to the other about a match that had been on the day before.

'I'd a small errand to run,' said Neil.

'A small errand. Did your devoted wife run out of fags?'

Neil acted as though his father hadn't said anything that concerned him, all his attention apparently focused on the task of emptying the dishwasher, drying the glasses and putting them back in their place. This was always how he'd acted when his father had a go at him, when Sarah used to work there. The same dance playing out – the father antagonising, the son pretending it wasn't happening. Even back then, she'd understood without it being spelled out for her that this was the best approach for him to take, something he had probably learned the hard way. It had seemed to lift briefly, after he'd gotten engaged to Jane, and for the first time it occurred to her that maybe that had been an effort to win his father's approval. Everyone had been so impressed by her at the start, her beauty, her past career in marketing. The wedding had been talked about as though they were celebrities, and in a way they were, at least to the people of Crookedwood. Until the rumours started, maybe a year or so after they married. About the terrible arguments first, and then her drinking. And then her having an affair with someone she used to go out with.

'Go on over to the girls,' said Neil, turning to her. 'I'll bring you that round.'

'Thanks.'

A while later, it was just the girls and Neil left in the place.

'I'm going to have to kick you out, ladies,' he said. 'Especially with your fella a guard,' he'd added to Ursula.

'I'll help you clean up,' said Sarah.

'You've done enough.'

'It won't take long.'

After the girls had gone and the cleaning up was finished, he poured them each a drink and, for a while, they had sat there at the bar.

Almost friends.

'That was decent of you,' she said. 'Not saying anything to your father about Jim Byrne. Whatever was going on with him.'

Neil made a face. Drained his glass.

She couldn't help herself. 'What *was* going on with him?'

'Can't say.'

'I won't tell anyone.'

'I know you won't. Still.' He threw her a glance. 'He had some personal trouble, shall we say. All resolved now.'

Personal trouble. She looked at Neil again, but he shook his head. Don't go there.

'I hear you dropped out of your studies,' he said, raising an eyebrow at her ironically.

'That was ages ago. And, technically I failed the exams. Rather than dropped out as such.' She hadn't meant to be funny but as soon as she had said it the two of them were laughing. It took a while before they could stop. She looked into her glass ruefully. 'I never wanted to do it.'

'Agricultural science. Who would, in fairness?'

'Nancy,' she said. 'Nancy would have been top of the class.'

'Maybe she should have done it.'

'Maybe she should.'

They lapsed into an easy silence.

'It's not like you're short of brains,' he observed.

'I didn't give a damn about it.' She looked at him. 'I'd been practically full-time in the restaurant for the last year of it.'

'You're still in the same place?'

'I'm a station chef now.'

'What's that when it's at home?'

'You're basically in charge of a particular area in the kitchen.'

'What's your part?'

'I used to be on vegetables. Now I'm the saucier.'

'Sounds naughty.'

An urge came over her then to confess to him her crush. Until she remembered, with a mild shock, that he was married. His wife was so rarely around, it was easy to forget about her.

'I do the sauces and the sautéing. All that stuff.'

'That actually sounds kind of important in a place like that. How long have you been doing it?'

'Just over a year. Jack, the head chef, said I'm next in line for sous-chef.' She made a face. It's the first time she's told anyone besides Nancy.

'What's a sous-chef?'

'You're basically directly under the head chef. You know, you manage the kitchen, oversee everything. It's tricky, I think, because you have to delegate but do a bit of everything yourself.'

'Jesus, that's fantastic, Sarah. Crookedwood girl made good.'

'Pity Nancy doesn't see it that way.'

'I've a lot of time for your mother.'

'But.'

'Since your father died, has she been at a loose end?'

'I suppose,' she said, 'you could put it like that.'

'All these campaigns. Why doesn't she get a job?'

'She has her widow's pension.'

'A pittance, surely.'

'She still has this idea of us keeping the place on. She's sort of clung to it, I suppose.'

'Why? Anyone could tell her that's a fool's game, these days.'

'Dad, I suppose. You know. He worked so hard to keep the place going.'

'But it's to be sold.'

'I think part of her's still hoping I'll change my mind.'

'She's persistent, I'll give her that. She must be mad thinking she could tempt you into that for a future.'

'Yeah.'

He looks at her curiously. 'Pat Doyle thinks she's selling it to him,' he said. 'He was in here the other day saying he'd finally persuaded her. He was practically rubbing his hands together.'

'I suppose I feel a bit guilty,' she said. 'The cost of that degree.' It was the first time she had admitted this to anyone.

'Sure you paid your own way more or less, didn't you? Along with the grant. It can't have cost Nancy that much.'

'True.'

'Stick to your guns, Sarah. The years pass quickly,' he added, and she thought she caught a trace of bitterness in his voice.

'Jesus. What age are you? Thirty-five, thirty-six?'

'Around there.'

'You're hardly old. You're *young*.'

'No, but ...' he looked at her, looked away '... at your age, time feels different. Like you can just keep bouncing along. But when you get to my age—'

'"My age". Sure, you're only ten years ahead of me.'

'—you realise mistakes add up,' he continued. 'They kind of set around you. It gets harder to change things.'

'Cheery.'

'I'm not messing.'

'Jesus. You're in a great mood.'

'What do you love about it so much, anyway?'

'The restaurant?' She searches for the right way to put it. 'It's hard to explain.'

'Try.'

'It feels. I feel – alive when I'm doing it. You know? Like I've disappeared. Okay, that makes no sense. I just love the process. The way the kitchen is so hectic but it all comes together. And the things you can do with different ingredients, like you could keep learning for ever but there are always new ways of doing things, little changes that make something different.'

'You're good at it,' he said.

'I am. I love it.' It didn't feel like boasting with him. It felt like together they'd put their finger on it.

He smiled into his drink.

'What?'

'Your face all lit up there. It was nice.'

'What about you?' she asked.

'What about me?'

'Do you feel like that about anything?' Her voice faltered as she asked the question.

'No,' he said brightly. 'I most certainly do not.'

'You did an English degree, didn't you?' she asked him.

'The son of Padraig Hart has to have a university education, don't you know. I even got to do what I wanted.'

'But he always meant for you to come back and take over here.'

'Cormac, on the other hand, was destined for greater things.'

'He's a small-town solicitor,' said Sarah. 'It's not like he's going to show up in that *Who's Who* list any time soon.'

'Don't let my father hear you saying that.'

'Can't you just jack it in? I mean, what can he do?'

'It's complicated.'

'And you lecturing me.'

'Well, there you go.'

'Neil?'

'What?'

'Why don't you leave her?'

He gave her a look. She couldn't believe it herself, that she'd asked the question.

'It's not that straightforward.'

'Maybe it is, though.'

'Look. She has problems. She needs me. That's it.'

That was when it occurred to her that Jane taunted him in just the same way as his father did. But she didn't say this. She'd already said enough. Still, all week she found her mind going back to him. How he'd helped out Jim Byrne, and not told his father despite what he had said to him. How he'd stayed with Jane, even though doing so clearly brought him no happiness. How he never seemed to stand up to his father. How he always seemed to try to please others, instead of himself. The old crush reasserted itself. She started to find herself daydreaming about him.

So, when she came out of the restaurant on the following Friday to see him standing there, outside the pub across the road, an embarrassed, unhappy smile on his face, she felt as though she'd been expecting him.

'Really?'

'Why?'

'Why don't you [illegible]?'

He gave her a look: she couldn't believe it herself, that she'd asked the question.

'[illegible].'

'Maybe I [illegible].'

[illegible]

That was when it occurred to her that [illegible] just the same way as his father did, but she didn't [illegible] about [illegible] enough [illegible] And he [illegible] going back to [illegible]. How he'd [illegible] rather [illegible] that he [illegible]. How he'd [illegible] even though [illegible] so clearly brought him [illegible]. How [illegible] to his father. How he [illegible] to please [illegible] instead of himself. [illegible] The [illegible] him.

So [illegible] out of the [illegible] on the following Friday [illegible] standing there, outside the [illegible], a [illegible] smile on his face, she felt as though she'd been expecting him.

PART IV

24

Joe's at his kitchen table, the paper spread out before him and rollie in hand, all his attention on whatever he's reading until he abruptly turns and is taking in the sight of Sarah, standing at his back door, looking in at him through the glass.

'What, in the name of God ...?' he says, when he's opened the door. 'What's happened?' he says. 'Come in.'

She follows him inside. Even after what has happened, she can't help noticing the difference in his kitchen since she was last there. The dresser is still chock-a-block with its clutter, the ashtray on the table full, but there are no dirty plates stacked in the sink or on the draining-board, and the floor is not tacky underfoot like it had been then. There is no mouse trap beneath the sink, a piece of hardened cheese in its jaw. No wine bottles or naggins on the table, or in a plastic bag by the door. Just one empty whiskey bottle on the windowsill.

'What's happened to you?' he asks again, pulling out a chair. 'Did you crash?'

She shakes her head. No.

'You're cut,' he says, aghast, looking at her hand, where the skin on her knuckles had torn against the stone wall. 'Sit down.' He pulls off a couple of sheets of kitchen towel, wets it under the tap and starts to dab at her hand.

'What happened?' he asks again, as he takes another sheet of dry kitchen towel, presses it down on her fingers.

'She went for me, Joe.'

'Who went for you?'

She doesn't answer.

'You were mugged, is that what you're saying?'

'Maybe,' she says, 'you could call it that.'

'Did you go to the guards?'

'No.'

'Why not?'

She doesn't answer.

'Are you hurt anywhere else?'

'Don't think so.'

'A bit of sugar into you,' he says.

He fills the kettle, clicks it on, pulls a packet of Digestives out of his cupboard, which he spills onto a saucer, places on the table beside her. She keeps her gaze on him, watches him throw the teabag into a cup, half the boiling water spilling over the side as he fills it, the fat spoon of sugar and blurt of milk that follow.

Then he sits down beside her, waits until she's sipped her tea.

'Where did this happen?' he asks.

'In Dunlone, under the bridge by the castle.'

'A woman?'

She nods.

'This woman just attacked you. She didn't even take anything off you, like your wallet?'

'No, no.'

'Did you get a look at her?'

'I didn't need to.'

'You didn't need to?'

He searches her face, as though he'll find an explanation there.

She looks at him miserably. 'It was Jane Hart,' she says.

'Jane Hart? As in Neil Hart's wife?'

'Telling me to stay away from her husband.'

He's mystified. Until suddenly, his eyes are widening and he's looking at her differently. And then he's staring at his ashtray. Absently stubbing out his cigarette.

'How long?' he asks, as he starts to roll another.

'January.'

He looks at her again. 'You and Neil Hart?'

'Yep.'

He looks back at his rollie. Licks the paper.

'That night back at Christmas, when I helped him in the pub. Nothing happened then, but we got talking after. He came up then, a couple of weeks later.'

'To Dublin?'

She nods.

'Christ.'

'I know.'

'It doesn't bother you he's married.'

She raises her eyebrows at him.

'I know I'm not in a position to judge.'

'Hardly.'

'I'm not judging you.'

'You're angry with me.'

'I'm not angry with *you*.'

'He's married to someone who doesn't love him. There isn't a soul in this town who doesn't know that.'

He considers this.

'She's probably seeing someone else herself,' adds Sarah. 'Everyone knows she was having an affair that time.'

'Do *you* love him?'

The question throws her. 'Do *I* love him?'

He nods.

'I mean, yeah. I do.' She looks at his tobacco pouch. 'Roll me one of those, will you?'

'I will not. Destroy your lungs.' He takes a drag.

'You're such a hypocrite.'

'And she – beat you up.' He frowns. 'I can't see it.'

'Well. She pushed me against the wall. Pulled my hair back.'

'She'd have to have been following you. What were you doing under that bridge anyway?'

'We'd arranged to meet there.'

'Who? You and her? No. You and Neil?'

'Me and Jane.'

'You and Jane?'

She looks at Joe helplessly. 'What exactly happened that night back at Christmas? When Jim Byrne showed up in the pub?'

Joe sits back in his chair. 'What's that to do with anything?'

'Just tell me. And then I'll tell you everything that's been going on.'

He regards her for a moment.

'He'd ended it,' he says then, heavily. 'I told you that.'

'Byrne.'

'I was out of my mind with the drink that night.' His eyes fill with shame at the memory.

'You went round to his house,' she says.

'Nearly banged the door down. Told him I'd tell the wife. All this.' Briefly, he rests his hands on his head. 'Luckily, she was out.'

'So Byrne got Neil over to talk you down. Before she came home.'

'That's it.'

'And he's the only other person who knows. Neil.'

'Correct.'

'And he's never told anyone.'

'Not a soul, as far as I know.'

'What did he do that night?'

'I can hardly remember it, sure. He got me back here and into the bed, I know that much. Checked in on me the next day. Made me promise I'd not do it again. "It'd be the end of him," he said to me. Sure, he didn't have to tell me.'

'No.'

'Told me to knock the drinking on the head.'

'It was decent of him, wasn't it? To do that, and not tell anyone. He didn't even tell me. And you should have heard the hard time his father gave him, when he came back into the pub. The place was heaving that night. He was gone nearly two hours.'

'It was,' he admits. 'It was very decent of him. Now. Your turn.'

She starts with her encounter with the guy in the woods and his dog and doesn't stop until getting Jane's number off Neil's phone, and the message she left on her phone.

There's a long pause.

'I suppose he knew what he was talking about,' says Joe. 'When he said it was a bad idea to talk to her.'

'I suppose.' She looks at her grazed knuckles.

'But you wanted to speak to her. And he wasn't going to agree to it.'

'He wasn't.'

'Who else have you told all this to?'

'Besides Neil?' She thinks about it. 'Ursula, her husband, Paul. He's a guard.'

'You reported it?'

'I just went around to their house. I didn't even tell him about the time in my car. You're the only one who knows everything.'

'What's his take on the guy in the woods?'

'He thought it might have had something to do with the sports shop being robbed.'

'I heard of that.'

'But he didn't find anything down there.'

'And Neil?'

'He says Jane is dangerous. He thinks she wrote "slut" on the wall. That that guy might even have something to do with her.'

'It's hard to believe.'

'Isn't it?'

'She'd planned some sort of vengeance on you down there, with some dodgy lad. Waited there on the off-chance you'd go for a walk.'

Joe sits back in his chair, stares at her, until the rollie burns his finger and he lets it fall onto the saucer.

'Roll me a cigarette, Joe. Please.'

'I won't,' he says mildly.

She glares at him.

'She's known for taking long walks, Jane Hart,' he says. 'I wouldn't read too much into the bracelet. It's a coincidence.'

'I asked Mary in the newsagent's about her. She was really weird with me.'

'That's your guilty conscience at work.'

'She said Jane hadn't been into the shop all week.'

'That's funny.'

'What?'

'I was picking up some clothes off Maisie Dolan the other day. You know, the dressmaker. And she was saying she'd a bag of stuff there belonging to Jane Hart that she was supposed to pick up a week ago. She was just giving out, you know, about people not picking up when they said they would.'

'What's going on?'

'It was definitely Jane Hart under the bridge?'

'Who else would it have been?'

'But you actually saw her face?'

'Well, no. But ...'

'You didn't see her face.'

'No,' she admits.

He sits back. For a second, she thinks he's going to say they're getting carried away and it's just stress talking. That after a good night's sleep everything will seem better.

'I wonder,' he says slowly, 'did that charming fellow say something down in those woods. On his phone maybe. Something you didn't hear, but he doesn't know whether you heard it or not.'

The quiet way he says it frightens her.

'Like what?'

'I don't know. Something incriminating, maybe.'

'Jesus, Joe.'

'Your mother doesn't know any of this.'

'Of course not. And you can't tell her.'

'She might be more help than you think.'

'That's a joke, right? She'd probably drag me to the church to confess my sins.'

'You shouldn't be so hard on her.' He taps his new rollie against the ashtray. 'Your grandmother,' he says benignly, 'was a terrible woman.'

'Say what you really think.'

'I remember one time, you weren't even born yet, she didn't speak to your mother for a whole week because she wore a pair of trousers to Mass. And your mother married to your father by then. When your mother was young, she used to make her go to six o'clock Mass every morning before school.'

'I never knew that.'

'How would you? You were only a wee thing when she passed.'

'Four.'

'Your father then going a few years later.'

'Yep.'

'She's stopped going to Mass, you know.'

'Mam? No.'

'She has.'

'Why?'

'She told me she didn't believe any of it any more.'

It's impossible to conceive – her mother minus her religion.

'She's finished with it all, she said. No more Mass, no more confession, no more Stations of the Cross. None of it. I believed her too, the way she said it.'

'Really?'

'Even if I was drunk at the time.'

Sarah's gaze falls on the whiskey bottle on the windowsill.

'I keep that lad there to remind me of that night. Didn't I have it with me when I went down to his house?'

'You hadn't thrown it out.'

'I used to hold on to the empties,' he tells her. 'To keep an eye on how much I'd drunk. That won't make sense to you.'

'Are you saying you're off it?'

'Twelve days. There isn't a drop in the house.'

'That's good.'

'Since you cooked me that steak. And I tell you what you need to do now,' he says. 'You need to call the garda station.'

'It'll be closed.'

'Well, call Ursula then. Ask to speak to Whatshisname.'

'Paul.'

'Paul. Tell him the lot.'

'He gives me the creeps,' she says, hearing how childish she sounds.

'Well, that's neither here nor there. You can't be holding on to all this yourself.'

'I'm not telling him about me and Neil.'

'Well, you can tell him everything else.'

With Joe watching, she calls Ursula. Tells her as briefly as she can about what happened in Dunlone and asks if Paul can come out to Joe's house. When Ursula says of course, that he'll be out to them straight away, there's the feeling of something lifting, if even just a little. The feeling strengthens when Paul arrives and is sitting at the table with them, listening as she relays it all, seeming to take her concerns more seriously this time, looking at her sharply and taking notes. And when Joe, after an apologetic look her way, interrupts her to tell Paul that there's another part of the story he needs to hear, and if Sarah won't tell him he will, instead of feeling angry she's relieved. With only the faintest trace of guilt at breaking her promise, she tells Paul about her and Neil, and how she had found Jane's bracelet in the woods, and Jane approaching her that time at the Project. How Neil is certain she must have written the message on the wall and how the paint matched that on Neil's sign by the woods.

'What I'm wondering, though,' says Joe, 'is if it really was Jane Hart who went for Sarah there in Dunlone.'

Paul taps his pen on his notebook, frowns at it. 'Hm,' he says.

'Like, what if it was an associate of this fellow who threatened Sarah? Someone who for whatever reason wants her to think it was Jane. We know he knows about her and Neil.'

Paul nods, frowning.

'Maybe he's using it to scare her off. You found nothing down there?'

'Not a thing,' says Paul.

'I wonder,' says Joe, 'should I ask around about him? Someone might know who he is, or have seen something. If I tell people what's been going on, they'll keep an eye open for him. There's that as well.'

Paul grimaces. 'I wouldn't,' he says. 'Not yet. Now I have Sarah's statement, we can start investigating this properly. Asking around might draw the wrong attention.'

'He's right, Joe. That's the last thing we want.'

'A couple of discreet enquiries is all I meant,' grumbles Joe. 'Someone like that, you want eyes in the back of your head.'

25

She finds her mother out in the yard, pounding the rug from the sitting room against the wall of one of the outhouses. Beside her on the ground lie the rug from the hall, the one from Nancy's bedroom upstairs and the small mat that's usually at the back door in the kitchen.

She is pounding the sitting-room rug as though she's trying to kill it.

'Mam,' Sarah calls. 'Mam!'

Nancy stops beating the rug and stares as Sarah raises a hand. It occurs to her that Nancy would be surprised to see her, having not heard the car. She has parked down a nearby boreen, at a spot where it's not visible from the road, like an advertisement that she's home to anyone who might be passing.

'Are you hungry?' she says. 'I could make us dinner.'

'You sort yourself out,' says Nancy.

'You're sure?'

Nancy returns to her task.

Thump. Thump. Thump.

'Do you need a hand?'

But Nancy doesn't answer. Just keeps whacking the rug, even though surely by now all the dust has been well knocked out of it.

Back inside, Sarah makes herself an omelette, which she eats at the table. All the while, Nancy's thumping continues outside. When it finally stops, she looks up at the door, expecting Nancy to come in any moment. But she doesn't. And when she goes to it herself, opens it, she sees that Nancy is now leaning against the gate that separates the yard from the field. And, to Sarah's amazement, she's smoking. Sarah has never before seen Nancy with a cigarette in her hand. Not once, not even when she was a child. What's more, despite the sharp cold, she's still only wearing her short-sleeved dress. There's a large patch of sweat on the back of it and a thick strand of hair clings damply to her neck. Standing there like that, she strikes Sarah as strangely youthful, like she might have looked when she was a young woman, before Sarah was born.

She puts her coat on, goes outside and walks down to where Nancy still stands, still looking out at the field, not even turning when Sarah is standing beside her, her own arms pressing against the cold metal of the gate.

It's nearly the same time of day as it was that evening Sarah walked down into the woods alone, but now she can make out the outline of its individual trees.

'You can really feel the stretch in the day now,' she says. When Nancy doesn't answer, she looks at the heavy sky. 'Though it looks like it might snow.'

Again, nothing.

'No sign of that paperwork yet from the council. I'm starting to wonder if we'll ever get it.'

'It'll come.'

'I suppose. The calving would be starting up around now, wouldn't it? If we still had the farm going.'

A slow nod.

'I suppose we'd take turns,' she says. 'You checking on them one night, me the next.' She looks at her mother. 'So, is the challenge in?'

A curt shake of the head.

'Are you not freezing? Will I get your coat?'

'No, thank you.'

'Are you sure you're not hungry? I could do you an omelette.'

'No.'

'Were you expecting me back sooner? I can't remember what I said.'

Nancy takes a drag and blows the smoke into the still air.

Sarah smiles at her nervously. 'When did you start smoking?'

For a long moment, Nancy says nothing. Then: 'Before you were born.'

'It's the first time I've seen you do it.'

'I gave up,' she says, 'when I got pregnant with you.'

'So why start again now?'

Reluctantly, it seems, Nancy finally turns to face her. Her gaze is so severe, Sarah looks away.

'I miss it,' she says, her voice icy. 'I thought to myself, why not?'

'Well, I don't know, lung disease?' says Sarah. 'Cancer? The way they make everything smell disgusting? The way they can give *other* people cancer?'

Nancy takes another drag, laughs angrily to herself. 'My daughter,' she says. 'The saint.'

'I thought you were happy with how the meeting went.'

'Happy. Oh, yes, I was very happy.'

'Okay. Well, I think I'll get an early night.'

Sarah has started heading back to the house, when the question is thrown out, Nancy's voice breaking on the word.

'Why?'

She turns back to her mother, who is now looking right at her, all frightened rage, like a cornered animal. Sarah thinks of that time years ago with the pregnancy test.

'Why what?'

'Why did you do it?'

'Why did I do *what*?'

'You and Neil Hart. Carrying on.' Nancy spits the words out, her face contorting as she speaks.

Sarah laughs, in a kind of shock.

'I said to Bill, it can't be true. That you'd never do something like that.'

The way she's staring at Sarah, it's like she's still hoping this might be true. More than anything, Sarah wants to reassure her mother that it's a lie. That there has never been anything between her and Neil Hart. 'I was going to tell you,' she says.

'She was going to tell me. The whole town probably knows by now.'

'Who told you?'

'Bill. He heard it from Mary in the newsagent's, and you know who she heard it from? She heard it from Cormac Hart's wife, who knows the whole story. Who told Mary all about it, apparently. How he got you pregnant. They're saying you went to Liverpool for an abortion.'

'Wait – what? None of that happened. Who told you that?'

'You're saying that didn't happen?'

'I promise that's all lies, Mam.'

Nancy stares at her. 'But you were with him. You admit that. You've been seeing him this past year.'

'It only started two months ago.'

'That's not what I was told.'

'I swear. It started after Christmas. I know he's married, but it's serious. We – we love each other.'

'Love each other? Are you crazy? Sure, he's been using you. He's been using you to get at me. To destroy the campaign.'

'No.'

'Sure, they're saying I swore I'd get my own back on him. That he'd be sorry when his planning application met the fight of its life. How could I have said any of that and I only hearing about this now? He's used you, my girl. For his own ends.'

From the far side of the field, a herd of cattle is making its way up towards the gate, behind them Pat Doyle the dairy farmer. He will be herding them to his milking parlour, up the field and across the road, where their milk will be removed from their bodies for the second time of the day. Afterwards, he'll bring them to the barn where they'll sleep until morning and the cycle starts again.

'At the open house,' continues Nancy, 'you were doing his bidding. They're saying my whole campaign is down to me wanting to get back at him. Seventeen people have called me in the past couple of hours, asking to have their name taken off the petition. Emails flying in.'

Sarah looks at her mother helplessly.

'Sure, you played straight into his hands. Everyone was there. They'll all remember that. And that comment Walsh made, about there being a personal factor. That makes perfect sense now. Everyone will remember that and think now this is what he meant. What else are they supposed to think?'

'He wouldn't.'

'You made a fool of me.'

'There's been a mistake.'

'You still don't see he used you to destroy my chances?' Nancy laughs. 'I have to hand it to him, it was the perfect solution. No one's going to support a campaign if they think it's based on a personal grudge. Are they? Are they?'

'No.'

'And you went along with it. I don't know which is worse, how stupid you've been or your – your immorality. What would your father say, God rest him? But you don't think of that. You don't think of me, on my own, doing my best with you all these years.'

'Well, maybe,' says Sarah, 'if your best hadn't been so shit.'

Nancy stares, her anger punctured for a moment. 'Excuse me,' she starts.

'How could I ever have told you about him? You never explained sex to me. You never even told me about periods. I had to find out about that from the girls in school. Everyone thought I was ridiculous. Look, now you can't even bear me saying the word.'

After Nancy has gone back inside, Sarah stays by the gate, watching the cows and the farmer continue to make their slow way up the other side of the field. She stays there until a memory of her father comes to her. She's about six years old and she is standing right here, looking out at the field and crying because she didn't even come third place in the Feis for saying her poem, didn't even get a certificate. Her father, coming out and finding her, had put his arm around her and told her he didn't understand it either. That, as far as he was concerned, she'd been the best of all of them. That maybe the judge had made a mistake. Feeling his love for her when he said that – how strong and vast it was. Something that could never be taken away.

It's like the ground is shifting beneath her. As though at any moment there might not *be* any ground beneath her and she will just be in freefall. Maybe, she thinks, this is what it feels like to lose your sanity. Because people who go mad can't realise that's what is happening to them. If they did, they wouldn't be insane. And for a second, when her phone rings, she feels that it's a kind of confirmation. That it's ringing to say, yes, you are mad.

But it's the woman from the council. Valerie, she says her name is, her voice all brisk and business-like, as though everything is as it always was and as it should be. 'I have that paperwork you've been after here at the desk. We're closing now but you can pick it up in the morning. Okay?'

The cattle and the farmer have reached the gate that leads out onto the road. As she watches him swing it open, snow starts to fall, some flakes swooping this way and that, or twirling, others cutting thin white lines through the air, making a straight cold path to the ground. Almost as soon as they start, the flakes get thinner and lighter, turning quickly to sleet, individual drops coming too fast and small now to be distinguishable, so that all that can be seen besides an occasional flake is the blur of rainfall, against the grass and hedgerow, the cows and farmer, and, beyond, the long, dark knot of trees.

26

The nightmare wakes her at four in the morning. Even though it's years since she last had it, it is exactly the same as when it used to recur, in the years following her father's death, when she was still a young girl. In it, she is walking home, except that the road seems to twist and wind for ever. All she knows is that her father is in the house, waiting for her, that he is unwell and needs her, that it is a matter of great urgency that she get to him. But the road keeps twisting on and on, far longer than it ought to. Until, suddenly, she's at the cottage, and she's looking in through the window of the sitting room, to see him lying there on the floor, dead, his face all horribly fallen in on itself. It's at that moment she always used to wake and she's woken at now, her pulse pounding rapidly in her ears, her heart doing its painful, wonky thuds, with the need for deep breath after deep breath, as though she'd been under water.

Getting out of bed, she goes to the window and pushes back the curtain. It's still that inky dark of night you get in the countryside, like a heavy blanket. Even when she still lived here, before she moved to the city, she had found the deep darkness oppressive, of the dark half of the year, as her father used to call it. The way it seemed to turn their small home into a full stop where nothing could happen.

Her mind is full of agitation, not just from the terrible dream, but also from the memory that was there with her when she woke as the dream dissolved. A memory that must have been there all those years but which she has somehow managed to keep from herself until now. Of when she left Ursula alone in the woods with that boy, knowing what would happen to her. No wonder Ursula hates her. And alongside this old, surfaced memory hums her new understanding of Neil. It's as though the two are made of the same stuff. What happens in the night-time that we wake to find ourselves without our defences against the things we don't want to face?

Out on the tiny landing, the house feels so empty. She opens Nancy's door a crack, and listens until she hears her steady breathing. Then she goes down into the kitchen and makes herself a cup of tea. Finds Nancy's cigarettes and sits on the step of the back door, Nancy's coat around her shoulders. Besides the flinty drone from the motorway, at this hour not unlike the sea, the world is quiet. The birds haven't even started up yet, though a dim, pre-dawn light is growing in the sky behind the woods.

She cannot believe that there was never any real feeling between her and Neil. That night in the pub, when they'd talked about everything. That drive out to Howth, when they'd run away with themselves imagining their lovely futures. That first time he came up, when she walked out of the restaurant and there he was, smiling sheepishly across the street at her.

His evident guilt had made sense, of course. He was married. It had never occurred to her before now that there might have been something else behind it.

27

She gets to the council early. It's the same woman behind the vast wooden desk. Valerie.

'Good things come to those who wait,' she says to Sarah. 'Where is it, now?' She picks up an A4 envelope, goes to hand it to her. 'Do you want to check it's all there?'

'I suppose I should.'

Watching her delicately pull out the couple of sheets of paper, Sarah feels gratitude towards the woman. A stupid tightness grows in her throat.

'There it is.' She holds out the document: planning permission for the decommissioning of an old septic tank on the land, for the instalment of a new treatment system.

'All above board. Your father did it properly. Unusual enough in those days.' She shakes the sheets back in, hands the envelope to Sarah.

'Thank you.'

'You're welcome, love.'

She's about to turn away when the thought occurs to her. Silly from-nowhere idea. Still, she turns back to the desk. An olive branch for Nancy. That she even asked.

Valerie raises her eyebrows expectantly.

'I was just wondering. Maybe you can't tell me.'

'Try me.'

'You don't know if any planning applications have gone in for re-zoning farmland around Crookedwood?'

'Well. People are obliged to put up a notice, if they've applied for planning permission.'

'I know. I suppose it was just in case we'd missed anything. Never mind.'

'Well, hang on till I check.'

'Are you sure?'

'It's no skin off my nose.' She sits down at a computer. 'Crookedwood,' she says, as she types. 'Let's have a look.'

After a few moments, a map comes up on the computer screen. A thin red line demarcating Neil's site, slicing it off from the rest of the land.

'There's one for a mixed-use development down by the motorway.'

'I know about that one.'

'I think that's it. Let's just double-check.' She pulls up a Word document. 'Crookedwood, Crookedwood. Just a couple of small applications. Someone's moving the entrance to their property. Yes, just that one for Neil and Ursula Hart.' She looks up at Sarah. 'That's the only big one. The only one looking for re-zoning.'

'Sorry,' says Sarah. 'Did you say Neil and Ursula Hart?'

'That's it. The re-zoning one.'

'Those are the names on that application. Both of them.'

'That's right.' She's looking at Sarah curiously now. 'Are you all right, love? You're after turning pale.'

'I'm fine.'

'Did you have your breakfast?'

'Ursula Hart's name is on that re-zoning application. Neil Hart's one. You're sure?'

'Sure as sure.' Valerie looks back at her screen. 'Isn't it there in black and white?'

When she gets to Joe's, the first thing that tells her something is wrong is the way the curtains of his bedroom window, to the left of the rarely used front door, are still drawn. The only other time she has seen them closed in the day was that time Joe had his breakdown you weren't allowed to call a breakdown.

She gets out of the car. The place feels eerily quiet, and though there's no particular reason to expect it to be otherwise, as she takes in the white front of his cottage, the grey-tiled roof freckled with limescale, Sarah feels a trickle of fear. Reluctantly, she walks across the gravel to where the laurel ends, a couple of feet shy of the house, leaving a gap onto the tractor path that runs parallel to the driveway. As long as she's known him, which is to say as long as she's known anyone, this is how you visit Joe: pick your way across onto the mucky tractor path and up through the yard to the back door. Not once has she rung his doorbell or entered through the front door.

She's on the yard when she hears a man's voice, yelling out what sounds like an order, and he's answered by someone else. The voices, neither of them Joe's, are coming from the shed where he keeps the cattle in winter, the one over the slurry pit. Looking towards it, she sees its door is open and that inside it a cow is lying on her back. She can see her front legs and hoofs, her head flat on the ground, tongue lolled out.

Entering the shed, she finds the men by the slats, down at the far end. The slats are open and both men are wearing a kind of breathing apparatus over their faces. As she watches, they start to pull something through the open slats, out of the slurry. They drop it onto the ground. Though it's covered with muck, it's clear that it's a human body.

For a moment, the idea occurs to drive home. Come back later, to find Joe sitting at his table again, or out here in the yard.

One of the men is walking towards her now. He takes her arm, leads her back outside. There, he takes off his breathing thing. She recognises him as Joe's neighbour.

'Now,' he says to her. 'That's not for your eyes.'

She tries to get past him, back into the shed.

'It still mightn't be safe in there,' he says, his hand firm on her arm. 'I'm so sorry, Sarah. Go back to your mother. She'll need you now.'

She looks at him furiously. In that moment, it feels as though this man, this neighbour, whom she only knows to have been a good neighbour to Joe, is entirely to blame.

'I was with him yesterday. Just yesterday evening,' she says. 'We were there in his kitchen.'

'It was this morning it happened. I heard the agitator on and came over. The fumes would have got him in a second. Come on, now.'

'Joe knows about those fumes better than anyone.'

'That'll be the ambulance,' he says. 'Go on now, love.'

She turns to see an ambulance driving up Joe's tractor path. It's one of the most incongruous things she's ever seen. Up it comes through the yard and parks beside them, by the shed.

'Come on now,' says the neighbour again. His voice firmer now. 'Go home to your mother. You don't want to see this.'

28

There are two other cars parked out front of the cottage besides Nancy's. One Sarah recognises as Olive's and the other is a garda car. Together, they leave no room for Sarah's, so she parks on the verge, the strip of grass on the roadside of the garden wall.

She turns off the engine and gets out of the car, only to find she can't go in. Not yet, not straight away. So she leans against the car door, takes in the downy fir tree her father planted across the road, when she was little. It must be four times the height of the tree he planted. Maybe five. She doesn't know when it stopped growing. Maybe it still has growing to do. When she was younger, she would look out at it from the sitting-room window, waiting for a bird – a crow or a blackbird or sometimes a magpie – to land on one of the thin, swaying branches at the very top. The branch would bend under their weight but they would hold on, effortlessly it seemed, as they surveyed the land beneath them. Now, as she looks at it, a magpie lands on one. It looks around, opens its beak and emits an ugly cry, like a cough, before flying away.

She pulls up Neil's number on her phone. It would be so easy to hit the call button. She even lets herself imagine him answering and them talking like they used to. He would know what to say now. He would know what to do.

She exits out of it, puts the phone on silent.

She hadn't left Joe's when the neighbour had asked her. She had stayed there on the yard, watching, until they'd fully loaded Joe's body – because that is all he is now, a body – onto a stretcher and into the ambulance. The ambulance emitting a stupid beep all the way as it reversed down the tractor path, before driving away. He was to be taken straight to the morgue, the neighbour told her, in the hospital in Dunlone. Afterwards, instead of coming straight home, she'd driven around, aimlessly, back roads, for she doesn't know how long, before getting back here to her mother's house.

'Sarah.'

It's Olive, standing at the doorway.

'You heard.'

Sarah nods.

Olive walks down to her. Her eyes are red.

Sarah lets her hug her.

'The two of you were so close.' Olive is crying now.

'We were,' says Sarah. A wave of hate passes through her.

'You're in shock,' says Olive. 'Come on in out of the cold. Paul Scully is here asking questions. Who told you about it?'

Inside, Nancy is sitting on the couch, in the corner, Paul Scully in the armchair, a notebook on his knee.

'Sorry for your loss,' he says, rising and nodding respectfully at her before lowering himself back into the chair.

Nancy doesn't say anything. Doesn't even look at her. She is staring across at the fireplace, her pursed lips twitching, cigarette burning between her fingers. Like she's mumbling a prayer to herself. Or a curse, Sarah thinks. It's more like a curse.

'Hard to believe,' says Paul, 'that we were out with him only yesterday.'

'I went to his house just now,' says Sarah, looking at Olive. 'That's how I found out. I went to the council first and then I went up to him. I got that paperwork,' she says to Nancy.

Nancy looks up at her, her expression blank, as though she doesn't understand.

'I saw them pulling him out.'

'Oh, God love us,' says Olive.

Paul shakes his head. Eyes closed. Like he can't bear to think of it.

'They're saying the fumes probably got him while he was agitating,' says Olive. 'And that then he just fell in.'

'That's what it looked like,' says Sarah.

'At six in the morning, he was at this.' Nancy hisses the words. 'He hadn't opened the doors for ventilation. And not a breeze.'

'You think he was drunk,' says Sarah, quietly.

'I *think* he was drunk?' Nancy makes an ugly noise. 'You saw the state of him the last time he was in this room.'

'At the committee meeting,' says Sarah. She looks at the armchair where Joe had sat, where Paul Scully is now sitting.

'Out of his mind,' Nancy says to him. 'Talking nonsense. Making a show of himself.'

'Ursula mentioned that all right,' says Paul. 'That he'd a few on him, I mean. She heard it off someone.' He looks sympathetically at Sarah. 'I'm just calling on people who saw Joe yesterday. You might have been the last person to see him.

'No doubt he woke still drunk from the night before,' says Nancy

'He didn't wake drunk,' Sarah starts. And then she stops. Looks at Paul Scully. 'Is that what you think?'

He makes a face as though he regrets having to say it. Speaking ill of the dead.

'I noticed yesterday,' he says, in a reluctant kind of way, 'there was an empty whiskey bottle on the windowsill. You must have seen it yourself.'

'But that—' Again, she stops herself. 'It was empty,' she says.

'I suppose you have to imagine drink was a factor.'

'He told me he'd stopped drinking.'

Paul Scully looks at her.

'Pah,' says Nancy.

'You're assuming, then,' she says, 'that it was an accident.'

'Of course they're assuming it was an accident. What else would it be?' says Nancy.

'Yesterday,' he says. 'Did he say anything to you?'

'Like what?'

'It's not his fault,' says Nancy.

'She's fine, she's fine,' he says. 'She's had an awful shock.'

'Will you not sit down, Sarah?' There's a note of anguish in Olive's voice.

'I'm grand.' She looks back at Paul. 'He didn't say anything that struck me as strange. Did he say anything that struck you as strange?'

He frowns at the question.

'Was he drunk then, Sarah?' Olive asks gently.

'He didn't have a drop on him. I told you, he said he'd stopped. Hadn't touched the stuff in twelve days, he said. We were drinking tea.'

Olive and Nancy look at Paul then, who starts writing in his little black notebook. Sarah has the distinct impression he hasn't written any actual words. That he's just pretending to write something.

'What time was that?' asks Olive.

'About six, maybe.'

'Isn't that strange?' says Olive.

'I suppose,' says Paul, all reluctance again, 'if something had upset him, or ... He might have ...' He leaves the sentence unfinished.

'What are you saying?' asks Sarah. 'He got drunk after I left and that was my fault?'

'Of course not.'

'There's no need to be rude,' spits Nancy.

'Sorry,' says Sarah. 'I didn't mean to sound – rude.' She returns her gaze to Paul. 'What's happening now?'

'You mean, with the body?'

She nods.

He purses his lips, frowns at his watch. 'He'll probably be with the coroner by now,' he says. 'For the post-mortem.'

'Will that show it?' Olive asks.

'If he had drink on him? It would all right.'

'How long will that take?' Olive asks him.

'Depends how busy he is. Usually the body isn't returned until the following day. But it was brought there early enough. If it happens to be quiet for them, it might be released back to the house later today.'

'Right,' says Olive, looking anxiously at Nancy. 'We might be having the removal tonight if that happens.'

Nancy squishes her cigarette into her saucer and starts fishing out another.

'You could give them a ring,' says Paul. 'They should be able to tell you.'

'That's what I'll do. I'll get onto the funeral home as well.' Olive stands again, starts putting on her coat.

'I'll be going myself,' says Paul, standing too and putting his garda cap on. 'I'll be back later on, Nancy, okay?'

'Thanks,' Nancy says to him. 'Thanks, Olive.'

'Take care of your mother,' she says to Sarah at the door.

After they've left, Sarah stands at the doorway of the sitting room. For a while, neither she nor Nancy speaks. Then the two of them are saying something at the same time. Abruptly stopping at the same moment.

'You go,' says Sarah.

Nancy glances sharply at her. 'We'll have to clean out the house,' she says.

Sarah doesn't understand.

'Joe's.'

'Joe's.'

'For the wake.'

'Oh.'

'What were you going to say?'

'I was going to say ...' She pauses. What had she been going to say? It's like the air has gotten thicker, making it harder to think. 'I was just going to say that I really don't think he was going to drink after I left.'

Nancy glares at her. 'Well, he didn't do that sober.'

'No.'

'So what are you saying?'

'Nothing.'

'Alcoholics are always lying. Everyone knows that.'

There's a heavy pause.

'That empty whiskey bottle. He left it on the windowsill to help him stay off it. That's what he told me.'

'And you believed him?'

'I did.'

'Well, if he wasn't drunk, how in the name of God did it happen?'

'I don't know.'

'The post-mortem will show it anyway. Isn't that what he said?' Nancy starts to cry.

She ought to sit by her mother, put an arm around her. She knows this. They ought to share their grief. She tries to remember what happened after her father died. Did she and Nancy hold each other then? She can't remember.

'Give Olive a ring there and tell her it's to be a wake,' says Nancy. 'She might come up and give us a hand.'

Joe's body laid out in the front room. People queuing up to pay their respects. The priest saying his prayers. The same priest who would have had no problem in telling Joe, should he ever have asked, that his having sex with another man was sinful, that it was an act of depravity or some such bullshit. And all the while Nancy's fury with Sarah humming away.

And this thing, still growing and turning in her mind even though every time she tries to look at it, her thoughts grow woolly and she can't see anything. Too dark and murky even to be an idea, more a feeling, but one she can hardly bring herself to acknowledge, let alone try to understand.

She looks at the armchair where Paul Scully had sat. Where Joe had sat less than two weeks ago.

'You don't think a removal would be better,' she manages.

'It'll be a wake. Up at his house.'

29

Kathy and Lisa look up in surprise when Sarah walks into the office at the Garden Project.

'Sarah,' says Kathy. 'We weren't expecting you.'

'I know,' she says. 'Sorry.'

'Not at all,' says Kathy, standing uncertainly. 'We heard about Joe. Awful.'

'Yeah.'

'I'm so sorry.' Kathy crosses the room to her, presses her arm. 'You've already had too much loss in your life, for your age.'

'Yeah. Well.'

'Will you have a cup of tea?'

'You're grand. I just had one.'

All afternoon, she's been in Joe's house with Nancy and

Olive, working through all Joe's stuff in the downstairs rooms, the books and magazines, his smoking paraphernalia, filling boxes and rubbish bags with them, then carrying them upstairs. Spraying down and wiping his surfaces, until it could be anyone's front room or anyone's kitchen. Slowly and steadily emptying the place of him. All the while, trying not to look out to the yard, which now looks pretty much like it ever did. Trying not to feel as if they're just waiting for him to come back, every now and then glancing out a window as though expecting to see him, only for it all to return. And then Paul Scully sitting in the armchair coming back too. The way he'd been so certain that Joe had been drunk. The way he'd spoken of the whiskey bottle. As though that was all the evidence they needed.

As though it had been a gift.

'Do you want to sit down?' says Kathy.

'That guy I was asking you about, the last time I was here.'

'Yes.'

'He showed up after I left. Got into my car, got me to drive onto the overpass. He threatened me.'

'Oh, my God. Why would he do that?'

'That's what I'm trying to figure out.'

Kathy turns to Lisa, who looks back blankly.

'That's terrible,' she says. 'What – he was just out in the car park, like?'

'Yeah.'

'He wasn't in the records,' says Kathy.

'No, he wasn't. I just wondered if he'd shown up since.'

Kathy shakes her head. Looks at Lisa, who shakes her head too.

'Did you go to the guards?' asks Kathy.

'I did.'

'Well?'

Sarah shrugs. She doesn't know what else to say to Kathy. She doesn't want to get into all that with her. At the same time, she doesn't want to leave. At the same time, she wants to tell her everything.

'Sarah,' says Kathy.

'I'm grand,' she says. 'I'd better go.'

By the time she pulls in on the overpass, somehow day has become evening and soon it will be dark again. She has been driving around for the best part of an hour, into Dunlone, then back out again, over and over, always staying on the motorway. She hasn't eaten since this morning. She feels light-headed, almost dreamy, her mind replaying everything at a remove. Until suddenly she's being overcome with the memory she woke to that morning, which seems so far away now. Of Ursula, and how things had changed between them in their last year of school without Sarah understanding why until now.

Except she must have understood at some level. Because that memory has been with her all along.

She's still there on the overpass, looking down on the passing cars, when a hearse drives past, going in the direction of Crookedwood.

30

Sarah did what she'd done that other night, back at the start of the summer: she hung back in the trees for a minute or two, watching the others around the fire. She was properly late this time and everyone else was already there, along with a couple who'd not been before. Girls from their class Sarah hadn't known were invited, as well as a couple of other guys from the football team.

David Fitzpatrick was sitting close to one of the new girls, talking to her. The last time Sarah had seen him was outside the school gate on the last day of term. It was just a week after they'd been together, and he had turned around, registered her, then turned back to his friends. He'd said something she hadn't caught and all his friends had laughed. Everyone had seen this.

There was a coolness in the air that said the summer was ending. In an hour or so, it would be cold. She was glad she had worn her fleece, unlike Ursula, who was wearing only a vest top over her jeans. She was the only person by the fire who was standing, a beer can swinging from her hand.

'We didn't even go to bed that night,' she was saying. 'We stayed on Sue's roof and then went to this place for breakfast. They do amazing poached eggs. And the Bloody Marys are to die for.'

She was talking about one of the times she'd stayed with her student sister on the university campus in Galway. Sarah had heard about the poached eggs and the Bloody Marys more times than she could recall. Whenever she could, Ursula was bringing up Galway. The music, the drinking, the late nights. Sometimes making vague allusions to a guy, managing to imply she had a boyfriend there whom she'd slept with, without ever actually saying as much. Watching her, it occurred to Sarah for the first time how convenient this was for Ursula. It allowed her to avoid being called frigid without having to sleep with anyone. It wasn't as though she could be challenged on any of the detail. For all they knew, she spent her Galway weekends on her own in some damp flat, waiting for her sister to get back from wherever.

'Amazing poached eggs,' repeated one of the guys, and they sniggered.

'What else did they do?' asked another. A tall guy with shoulders bulging beneath his T-shirt. His question was met with more laughter, this time from the girls as well as the boys. For a moment, Ursula looked wrong-footed. It was an unusual sight. But she recovered quickly.

'I hope you're not implying anything.'

'You tell me.'

'She has a boyfriend in Galway,' said Marie. 'Or had.' She looked at Ursula. 'Has or had?'

'Let's just say I had an education of my own when I was there.'

'Is that so?' asked the guy with the shoulders.

'Well,' said Ursula, 'maybe that's for me to know and you to find out.'

He made a sad face. 'You're not going to share your new-found knowledge?'

Ursula laughed uncertainly.

'That's mean,' he said.

'Or maybe,' said David Fitzpatrick, 'she's full of shit.'

'Frigid, like the rest of them.'

Ursula looked at the guy who'd said this. The guy with the shoulders again. He was looking brazenly back at her.

'You take a walk with me anytime, I'll show you who's frigid.'

There were a couple of wolf whistles at this. Geraldine let out a shriek. Stepping into the clearing, Sarah told herself that she would never come down here again.

Everyone looked up at her, including David Fitzpatrick and the girl he was talking to.

'They're not all frigid,' said the one with the shoulders said, and the guys all laughed. A couple of the girls smiled.

'Sarah,' said Ursula, going over to her and hugging her. She reeked of drink. Then she glared at David Fitzpatrick. Sarah closed her eyes, shook her head. *Don't do that.* But if Ursula noticed, she ignored her.

'You come and sit with us.'

No one said anything as Sarah followed Ursula, sat between her and Geraldine by the fire.

'Neil Hart's wedding is next week,' said Geraldine, in a bright voice.

Sarah looked at her gratefully. 'That's right,' she said.

'Do you still have a crush on him?' said Marie.

'I never had a crush on him,' said Sarah.

To her relief, Marie dropped it and, for a while, they talked about the wedding. How many people were attending, what her dress might be like. But as soon as there was a pause, Ursula was throwing a dirty look David's way again.

'Prick,' she whispered to Sarah, loud enough for everyone to hear. Then, in a louder voice, 'Some people aren't worth the time of day.'

Sarah tried to smile. 'It's fine,' she hissed. She looked at Geraldine again.

'I heard they're going to Nice for their honeymoon.'

'It's not fine.' Ursula's eyes were full of indignation.

'Seriously.' She gave Ursula a look. *Drop it.*

'Getting what he wanted out of you, then dumping you.' She glared at David. 'She's not a prostitute, you know.'

An eruption of laughter.

'Ursula!' said Geraldine.

'You can't treat my friend that way. That's all I'm saying.' Ursula turned to Sarah. 'You shouldn't feel bad.'

'I don't.'

'No. Why would you? It's not like it makes you a slut, just because you slept with him. Unless you *have* slept with someone else. Have you?' she asked, in a faux-sincere voice, like she really was just curious. It was plain as day what she was actually doing. Moving the focus away from herself and onto Sarah. It occurred to Sarah then that had it not been for Ursula she might not have slept with David Fitzpatrick that night. And if she hadn't slept with him that night, maybe she would never have slept with him.

Ursula, who was probably still a virgin herself, who had gotten all the way through school without ever experiencing what Sarah had.

'I heard they spent over a thousand on the flowers,' said Geraldine.

'The dress is from London,' said Marie.

As soon as she was able to do it without being noticed, Sarah wandered away from the others, down towards the end of the wood, the bit that bordered their big field. She was going to walk home through the field. No one would notice. She had almost reached the point where she could cross into it, when she heard someone walking through the thick bracken to her.

'There you are.' It was Ursula. 'You're not going, are you?'

'I'm on in the pub tomorrow.'

'Don't.' Ursula, contrite, put a hand on Sarah's arm. 'I'm hammered,' she said.

'See you.' She was about to make the long step over the gully when the sound reached them of someone else walking through the bracken.

'Ladies.' It was the new guy. The guy with the shoulders. He looked even bigger standing.

'What are you getting up to?' He put an arm around Ursula, passed her a hip flask, watched as she took a long swig. When she gave it back to him, he didn't offer it to Sarah.

'Let's go back up,' said Ursula, brightly.

'Hang on just a second,' he said. 'I thought you said you'd things you could teach me.'

Ursula laughed nervously. She looked frozen, like she couldn't move, even if she wanted to. Maybe, thought Sarah, she couldn't. His hand seemed planted so firmly on her shoulders. Like she was a thing that belonged to him. Sarah almost said it. *This is a private conversation. Do you mind?* Because even he wasn't going to try anything while she was still there. He wouldn't like it, but between the two of them they could get him to leave.

If Ursula was on her own, that would be a different story. There were rules that had to be followed. If you say things to a guy like Ursula had said to this guy, then find yourself alone with him, you can't reasonably object. You have given permission. You have crossed a line and now you have to go along with it. Whether you still want to or not is neither here nor there. Whether you ever really wanted to.

These were rules that Sarah knew well. Rules that Ursula had made sure she knew and that Sarah had followed. That she now wished she hadn't followed. That Ursula has somehow managed to get away with not following.

Up to now.

'I guess I know when I'm not wanted,' said Sarah.

The guy laughed.

Ursula's eyes were so big on her. *Stay*, they said. *Don't leave me with him.*

'Don't do anything I wouldn't do,' said Sarah.

'Don't worry about that,' he said.

She cleared the gully into the field in one step. The light was on in the kitchen window. She started walking towards it.

PART V

31

The people gathered by Joe's front door watch as the undertakers silently open the back of the hearse and unload the coffin, everyone blessing themselves when they pull it forward. Everyone except Nancy, who is staring at it as though it might hurt her, her face rigid. It is a shockingly solid thing, its wood dark and gleaming. The undertakers nod at the men who have edged forward, and they flank it, three on each side. Then they hoist it onto their shoulders and carry it through the front door. The others follow.

Sarah stays where she is, by the laurel lining the driveway, from where she can see into the hallway. She waits until she sees everyone has gone into and come out of the front room, where they brought the body. Only when she's sure they've all gone on into the kitchen does she make her own way to the front door, where a lit candle wavers in the window of the small porch. There's a book there too, where people have signed their names. Nancy must have put these things there after she'd gone. Sarah holds her hand over the flame, keeps it there until the warmth turns to a hard burning, and she pulls it away.

She can already see the lid of the coffin, resting against the wall. Another step, into the hall, and she can see the coffin itself, in the middle of the front room, on what looks to be the table from the kitchen.

More people arrive. She can hear them behind her without looking around. Waiting to pay their respects. She walks up to the coffin and looks in at Joe.

Joe's body.

They have him in his only suit, the one he kept for weddings and other people's funerals. Eyes closed and rosary beads wrapped around his hands. His face is bloated, so that it's like him and it's not like him. She puts her hand on his cold, interlaced ones, and feels nothing. She kisses his cold, hard forehead.

Back in the hallway, she sees Ursula Hart is among the newly arrived mourners.

'I'm so sorry,' she says, squeezing Sarah's arm, her eyes all pity. 'We'll talk to you later,' she whispers.

In the kitchen, a woman is describing how, years before, she'd once come across Joe and Sarah's father on their way back from a dance. Joe had only one boot on, she is telling them, and when she asked what had happened to the other they confessed they didn't know.

Everyone laughs uproariously.

'That'd be the pair of them all right,' says Nancy.

'Pair of eejits,' says Olive.

They're all talking in this heightened way. No one notices her until she's at the back door.

'Sarah,' says Olive.

'Where are you going?' says Nancy.

'I'll be back in a second,' she says.

Outside, it's not yet fully dark. She can make out the field to the left and, though the blinds are down, there is enough light from the kitchen window and door for her to see that all looks just as it did the evening before, when she came to him for help.

The door to the shed is closed. But when she crosses the yard, and presses the handle, it swings open. She looks back at the house. Then she takes a step inside. When she was a child, she was strictly forbidden to go near this shed, let alone enter it, warned of a terrible danger. The feeling is not unpleasant as she stands there now, taking in its dark quiet. Only about half the usual number of cows there, the others all having died from the poisonous fumes.

The slat where they found Joe is closed. As though nothing has happened.

Joe, who will never again roll himself a cigarette or get himself worked up about something or read a newspaper or butter a slice of bread or help a cow calve, or worry about his future or his bills or his health, or feel the pleasure of warmth from the sun on his skin or getting back into bed in the middle of a cold night. Never eat eggs again, or sit at the bar, or do a crossword. Joe, stopped for ever.

She takes herself through it again. The version everyone is saying happened. For that to be true, he'd have had to drive down to the petrol station to buy whiskey or maybe a couple of cheap bottles of wine after she and Paul Scully had left, unless he'd been lying to her when he said there wasn't a drop in the house. Then he'd have to have drunk them, probably there at his table. Then he'd have to have woken in the early hours, deciding in his still-drunk mind he ought to get up. A cow due to calve that needed checking on, maybe. Then he'd have to have come outside – not even getting dressed, just throwing his coat and boots over his T-shirt and underwear – and decide on a whim, there in the still-dark, to check on the slurry. And then noticing there's a crust, he'd have had to decide to agitate there and then. Without evacuating the animals or making sure it was properly ventilated or anything. And it was a still night, they were saying. Not a breeze to be had. The worst conditions to do it, not that she had to be told that, because Joe had told her, more than once. Yet according to this version of events, which everyone has accepted, Joe stood right there beside the machine, and he stayed there all the while it churned up the slurry, releasing its invisible poison into the air. A single breath of it would have been enough to kill him, destroying his nervous system and making it impossible for him ever to breathe again. So that he'd collapsed, right there, into the pit.

She tries to lift up the slat, knowing that by now there will be little to no danger of any fumes still being in the atmosphere, even in there. Hours have passed since the agitator did its damage. But it seems to be jammed, or locked in place, until suddenly it jolts loose, so that she almost falls back. Then she's looking down into the slurry, dark and deep.

She's still staring down at it when the kitchen door creaks open, clicks shut. Then she hears clip-clopping into the yard.

'Sarah?'

It's Ursula. As though on cue, Sarah's heart starts up its wonky hammering, harder than ever.

'Sarah? I know you're out here somewhere. Your mother sent me to check on you.'

'Here,' she says.

'Where?'

'In the shed.'

'The shed!'

More footsteps, and then Ursula is in the doorway. Sarah can see only her outline.

'*There* you are,' she says. She walks over to her. 'You poor lost lamb, come here to me.'

'I'm fine.'

'You're not fine.' Ursula puts her arms around her. Too tightly, as always. When Sarah's released, she steps back and looks at Ursula. She looks at her until she can make out her face.

'I owe you an apology,' she says then.

For a moment, Ursula seems frightened. 'What are you talking about?'

'That time in the woods. When we were still in school. I left you with that guy. You must remember.'

Ursula stares.

'I'd managed to forget it all these years. I don't know how. It was awful of me.'

'Well,' says Ursula, 'it was a long time ago.'

'I'm sorry.'

A bitter expression has crept over Ursula's face. A kind of angry pride. 'Don't worry about it,' she says. She looks down at the slats. 'So this is where it happened?'

'Yes.'

'Poor Joe.' She puts a hand on Sarah's shoulder. 'Don't cry,' she says.

'I'm not crying.'

'It's the fumes that do the damage, they say.'

'That's right.'

'A couple of seconds and it'd all have been over. All his worries gone for ever.'

Sarah takes a step back, away from the open slats, away from Ursula. 'Do you think he was drunk?' she asks.

'It seems the most likely explanation. I heard he was agitating and it still dark.'

'You don't think there's a chance of foul play?'

'Foul play?'

'It's a silly idea, isn't it? My mind must be playing tricks on me, to entertain such a ridiculous thought.'

'The shock, maybe.'

'Maybe.'

Suddenly, light is drenching the yard and then another comes on, lighting up the inside of the shed where they're standing. They blink and squint. They shield their eyes with their hands.

'What on earth.' Sarah recognises the voice as belonging to Joe's neighbour. The man who'd been there that morning.

'Sarah Flynn,' he says, his voice all astonishment. 'Ursula Hart. What in God's name are ye doing? The two of you should know better – was this open?'

Sarah closes the slat. It slams loudly shut.

He strides into the shed, towards them, looks at the slats, then back at Sarah. 'You of all people know how dangerous that is,' he says to her. 'Your father would have taught you that. Joe as well.'

'I thought it had been well ventilated by now.'

'Well, it has but better safe than sorry.'

She doesn't know what to say to him. 'I just wanted to see.'

'See? Sure, what is there to see?'

'She was very upset,' says Ursula. She shakes her head at him, as though to say she hadn't known what to do.

'The priest is in there,' he says. 'He'll start the prayers any minute. They're all in the front room, come on in now.'

Inside, the priest has started a decade of the rosary and people lining the hall stand back for her to go on into the front room, which is now filled with people standing, and where she sees Nancy. Everyone is facing the priest, repeating his prayers. No one seems to notice when, instead of going on into the room, she makes her way down the hall and back outside, where more people are arriving. Among them Sarah sees Cormac Hart, with his wife. He comes over to Sarah, takes her hand. 'So sorry for your trouble, Sarah,' he says.

The wife is looking ahead, at the door. For a moment, Sarah is filled with a cold desire to push her hard.

'Are you heading off?' asks Cormac.

'Am I heading off?' she repeats. He's looking at her so closely. Anyone would say he was worried about something.

'Just for a minute,' she says. 'We're low on plates, Nancy asked me to run down to the house and grab some.'

'You're probably staying down for the funeral in the morning.'

'That's right. Straight back to Dublin then. Goodbye, Crookedwood, for a long, long time, I think.'

'Dead right,' he says. 'And sure it won't be too long before your mother has moved into the town. Much better for her there.'

'That's right.'

'I hate to ask but I rang the council earlier on a bit of a whim.

They said you picked up that paperwork about the septic tank there this morning.'

'Oh,' she says. 'I'd forgotten all about it.'

'Very understandable. It's just if I get it off you now, I won't have to be bothering you about it again, and we can get the whole thing sorted within the week.'

'Well, it's not in the car,' she lies, 'but I'll bring it back up with the plates.'

'Good woman,' he says. 'The sooner we have your mother set up in town, the better. Especially after this shocking business. The change will do her good.'

'I'm sure you're right,' she says.

Her car, which she'd parked on the road, is no longer the only one there. There are four in total, one of them parked down at a gate to a field. Although by now it's almost completely dark, she can just about see that it's a black Peugeot. The black Peugeot that has been following her. There is no doubt about it now. She goes to it, presses her face up against the window until the inside is revealed. There on the passenger seat lies Ursula's bag. She sees it and doesn't feel shocked, or even surprised. Instead, she feels fear, cold and liquid, starting up inside her. And another feeling that has her hands forming fists. She runs her hands down the windscreen until they reach a wiper, tucked in where it's supposed to be. Squeezes her fingers through until she's grasping the thing, and then she pulls and pulls she knows that if she pulls anymore, it will surely snap in two.

She lets it go.

32

It's as though someone has told Sarah that the faster she drives, the sooner she'll be able to see. As though she has reason to believe that the truth is waiting out there, somewhere in the darkness, for her to come to it, that any moment it might evaporate. Because she knows now, as well as she knows this narrow twisting road, the loping dark branches of that dead ash tree caught in her headlights, that Joe's death wasn't an accident. That someone wanted him to die and then made it happen. And that it has something to do with Ursula and it has something to do with Paul and with Neil, and with Jane, and with the guy in the woods.

And that it has something to do with her.

Tearing down the road, towards the town, she tries to tear through the events of the past few weeks in that cold month of March, feeling for a weak spot somewhere, a place she can go back to and prod and poke until something comes loose and she can see what's going on. But nothing comes. She can't form a thought at all, her mind reduced to this useless rage. Until she's passing the entrance to the Heights, on the other side of town, and her thoughts go to the Garden Project. Where the guy had found her. And the feeling of being lied to there, everyone insisting they hadn't seen him. If only there was some connection between the Project and the others. But none of them has ever even been there, as far as she knows. She hadn't even told Neil she was taking that class.

And then she's remembering, suddenly, that she did mention it to Ursula, that time they had coffee in the hotel. She's remembering how indignant Ursula had been, that Nancy had signed her up to do it without asking her first. Even then, her reaction had seemed out of proportion. And she had asked Sarah, hadn't she, what time her class was on at. She's sure that she asked her that. So there was a link. Because it was after that class that he'd been waiting for her, by her car, the first time. Ursula, she understands, must have told him to find her there. He would probably have gotten into her car and threatened her there and then, had Lisa not been with her.

Lisa.

Another realisation. She slows down, relaxes her grip on the steering wheel. She pulls over, turns off the engine.

Lisa.

The way she'd been so awkward and cold, her eyes firmly on her computer screen, both earlier that day and the last time she'd been down at the Project. Carefully avoiding Sarah's gaze.

Lisa, who had advised her once to go back to Dublin and stay there. Lisa, who *must* have seen him that time in the car park. It never made sense that she didn't see him. She has started up the engine even as she's seeing all this. Doing a U-turn back towards the town. Driving in through the entrance to the Heights.

It takes a couple of drives through the estate before she recognises Lisa's house, from the time she'd given her a lift home. A narrow two-storey terraced place, with a flimsy white door, just like all the others in there. She can hear the low murmur of the TV from inside, and when she presses her finger on the doorbell, she hears its loud ring.

'Is Lisa in?' she asks the man who answers it.

He blinks in surprise at her. Stares as though at a ghost.

'Lisa,' he repeats. 'She is,' he says. 'She is, all right.' He looks up the stairs. He calls her name, then looks back at Sarah. 'Sorry,' he says. 'Who will I say it is?'

'Sarah. From the Garden Project.'

'Ah,' he says.

'Sorry about this,' she says. 'Sorry.'

'You're all right,' he says.

A door opens then and a little boy in his pyjamas walks out of the room where the television sounds are coming from. He stands close to the man, as he stares solemnly at Sarah.

The man puts a hand on his head. 'We're supposed to be brushing our teeth. Isn't that right?'

'No,' says the boy. 'No, Granddad.'

'The rest of them are out at some dance thing in the community centre. Salsa or one of these.'

'Zumba,' says the boy.

'Is that it?' He goes to the stairs, calls Lisa's name again. 'What is she at? Sure, come in out of the cold.'

Sarah steps into the warmth, closes the door behind her. The little boy's eyes seem to grow bigger as he takes in this development. He moves even closer to his granddad.

Sarah makes herself smile at him. 'The last time I met you,' she says to him, 'you were just a baby.'

'Now,' says the granddad, looking down at him.

The boy shakes his head. 'I was not a baby,' he mutters.

'You weren't a baby,' repeats the granddad, indignantly. 'Of course you were a baby. Everyone was a baby.'

'I was not.'

'I was a baby,' says the granddad.

The boy stares up at him. Then his face creases into a grin at this ludicrous idea. 'No,' he says.

'Ga ga, goo goo,' says the granddad.

The boy laughs. A lovely belly laugh. Sarah finds herself really smiling.

'What is she at?' says the granddad again. He goes up a couple of steps. 'Lisa,' he shouts. 'You've a visitor.'

Silence for a second, then the sound of a door upstairs opening, and then Lisa, making her way down the stairs. When she sees Sarah, she stops. She looks frightened. Then something in her expression changes.

It's still frightened, but it's as though she knew that it was only a matter of time before this happened.

'Lisa.'

'Hiya, Miss.'

Lisa takes the last few steps, gives her son a faux-stern look. 'Have you brushed your teeth yet?'

'We were just going to,' says her father. 'Come on, you.'

'Want to watch more *Peppa*,' says the boy.

'You've already watched enough of that.' She turns to Sarah. 'You'll have a cup of tea.'

'No, you're grand. There was just something I wanted to ask you about the Project. It won't take long.'

Lisa turns to the granddad. 'Sure, let him watch one more episode, Dad.' She turns back to Sarah. 'We'll go up to my room. That lot'll be back soon. It's the only place we'll get any peace.'

It's a box room, with most of the floor space taken up with furniture – a single bed, a tiny desk and chair, a wardrobe and a skinny chest of drawers. As soon as they go into it, she starts picking up clothes and stuffing them into the wardrobe. 'Sorry,' she says. 'This place is always a mess. There's not enough room.'

'Don't worry about that.'

Lisa gestures at the chair, sits on the bed. Sarah watches her pick up a book from her bedside locker and frown at it, as though she's never noticed it there before.

'Lisa.'

'What?'

'You know why I'm here, don't you?'

Lisa doesn't answer her. But she puts the book back on the locker. Looks at Sarah.

'Who is he?' asks Sarah.

'You're better off not knowing.'

'I'll be the judge of that.'

'Are you all right, Miss?'

'I just came from my uncle's wake.'

'That's right. Sorry.'

'Who is he, Lisa?'

'Reece Lawless, his name is. He lives four doors down.'

'You're kidding.'

'No.' Lisa looks suddenly alarmed. 'I hope he didn't see you outside here.' She pulls back a curtain, looks out, sits back on the bed, a trace of worry still on her face.

'No one saw me.'

'I hope not.'

'It's dark out.'

'I suppose.'

'That time in the car park. You saw him, didn't you?'

'I did, Miss. I saw him.'

'So, why did you pretend you didn't? Why did you lie to me?'

'Before you showed up for that class, he told us that if anyone asked, to say we hadn't seen him.'

'He did?'

Lisa nods.

'Kathy too?'

'She didn't see him. He just said it to me and the students in your class that time. They'd all know who he is too.'

'So, what, he just went up to ye—'

Lisa affects his voice. '"Don't breathe a word to anyone ye saw me here. I don't have to warn ye twice."'

'He said that?'

'To be honest, Miss, I think he's a bit of a fucking eejit. Likes to big himself up, you know.'

'I do know.'

'At the same time, you wouldn't want to cross him.'

'No. Why would you not want to cross him?'

'Oh, he's well dodgy. Deals and all,' she says. 'He breeds dogs. Sells them to these heads. They come from all over. Lads from gangs in Dublin and all. My brother says he rents them out too.'

'Rents out *dogs*?'

'Dangerous dogs. He's mean to them, to make them that way. They're illegal breeds as well, some of them. Pit bull terriers, like that. He started all this a couple of years ago. My brother Darren was in school with him. Says he thinks he's a big deal now, because these gang types are buying his mutts off him.'

'Do you know, has he ever done anything ...' Sarah searches for the word, '... worse.'

'Worse?'

'I don't know. Violent.'

'Violent?' Lisa frowns. 'Actually, Darren did say he'd been going on about being paid to do some heavy shit. I told Darren, you see, about him showing up in the Project. He said better do as he says, otherwise I probably would have told you.'

'Heavy shit. Like what?'

Lisa looks at her unhappily. 'Darren said he was making it sound like he was getting paid to, like, well, kill someone. But he reckoned it was just talk. It probably was. He really is an eejit, Miss.'

'Lisa. I won't be mad, I promise. But that time I called into the Project to ask you and Kathy who he was, did you tell him I was there?

'No.' Lisa's eyes are big. 'No way, Miss. I'm not that bad.'

'Sorry. I know you're not.' Sarah puts her hands to her face.

'I felt bad not telling you when you were asking about him.'

'I know you did,' she says.

'You don't know how come he has it in for you?'

'I came across him in these woods behind our house one evening, with one of his dogs.'

Lisa stares. 'That's it?'

'I think there was a woman with him. A local woman.'

Lisa's eyes narrow as she takes this in. She seems to Sarah to turn pale.

'When Darren said that about him saying, you know. When was that?'

'Not long ago. A few weeks, maybe. You don't think ...' Lisa's gaze darts back to the window. 'You know this woman?' she asks, looking back fretfully at Sarah.

'Jane Hart, her name is. I don't really know her.'

'But she would have been reported missing if anything had happened to her.'

'I've seen her since then.'

'Well, then.' Lisa folds her arms. 'Why are you looking like that, Miss? You're scaring me.'

'It doesn't mean he didn't intend to kill her.'

Lisa looks at her unhappily.

'What if he'd been about to kill her when I showed up? And then the dog got distracted by me, and she managed to run away.'

'You need to go to the guards,' says Lisa.

'I did.'

'What did they say?'

Sarah shakes her head. It's getting hard to think. Like a fog has come up out of nowhere.

'If I'm right,' she says slowly. 'What if he tries to hurt her again?'

'Surely she'll have gone to the cops herself, if that is what happened?'

Sarah frowns at this idea. 'I don't think so,' she says.

'Maybe she did.'

'Maybe. No. I don't think so. He would have told me.'

'Who would have told you?'

'He can't have known.'

'Who are you talking about?'

'I have to go. Thanks, Lisa.'

'Miss? Are you going to be okay?'

Sarah parks on Church Street, up by the hotel, and walks the couple of hundred metres back to the lane that leads to the house where Jane and Neil live. She passes no one – not on Church Street, and not on the lane. And the house when she reaches it is like it was before – no lights on, the curtains drawn, and only Jane's car parked out front. The night is deathly silent as, for a second time, she goes to the door and strains to hear anything from inside. She rings the bell and bangs the knocker, and when no one answers, she walks around to the back, a hand tracing the wall to guide her. There, she finds only more black windows and silence, the back door locked. She bangs on it too, anyway. She doesn't know what she will say to Neil, if he answers. Or Jane. She tries to think of what she wants to say to either of them, but finds she can't think of anything at all. When she's walking back around to the front and car headlights swoop the front yard, it's as though her mind has stopped working altogether, and now her body too. She stands, frozen, as the car comes to a halt and the engine cuts out. Then a door opens, clicks shut and footsteps announce a woman, walking to the front door. The knocker bangs. Then the woman calls, 'Jane? Are you home? It's me again, Jane.'

The voice is sharp and assertive, and it is tinged with fear. Sarah has heard it before.

It's Christine Flaherty. Jane's sister.

33

The inside of Christine Flaherty's car is all leather upholstery and new-car smell. They have driven around onto Church Street at Sarah's suggestion, parked by her own car, where there's just enough lamplight to see Christine's dark wool coat, her delicate face and fair hair just like her sister's, but cut into a short bob.

Christine turns off the engine and they regard each other warily for a second.

'You're the woman Neil is having an affair with,' she says coldly. 'It only occurred to me after we spoke on the phone.'

Woman. Her whole life, Sarah's only ever been referred to as a girl.

'How long?' asks Christine.

'Since January.'

'So it's a recent thing.'

'I used to work for him, years ago.' She nods in the direction of the bar, a few doors up. 'Anyway, it's over.'

Christine looks at Sarah closely. 'I dare say you're better off,' she says.

The back door of the pub opens and Yvonne comes out onto the street, lights a cigarette and leans against the wall.

'What were you doing at his house?' asks Christine.

'I was hoping I'd find Jane home.'

'Jane?'

'Or Neil. One of them.'

'One of them?'

'I need to figure out what's going on or I'm going to lose my mind.'

'Why do you think something's going on?' She doesn't just sound angry now, she sounds frightened as well. 'Tell me,' she says.

And Sarah tells the whole story again. Everything that's happened since the first night she took a walk down to the woods. Just as she told it to Joe. And then she tells her about Joe's death. And then she tells her what Lisa told her about Reece Lawless, him boasting about killing someone.

There's a long silence. Sarah can't even bring herself to look Christine's way. 'That's all I know,' she says. 'Probably it all adds up to nothing.'

'Usually,' says Christine, 'it's the husband. Isn't that what they say?'

'Neil's not violent.' She's shocked at how her voice comes out.

'No,' says Christine. 'I don't think he is either.'

The relief is almost painful.

'But it can't be easy, being married to Jane,' she says, her voice icy.

'Maybe,' says Sarah, 'she owed someone money.'

'Why did you call me that time? Why did you say you were worried about her?'

'Because I was.'

'Yet you never went to the police.'

'I told you, I made a statement yesterday.'

'That time in your uncle's house, to your friend's boyfriend? That wouldn't have been a statement,' she says. 'I'm pretty sure that's a more formal affair. It has to happen in the station.'

'He said it was.'

'Well, it wasn't.' She looks at Sarah sharply. 'And you're telling me you've reason now to not trust this Scully guy?'

'I don't trust him. His wife's been following me.'

'His wife being Neil's cousin?'

'That's right.'

'What's going on?' asks Christine.

'The woman in the newsagent's said Jane hasn't been there in a while. That's where she always used to buy her cigarettes.'

'Her phone doesn't even go to her voicemail any more, it's just dead.'

'Have *you* gone to the police? When Jane stopped answering.'

'Things have been bad between me and Jane for a long while now. I can't say it's unusual that I haven't heard from her. And when I called Neil last week, he said she'd been drinking more heavily than usual. That she was off her meds again.'

'You two had a falling-out,' says Sarah. 'You and Jane.'

Christine looks at her, like she's trying to take a measure of her. 'I don't know if you've ever known an addict,' she says. 'The deceit, it wears you down after a while.' She doesn't sound angry when she says this. She sounds tired. 'The amount of times over the years she promised me she was giving up,' she continues. 'She's stolen off me more times than I can count.'

Sarah shakes her head, a weak gesture of sympathy. Joe had had his problems with drinking, but he never stole from anyone.

'I suppose there isn't a person in this town who doesn't know about her drinking,' adds Christine.

'I doubt it.'

'She also suffers from depression.'

'Neil told me.'

Usually, she's okay once she's taking her medication. Though it has gotten worse in recent years. But when she's binge-drinking, like she has been lately, forget it.'

'Is it true she can be violent?'

'I suppose, yes. She still deserves better than being cheated on by her husband.'

'I've earned that, I suppose.'

'Of course you have,' she says dismissively, as though the point is so obvious it's barely worth mentioning. 'To be honest,' Christine says then, 'I don't know what went on in that relationship. No one does, except the two of them.'

'Would she not have gone to the police herself? If she was worried about anything.'

'Oh, she probably did go to them. Maybe she got your man Scully. Or maybe she was out of her mind and they took it to be the ravings of a lunatic. It wouldn't have been the first time she'd gone to them with some crazy notion.'

A man comes out of the chipper beside the hotel. He looks

down into his tray of curry chips, takes out a big one and puts it into his mouth. When some of the sauce spills onto his jumper, he regards it benignly, then wipes it absently with his hand, licking the sauce off his fingers in a contented way as he sets off down the street.

'What did she say,' asks Sarah, 'that time she called on you?'

There's a trace of guilt in the sister's expression now. 'They were after her, she said. She'd nowhere else to go. He wanted her dead. I've two small children. I can't be letting her in when she turns up like that.'

'No.' A feeling of dread has started in Sarah's stomach.

'God knows how she got up or where she was staying. And all this talk of people being out to get her. It's not like I hadn't heard it all before. It's not like I didn't know she wasn't just trying to find a way to get more money out of me. Though there was one thing she said.'

'What?' says Sarah. 'What did she say?'

'This was different. More specific.'

She looks at Sarah and the feeling of dread grows.

'What?'

'She said she'd found something that would land him in trouble.'

'Neil?'

'I think she meant Neil. I don't think he knew she'd found it.'

'What was it?'

'Some map or something.'

'A map?'

'She said he didn't know she had it, and if anything happened to her, I was to find it. That it was in a book on the shelves in the sitting room. That was the best place to keep it because he never actually read books any more, she said.'

'We need to go in,' says Sarah, 'and find it.'

'How are we going to do that?'

'I know where we can get a key.'

'You're serious.'

'I am.'

The pub is very quiet, as she had imagined it would be. Just a couple of men at the bar and Yvonne behind the counter, polishing glasses. One of the men is Pat Doyle, the dairy farmer who's buying Nancy's land. There is no sign of Neil.

'Quiet night,' she says to Yvonne.

'Dead,' agrees Yvonne. Then her face is all alarm. 'I was so sorry to hear about Joe, Sarah.'

'Oh. Thanks.'

'Such a lovely man. I always loved when he came in.'

Doyle and the other man nod her way. 'He'll be sorely missed,' says Doyle.

'A bad business,' says the other.

'A slurry pit can give you no trouble for decades, and then in one minute ...' Doyle shakes his head. 'You'll have a drink?'

'Thanks, I'd better not,' says Sarah. 'They're expecting me back up at the house.' She turns back to Yvonne. 'I'm to pick up the whiskey.'

'The whiskey?'

'For the wake. Did Neil not say it to you? He said he'd left out a couple of bottles behind the bar.'

Yvonne looks under the counter. 'There's nothing here,' she says. 'He never said a word to me. Will I ring him?'

'No, no. They're saying prayers up there. Let me think. I wonder did he mean out the back? Do you mind if I take a quick look?'

'Work away.'

The key to Neil's back door is there as it always used to be, hanging on the rack. After slipping it into her pocket, Sarah waits a moment before coming back into the bar.

'No sign of them there either.'

'That's weird.'

'Are you expecting him back?'

'Just at lockup. I think he was planning on staying up at the wake.'

'Yeah. Never mind. I'll go back and ask him. Maybe he put them in the boot and forgot. You know what he's like.'

Outside, the wind is sharp and the rain comes down in little bites that will soak her in seconds. There is no traffic and the street is deserted, except for Christine, who has gotten out of her car and is standing at the corner of the laneway to Neil's house, looking back at Sarah.

34

The key turns easily in the lock, just as it did all the times when Sarah worked in the bar and Neil sent her up to borrow his vacuum cleaner. No alarm, just as there was no alarm then. She goes inside, Christine following. She flicks on the light, as though the last time she'd done it was yesterday and not ten years ago.

In the vast kitchen, there is a solitary mug on the draining-board. A pair of his trainers by the island. His jacket draped over a high stool.

Christine opens the door into the hallway. She walks to the foot of the stairs.

'Jane?' Her voice warbles as she calls her sister's name.

Sarah follows her. 'She's not here,' says Sarah.

'I know.'

'I think the sitting room's through here.'

It's a big room, a suite of black leather, a faint stale smell of cigarettes. Heavy, expensive-looking curtains and dark wooden furniture. A pale pile of ashes in the grate. In the corner, a huge flatscreen television. On the side of the fireplace, a bookcase, filled with some hardbacks, which look like they've never been touched, and battered paperbacks.

Christine goes over to the bookcase, takes out one of the paperbacks.

'These are hers,' she says, sliding it back in with the others on its shelf.

'She didn't say which book?'

'No. You start with that row and I'll start here.'

They begin work, pulling out one book after another, leafing through each of them before returning it to its place. They're more than halfway up when Sarah finds it, buried in a fat volume. It falls to the floor when she leafs through the pages. An A4 page folded in four. Sarah opens it to see the whole page is filled with lines and words.

'It looks like a map,' says Christine.

'It is a map,' says Sarah, who has already recognised on it the motorway down at the bottom of the page, the triangle of land, marked in red, that is Neil's site. She's also recognised his handwriting in the words that dot the page. Apts. Houses. Shopping centre. Hotel. Apts. Plaza. Some, like 'Houses' and 'Shopping centre', are contained inside the triangle, and are in the same red ink that marks the site. Others, in pencil, are outside it, some coming up even as far as a little square that marks Nancy's cottage. Like they were added later. Lines here and there demarcating where an imaginary apartment complex would end, something else begin. They eat up all the farmland between the motorway and the old road that the cottage is on.

They are on both sides of the furry mark down the centre that must be the woods. She remembers then when she was very little her father once telling her that those woods weren't protected but should be. That anyone could cut the ancient trees down, if the land belonged to them and they had a mind to.

She remembers Nancy's mystery roundabout.

'What does it mean?' asks Christine.

Sarah traces the red triangle with her index finger. 'That's his development. What he's applied for permission for.'

'And the rest?'

'Who knows,' she says, 'what he was imagining.'

'It's like a town,' says Christine.

'It's worse than a town.'

Even after learning he'd been using her, it had never occurred to her that he'd planned anything more than the original application, with its social housing and its playground and its modest-sized supermarket.

'But he doesn't own all this land, does he?' asks Christine.

'No.' Sarah points. 'That's Corcoran's. That's Doyle's – he's a dairy farmer, he's supposed to be buying our land. This bit.'

'So this – plan. They must be in on it too.'

Sarah thinks of Doyle back at the bar. 'I don't think so,' she says.

'But how then?'

'I suppose Neil was hoping to buy their land off them down the line.'

Sarah looks at the map again. A bitter disdain comes over her. 'I think his greed might have got the better of him.'

'But what does it all mean? For Jane? How could she have thought this would be damaging to him?'

A sick feeling is growing in Sarah. 'Maybe,' she says, 'she was going to send it to a paper or something. If it came out before the deadline for challenges to his application, that wouldn't have been good.'

'But they're just scribbles on a piece of paper. She couldn't prove he drew this thing.'

'Still. Let's check upstairs.'

Before Christine answers, Sarah's back out in the hall and taking the stairs.

'Wait,' Christine calls after her. 'Let me shut off the lights down here at least.'

In the bathroom, empty toilet rolls litter the top of the cistern and the radiator. Soap scum furs the sink and a single damp towel lies on the floor. But there is a woman's shower gel on the bath ledge, and two toothbrushes in the glass. And when Sarah opens the cupboard behind the washbasin, there are jars of moisturiser inside, mascara.

'He could come home any moment and find us here,' says Christine, joining her. 'I'm telling you, we should get out and go straight to that garda station in Dunlone. That's what we should have done first of all.'

'Neil will be at the wake all evening,' she says, 'making sure everyone sees him do his Christian duty.'

The office is an unbelievable mess – folders and papers covering every inch of the table, as well as a couple of coffee mugs, the bin underneath filled to overflowing. The spare room has only a double bed, with no sheets on it.

'What are we even looking for?' asks Christine.

In the main bedroom, the air is stale and clothes are piled on top of each other on the armchair. All his as far as she can see. The rumpled sheets look like they haven't been changed in weeks.

'Only one person has been sleeping here,' says Christine.

There is no denying the indent on one side, how only that pillow is flattened.

'And these are all his,' she says, going to the armchair and lifting a sweater.

She goes to the wardrobe – which takes up all of the wall opposite the window – and starts opening the doors. There are four. She stops at the third, where a couple of dresses are hanging. What look like women's sweaters folded neatly.

'Her clothes are here,' says Christine. 'Some of them, anyway.'

They look at the bed again, as though it might offer a clue. There's a notebook on the bedside locker and Sarah picks it up – a spiral thing that looks well-handled, its pages matching the map they found downstairs. Leafing through it, she finds only wobbly columns of figures in Neil's handwriting. Some she recognises are to do with the pub, others make no sense to her. There's a biro beside it, and when she picks it up she sees his tooth marks on it. It was a habit of his, chewing his pens to bits. That night in the pub, after he'd helped Joe and Jim Byrne that time, he'd been absently chewing one as they sat at the bar talking.

She puts the biro into her pocket.

'I don't think,' says Christine, 'my sister is living here any more.'

'She might have left,' says Sarah. 'She might have been here yesterday, for all we know.'

They look at the bed.

'What has he done to her?' asks Christine.

'He hasn't *done* anything to her. You said it yourself, he's not like that.' But Sarah's voice, even to herself, sounds almost hysterical.

'Well, then, tell me what's happening.' Christine fixes her gaze on Sarah. She looks terrified.

But she's no answer for her. No new idea to make sense of things.

'I can feel it,' whispers Christine. 'I've felt it for the past week. Something's not right. Something's not right with my sister.' Her voice breaks on the word 'sister'. She goes to the wardrobe, grasps the skirt of a dress. 'Why didn't I go to the police when I started feeling like this?'

'Maybe she's hiding somewhere,' says Sarah, but it rings so weak.

'She would have come to me if she needed a place to hide.'

For a brief moment, Sarah manages to believe that none of it is real. It feels like she might be able to pull at the fabric of the room she's in, and break out of it into another, more reasonable reality. Back somehow to the right version of events. That seems more plausible than staying where she is. But then it's gone. She's back in Neil's bedroom with Christine.

'We're going to the police right now,' says Christine, 'the station in Dunlone. That's it.'

Sarah looks at Christine, whose face is full of defiance.

'Okay,' she says. She folds her arms, suddenly feeling the cold. 'Maybe you're right.'

They're leaving the room when Christine puts a hand on Sarah's arm. Her other hand is at her lips, her eyes wide and staring. She nods downstairs.

Sarah didn't hear anything.

But then she does.

Footsteps, smartly hitting the path outside.

And then a key turning in the lock of the front door.

35

Two sets of footsteps sound in the hallway. At first Sarah thinks they've gone into the sitting room but this is followed by such a long pause that for a moment she wonders if she was wrong and they've started to come upstairs quietly, knowing somehow that she and Christine are there.

Then Ursula speaks, her voice carrying from the sitting room. They haven't closed the door, so Sarah and Christine can hear her clearly.

'We need to hold it together, Neil,' she says. 'Now more than ever.'

And then his voice: 'It's a mess.'

'Nothing is a mess.'

'I should never have listened to you. I knew it at the time. I knew it. You made it sound like – like glass.'

'Glass.'

'So smooth.' His voice is straining, as if at any moment it will break away from him. 'If I hadn't opened my mouth to you that night at Christmas, none of this would have happened.'

'Calm down, Neil.'

'*She's killing herself anyway*. Do you remember saying that? *What difference will it make to her, when she doesn't value her own life?*'

'Neil,' says Ursula. 'I said you need to calm down.'

'*You won't get a penny for her dying from a destroyed liver*. Do you remember saying that? *But if she was to die from falling over and banging her head on a rock, that's a different story. There'll be enough money in her life insurance to turn that patch of land into a new future. If she dies that way, you'll get your life back*. Isn't that what you said?'

'And it would have worked perfectly,' says Ursula, 'if that bitch hadn't shown up in those woods that night–'

'Well, she did show up,' says Neil. 'And that moron fucking screwed up.'

'If that hadn't happened,' continues Ursula, her voice cool and hard, 'Jane would have died that night, and it would have looked like she'd fallen into that hollow, banged her head on the rock. Just as Lawless said it would.'

'He made it sound like it would be easy. It wouldn't have been easy.'

'She was drunk, wasn't she? Everything was just as it was supposed to be. No one around. That insurance money would be yours, now. But Sarah showed up. And he screwed up. And now we have to face those consequences.'

'I said no to you too.' His voice is calmer now. Sarah imagines him shaking his head at the injustice of it. How wronged he's been. 'That night in the pub, I told you you'd had too much to drink. I said you were talking like a madwoman. Didn't I?'

'You did.'

'What?'

'I said you did. But I wasn't the madwoman.'

'Jane hated me,' he says. 'I wouldn't mind but she hated me.'

'That woman,' she says, 'was ruining your life.'

'Well, I think we can agree we're square on that one now.'

'No one asked you to kill her that time. If you hadn't, we wouldn't be in this mess.'

'No one asked me—'

At these words, a low, strangled sound comes from Christine. Her gaze is bearing wildly down on Sarah, who takes her hand, squeezes it. A comfort and a warning. Do not make another sound. Do not move a muscle.

'I'm not like this, Urs,' he says.

'I know that.'

'The reason I ballsed it up is because I'm not a killer. I'm not like him.'

'You're a decent person, Neil,' she says, her voice soothing now. 'If anything, you're too nice. And see where that got you.'

'What about where not being nice got me?'

'There's still a way out.'

'You and him and Paul. You made it sound so easy, to make it look like an accident. And there she was, out of her mind drunk, at the top of the stairs. It was like she *wanted* me to do it. I nearly think she *did* want me to do it. One push, I thought, and it'd be over. You planted that idea in my mind. I'd never have done it on my own. All these years, the idea never entered my head.'

Sarah squeezes Christine's hand tighter, keeps her eyes locked on the other woman's, as though that might keep her frozen.

'No one's blaming you,' says Ursula. 'It was only a few days after Lawless's botched effort. You still had it fresh in your mind.'

'It was still fresh in my mind,' he repeats.

'And an opportunity presented itself. It *looked* like it was going to be easy. No one is blaming you, Neil. And, look, we've managed to bury her. It's over a week now and no one's noticed she's gone. And don't forget, people knowing about you and Sarah, that helps us here as well. You can just tell anyone who asks that you and Jane split up when she heard and she's moved to Dublin.'

A pause.

'I hadn't thought of that,' he says.

'You see? You're freaking out and not thinking clearly. We can still pull this off. The planning application is going to get through. That part of our plan has worked perfectly. Nancy's campaign is in pieces. And we might not need the insurance money. You'll get investors, with the permission.'

'Oh, God. Why did she have to go down there?'

'She went down there because she's never known her place.'

'And Joe. Why'd she have to tell him?'

'She can't keep her mouth shut. That's what I'm telling you. Who didn't she tell?'

'I didn't want to do that to him. God knows I didn't.'

'Paul said he put up a fight. When you were getting the whiskey into him.'

'Put up a fight? He nearly fucking tore the head off me. He nearly killed me.'

'At the wake,' says Ursula. 'She was acting so weird.'

'What are you saying?'

'Sarah. She didn't talk to anyone, just made straight for the yard. And the face on her. She went right up to one of the slats for the slurry pit and opened it. I think it was the one. You know.'

'You followed her out.'

'I did.'

'Why?'

'There was no one else out there. If that neighbour of his hadn't shown up, I would have done it.'

'You'd have done what? Pushed her into the same pit Joe was found dead in this morning? Half the town there inside in his house? Is that what you're saying to me?'

'People would have believed it. That she did it to herself.'

'For Christ's sake.'

Christine jerks her head towards the window, her eyes full of panic. But Sarah shakes her head. Her mind is strangely calm. She can see that trying to leave undetected is too risky. One squeaking floorboard is all it would take, or the window banging. The best thing is not to move unless either Neil or Ursula comes up the stairs, then get into the wardrobe. Hope the sound of their footsteps drowns any noise that would give them away.

'I would have done it,' says Ursula, 'for you. I would have taken the risk. Neil. Look at me.'

'What?' He shouts the word.

'We've given her enough chances to stay away. We've given her plenty of warnings. But she keeps coming back. Like a bad smell. You have to admit it.'

He doesn't answer.

'And at the wake. She definitely suspects something. She even asked me if I thought there was a chance of foul play. And Paul said she was weird with him when he went out to theirs.'

'I love her,' he says.

'Oh, for God's sake. You don't.'

'I want to marry her.'

'I told you what she did to me in school. She left me there with that guy. She knew what was going to happen and she just left me there with him. How can you love someone like that?'

'I do.'

'Neil,' she says. 'You know this as well as I do. We have to get rid of her now. There's no other option.'

'No.'

'Yes. It's not like we haven't warned her.'

'What are you suggesting?'

'Earlier,' she says, 'she left the wake without telling anyone where she was going. I won't be the only person to have noticed. Wouldn't it make sense if she went for a walk on her own? There isn't a soul in Crookedwood who doesn't know that she loved Joe.'

'So?'

'I have an idea,' she says.

'Of course you do.'

'This would solve the problem of Sarah. And it would solve another problem too.'

'Just spit the fucking thing out, Urs.'

'It's not just Sarah we have to worry about, is it? What if Jane's sister comes down asking about her? What if she reports her missing? What if they start searching for her around here? You'd be a suspect, Neil. You'd be a suspect right away.'

'Don't I know that.' Then he adds, 'The sister hates her.'

'She's still family. It will always be possible.'

'I *know* all this.'

'Well, what if someone else happened to die on the same spot as we buried Jane's body?'

'I'm not following you,' he says, but there's a new quality to his tone now. It's like wariness.

'What if someone else's blood was spilled there? Then if those dogs *were* ever down there looking for Jane's body, well, we'd have gotten rid of any last trace of it. No one would pay any mind to them picking up a scent there because they'd assume it was ... the blood from the other person.'

A long silence follows.

'How?' he says then.

'What if she happened to encounter a dangerous dog?'

If he answers, Sarah doesn't catch it.

'Paul can get that dog off your man Lawless right now if we need him to. He knows what to do with it. You give him something she's worn so he gets the right scent.'

'No.'

'All you'll have to do is hold her there while the dog—'

'Attacks her? Mauls her to death? Are you crazy? I'm not doing that.'

'Yes, you are. And I'll tell you why. If you don't, I'll report you. I'll tell them where Jane's body is and I'll tell them that you told me all about it and threatened to blame me if I told anyone.'

'You wouldn't do that.'

'Wouldn't I? If you think I'm going to spend the next however many years in prison, have my life ruined, and Paul's, because we tried to help you, you've got another thing coming.'

'You weren't just helping me. You were supposed to be benefiting from your plan too, don't forget.'

For a long moment, neither of them speaks. When Neil eventually says something, his voice is so quiet Sarah barely catches what he says.

'How would we get her down there?'

'Call her,' says Ursula, a new urgency to her voice now. 'Tell her you're out of your mind with worry. That you need to see her. She'll believe you.'

'And then?'

'Paul doesn't even need to tell Lawless what he wants the dog for. It'll just be you and Paul. Between you, you should manage it.'

'Manage it,' he repeats.

'It has to happen in the right place. Then, when he's ready, Paul will let go of the dog and he'll go for her.'

Sarah imagines him staring at Ursula, seeing himself holding her down while a dog mauls her to death.

'It'll be a few awful minutes and then it'll be over,' says Ursula. 'Neil. Neil. Look at me. I know you hate me now but you'll thank me in a few months' time. The summer. Think of the summer. Your planning permission through. You'll get the funding from somewhere. We don't need the insurance money. It can still work out. The future you dreamed of.'

'I feel sick.'

'You can do this. The slurry pit was brilliant. That was your idea, wasn't it? You just have to stay strong for one more day.'

'Call Paul,' he says.

'Good. Yes. I'll call him right now,' she says.

There's a pause.

'It's me,' she says. 'Get down there now. He's going to do it.'

Another pause.

'He's meeting us there?' asks Neil.

'He said he'll be there in five minutes. There'll have to be blood, Neil. Right on the very place. You have to get it right this time. We don't want a repeat of what happened with Jane.'

'I didn't know she'd fight back like that. Years of being a zombie and then it's like she's fucking possessed.'

At these words, another cry escapes Christine. This one is louder, like the sound an animal might make if it was in pain. There is no doubting that Neil and Ursula heard it down below. All silence down there, and now the stair light coming on.

Sarah opens the wardrobe door, the one containing Jane's clothes.

'They don't know you're here.' She mouths the words to Christine, who gets into the wardrobe, the door closing behind her just as footsteps sound on the stairs.

And then Ursula is on the landing. She's looking right at Sarah. Neil's footsteps sound on the stairs, and then there he is, behind Ursula. In his hand, he holds a knife. It gleams dully at her.

'You have to do it now,' says Ursula. 'There's no other option.'

The police will find me before they do it, Sarah tells herself. And if they do get her to the place where they buried Jane before Christine can call the police, before they can find her, she will kick and bite and scream. She won't let them take her. Anyway, she thinks, he won't do it, not when it comes down to it. He won't. He's not a monster.

His face, as he stares at her. He looks as though he would kill her right now if he thought he'd get away with it. And she's making a run for the window – in that moment she is going to push through the glass, she's going to throw herself out of it and hope to survive the fall. But before she reaches it he's grabbing her from behind, an arm across her torso, the knife cold and hard against her throat.

'We just need to get her into the boot,' says Ursula. 'I'll drive with the lights off. No one will see. They're all up at the wake anyway.'

His face is so close to hers. She can hear his breathing. She can feel his cheek against her ear. Smell his woody smell.

'We should put something in her mouth,' says Ursula, anxiously, and she looks around the room. Her gaze rests on the wardrobe.

'My scarf,' says Neil, nodding at the chair by the window.

Ursula grabs it, stares uncertainly at it, then wraps some of it tightly around her fist. She walks up to Sarah, who finds that, instead of screaming and pulling away, she has now frozen. She's completely unable to move, even as Ursula pushes the balled-up part of the scarf into her mouth and then, as they make their way, Neil pushing her forward, out of the room and down the stairs.

A crooked man, she thinks.

Now I see you.

You are all the decency you showed Joe over the years, maybe your wife and even me.

And you are all this too.

This, most of all.

A murderer.

This *is* you. *This* is who you are. It's who you have decided to become.

36

It is total darkness down in the woods, except for the sharp spread of stars visible here and there through the branches of the trees. Sarah and Neil walk slowly and awkwardly, every now and then one of them almost tripping. When they get to the hollow, they wait in the silence, his arm still across her torso, the knife still at her neck. Still she cannot move. She has never in her life before kept so still. She doesn't even try to spit out the scarf, even as she gags.

There is the sound of a car making its way down the road, then the engine cutting off, a door closing. Then footsteps sound out, as someone walks through the woods, towards them. There is a moment of hope, until Paul Scully appears in the clearing, with the dog. The same dog as the one that night, back at the start of the month.

'You took your fucking time,' says Neil.

'I couldn't have been fucking quicker.' He walks closer to them. The dog is snarling horribly, his eyes only on her.

'You need to get her on the ground first,' says Paul.

'How the fuck?'

'Just. I don't know. Kneel with her.'

Awkwardly, Neil pushes her to the ground, landing on top of her. Sarah can just about see the silhouette of the dog and Paul Scully standing behind him, looking down at her. She can barely make out Neil's face, even though he is kneeling on her legs now, facing her, the knife in his hand weakly gleaming again.

Rainwater trapped in the dead bracken under her seeps through the fabric of her clothes, making her skin wet and cold. Just as it did the last time they lay on that ground together, and as it had done when she'd lain there years ago while a different man had rested his weight on her, roots and pebbles pressing painfully into her back.

'Like this?' says Neil.

'Yeah.'

'You don't sound very sure. You'd want to be fucking sure.'

'I'm sure.'

'He's not going to go for *me*?'

'He has her scent now.' Paul sounds scared. 'He's trained for this,' he says.

Paul takes a step closer to them. The dog is straining against the lead. It's snarling, baring its long teeth.

'She's going to scream.'

'She can't with that thing in her.'

'Hang on. Hold that fucking mutt, okay?' Neil's voice is shaking, as he leans forward, tries to push back in some of the scarf that she'd managed to push out. For a moment, their faces are so close together she can see his eyelashes. She can see the pores on his skin. The last time they'd been that close, they had kissed. Now her heart is pounding so hard she wonders if she is having a heart attack, if that is how she will die.

And that's when it comes back to her, just like that, when she is about to be killed. In the car that time, on the way out to Howth, when they'd been talking so excitedly about their futures.

'When the insurance money comes through ...' It was a sentence he'd never finished. He'd interrupted himself with another, after a frightened glance her way. She hadn't understood it at the time but she had registered its wrongness. Like someone playing a pretty tune on a piano and hitting an off-key note in the middle. And yet she had taken that unfinished sentence of his and tucked it away, out of sight of herself.

Memories lying inside her like landmines.

And now she's going to die. And the men will wait until she's dead or close to it and then they'll return to the pub or the wake, where they can be sure people will see them. And even though Christine will report him and he will be caught for everything he's done, Sarah won't be here any more. She won't be able to follow her own life, which she understands now – in a way she never did before – belongs to her and no one else. That it's her future and not Nancy's or Neil's or anyone's. That it's something that belongs only to her and that only she should get to decide what she does with it. And she knows exactly what she wants to do with it. She's known ever since she set foot in the restaurant. And with this new understanding comes self-forgiveness, for what she did to Ursula that night long ago, for what she did to Jane, when she told herself the other woman's feelings didn't count. Clear and sharp as the stars.

If she tries to move, Paul will let go of the dog's collar. But if she doesn't, he'll do it anyway, any second now.

'Don't let her fucking move,' says Paul. 'When it starts, she has to stay here.'

He hadn't managed to push the scarf back, not properly. Now, without difficulty, Sarah manages to expel it from her mouth. And then she starts to laugh, a hard, mirthless laugh. When their eyes widen, she laughs harder.

'You're both screwed,' she says. 'So completely screwed. And Ursula.'

'What the fuck is she on about?' asks Paul.

'She'll have phoned 999 by now.'

'Who?' he says. 'Who?'

'Jane's sister, Christine. She was in your wardrobe. She heard everything.'

The hesitation comes – Paul looking in horror at Neil, but still holding the collar of the dog – and, with a strength she didn't know she had, she swings forward, her head cracking against Neil's sharp and hard, somehow dislodging herself in the same split second, before getting to her feet. She has taken one step away from them, towards the gully that separates the wood from the field and the dog is lunging at her.

He knocks her to the ground with a weight that is shocking. Now he's tearing at her.

She had imagined the pain would be in her skin, through

which his teeth are cutting. But it's not there at all – it's much deeper – heavy, muscle-aching blows as the dog's skull thuds into her soft tissue, first her thigh and then her stomach. Its teeth cutting into her flesh feels like being punched.

When she pulls the biro from her pocket, she doesn't know what she's planning to do with it until she's doing it – raising her hand above the dog's head like this, thumb at the base of the pen, and then thrusting it into his bare eye, and then, before he reacts, hammering it in further with the base of her hand, a jelly wetness spurting from the creature then, as he swings his head in that wild way, emitting this terrible cry.

And then she's pulling herself down onto the gully and up through the grass, towards the square of light that is the kitchen window of the cottage. The dog has left her alone and there are terrible gurgling screams behind her, which she understands before she takes one awful glance to be coming from Neil, the animal having thrown himself on his throat.

Then a bright, drenching beam is lighting up the wood. And Nancy is calling her name, over and over, from somewhere in there. 'Sarah. Sarah. My girl. Sarah.'

37

As soon as they get back from the graveyard, Nancy goes into the kitchen and starts making sandwiches, as though Sarah hadn't just said she's not hungry and doesn't want anything and will make something for herself later.

'Sit down,' she says, when Sarah follows her in. 'That'll have taken it out of you.'

'I'm grand,' she says. But she sits down anyway. Looks out the window. A clean square of blue.

That morning, she had gone across the road and, with the shears, cut two huge bouquets of mayflower. At her father's grave, she'd cried, the tears pouring out of her like they'd been building up for years. She had put her hand on the gravel, the closest she could get to him. Behind her, Nancy had reached out a hand. It had almost touched Sarah's shoulder. Then she'd gone over to Joe's grave, still a mound of earth and wooden cross, and she had cried there too.

Neil's grave they'd found at the far corner, by the stand where the priest says his decades of the rosary at a burial. Like Joe's, it is just a mound of earth, a wooden cross. Seeing it had pained her in a way she hadn't expected, his life suddenly so sad and small, like his grave. She'd stood there and been able to hold it all in her mind. That he'd hired someone to kill his wife. And when that hadn't worked, had killed her himself by pushing her down the stairs and then smothering her. That he, with Paul, had forced whiskey into Joe, thrust his head beneath the slats and then thrown him into the slurry pit. That he had intended to kill Sarah, by holding her in one place while a vicious dog tore her to pieces. That he'd been capable of all that as well as the decency she'd seen. And that if he'd never inherited that land, he might well have lived out his life without doing anything awful at all. Or if he had never married Jane. Or if his father hadn't treated him with such contempt.

Jane Hart is not buried in Crookedwood. When they took up her remains from the wood, Christine had them brought to Dublin, where she was cremated, her ashes placed in a crematorium. She herself was going to be cremated, she'd explained to Sarah. She wanted their ashes to be together. Sarah looked the crematorium up online. A vast place, out by the airport. As soon as she's well enough to get back to the city, she'll go out there. Maybe, she thinks, she'll do it en route to the airport, when she's leaving for London. Because the one thing that chafes at her mind in a different way from everything else is that she never once spoke to Jane. That she will never get to know her.

'Eat one,' says Nancy, putting tea and cheese sandwiches on the table.

Sarah takes a small bite from a sandwich, puts it back on her plate. She tries to think of something to say. It's been so weird with her mother since she came out of the hospital and moved into the cottage. All this walking on eggshells. It's like they have nothing to talk about, now they're not angry with each other any more.

Worse, Nancy keeps giving her these looks. Like she's about to do something awful, like apologise or try to talk about feelings or, even worse, sex.

'No Mass again this morning,' says Sarah. Since she was discharged, as far as she's aware Nancy hasn't once gone to Mass.

'I won't darken the door of that place again for the rest of my life,' says Nancy.

'Wow.'

'Except for a funeral. Or a wedding,' she adds, glancing quickly at Sarah at this last bit. 'If there's ever a wedding to go to. I'm not saying there will be. There doesn't have to be.'

Sarah suppresses a smile. 'Just like that,' she says.

'I woke up one morning and realised it's all a pile of rubbish,' says Nancy. 'That's it.'

'So you're one of these hardline atheists now.'

She throws Sarah a look that's severe and wry at the same time. 'I didn't say that,' she says.

'Are you looking forward to moving?' asks Sarah.

'I am,' says Nancy. 'A new start.' She nods at Sarah. 'Should have done it a long while ago.'

The sale of the farm has gone through. Nancy has been in and out to the recycling centre in Dunlone all week, getting rid of boxes and boxes of things. Her new little terrace house in town, Sarah thinks, will be like a nun's cell.

'I should never have put that pressure on you about the farm,' says Nancy.

'Oh, Mam. Forget about all that.'

'It was wrong of me.'

'It's grand.'

'I could have ruined your life.'

'Well, now, there's no need for drama.'

'I suppose not.' Nancy looks at her nervously. 'Are you looking forward to it? The new job.'

'I am.'

'You don't think it'll be too much?'

'It's still a good month away.'

'Well,' says Nancy, 'you deserve it.'

'And you and Olive are still going ahead with your café idea,' says Sarah.

'We need something to keep us out of trouble in our dotage. And she's out of a job now, of course.'

'They're saying Cormac Hart will get a couple of years.'

Nancy nods. 'At least a couple. They're saying he was in on it all along. Ursula will get more if there's any justice to be served. And that other fellow. But now there's no point in going there.'

'No.'

Sarah looks out the window again. It's still all blue out there. 'I think I'll take a walk,' she says.

'What?'

'It's lovely out now.' At the graveyard, it had spat rain, but the clouds are moving quickly this morning and the weather keeps changing.

'I'll come with you.'

'No need.'

'Where are you going?'

'Down the field.'

'Are you sure that's a good idea?'

'I am. I really will be saying goodbye this time.'

'Well, at least put on my wellies.'

'Okay,' says Sarah. 'Give us your wellies.'

Outside, the air smells clean and lighter after the rain. For the first time since she was discharged, she crosses the yard and goes through the gate. She starts the walk down the field.

This morning it's full of her father's absence. So heavy, it almost feels like a presence.

Almost.

It's probably the last time she'll walk down here. Her life in Crookedwood is over, as is her life in Dublin, the restaurant kitchen and her little flat gone, all let go like a kite into the sky, already out of reach. When she rang Jack to ask for her job back, she had done so knowing it would surely have been filled. She hadn't expected him to ring her back the following week to tell her a job in London was hers if she wanted it. Station chef, on vegetables again, but in the kitchen where Jack started out as a chef. The reference he wrote for Sarah still makes her wince, though she has reread it so many times she almost knows it by heart. He'd all but told the chef to give her the job. Sarah suspects it was followed up by a phone call, in which he *had* actually begged if not told him to give it to her. An old favour, maybe, repaid.

Her injuries are the only reason for this slight faltering when she reaches the end of the field, and steps over the gully and under the trees. Since the night she nearly died, her heart has stopped its wonky hammering. Even after the nightmares – no one can tell her how long they'll go on – coming fast and thick, always about the dog, his jaws always about to close on her as she wakes, shaking and wet with sweat. Even then, it doesn't come back. Looking through her diary one night after she was discharged from the hospital, she figured out that it started the day she and Neil took that drive to Howth, when he let slip about the insurance money and she in turn slipped it somewhere safe but out of reach. She has been half expecting it to start up here, down so close to the woods, but though her heart does start to race as she makes her way right up to where Neil had held her down, and where they had later found Jane's body, the thump, thump, pause, *thwack* doesn't come.

Standing there in the hollow, her mind can even turn to David Fitzpatrick. After it was all over the news, he'd sent her a text saying he hoped she was okay, but she hadn't replied. She has nothing to say to him. The person who vehemently maintains to himself as well as to her that he did nothing wrong, because he'd asked and she'd said yes, and whatever her body tried to say after that had nothing to do with anything. Of course, it had everything to do with everything. Her body takes care of her better than her mind ever did. Maybe if David Fitzpatrick paid better attention to what his body knows, he might not be so sure of himself.

She starts making her way back towards the field. In a month's time, an aeroplane will lift her high above this land, so that her ears will fill with pressure and she will look out her window and down at this network of green fields, growing smaller and smaller, and she will remember how she stood here like this, in the middle of it, how the birdsong is so sharp and clear down here, and how, beyond that, comes the clean, scraping sound of the motorway.

Acknowledgements

Warm thanks are due to my agent Darley Anderson and everyone in the Darley Anderson Literary Agency, especially Rebeka Sharp for her encouraging feedback and for reading all those drafts with such good grace. Particular thanks are due to my editor in Hachette Books Ireland, Ciara Considine, for her astute observations, suggestions and questions along the way, which were so helpful to me. Thanks again to my copy-editor Hazel Orme and proofreader Aonghus Meaney, for doing such a great job, and to Westmeath County Council for the arts grant they gave me to work on the novel.

Crookedwood was for the most part written during the first year of the COVID-19 pandemic and, during that strange time, I was buoyed up by the (sometimes bewildering) cheer and good spirits of the newer humans in my family, my own two but also my niece Mary and nephews Tim, Sean, Tadhg, Fionn and Oisín. Last but not least, I would like to thank my husband John for his unfailing generosity and honesty.

There is a real Crookedwood in Ireland – a small village north of Mullingar – but all I have taken from that place is its lovely name. The Crookedwood of this novel is an amalgam of any number of towns across the Irish midlands and needless to say all its characters are entirely imagined.